Ruby's Dream

Ruby's Dream

Book Two of The Crystal Warriors Series

Maree Anderson

ISBN-13: 978-0-9922498-8-5
ISBN-10: 0-9922498-8-0

RUBY'S DREAM
Copyright © 2011 by Maree Anderson
First print edition, 2014

Publisher: Maree Anderson

Cover Design: Rob Anderson

DEDICATION

This one's for any woman who's ever cringed at the thought of buying a new swimsuit, or had someone tell her she should join a gym.

And to all the Romance Writers of New Zealand Clendon Award readers who loved the first draft of Ruby and Kyan's story: Thank you!

A NOTE FOR READERS

This novel is set in New Zealand, and aside from the hero, Kyan, all characters are Kiwis—New Zealanders. American spelling has been used throughout, but Kiwi terms and slang have been used where appropriate. Although every effort has been made to make meanings clear via the context, to assist the reader a Glossary of Kiwi Terms & Slang has been included at the end of this book.

CHAPTER ONE

RUBY ROBERTS SLUMPED on the floor amid the remains of shredded wrapping paper. She stared at her brother's gift, so dumbfounded it took a minute to form actual words. It was like being slapped in the face with a stinky wet fish.

"Gee, way to make a girl feel good, Mike!" Her shriek echoed around the empty room, and those echoes were laden with the betrayal she couldn't help feeling right now.

She tossed the gift on the couch and rubbed her arms, blinking back tears. Her own brother. She'd always looked up to him. She would have forgiven him anything.... But this?

This shredded her heart. *This* slammed her already chronically low self-esteem into subzero territory.

"I get it, okay?" Her voice cracked. "There's no need to sodding well rub it in."

Even though there was no one to witness the gesture, she defiantly crammed another handful of salt 'n' vinegar chips into her mouth. Opening another present would cheer her up for sure because whatever it turned out to be, it sure as hell couldn't be any worse than the last one.

The gift she chose was from Lani, a motherly Maori woman Ruby had first met in a clay sculpture class. Lani's creations were *earthy*, to say the least. But this couldn't possibly be one of Lani's pieces because—

The wrapping fell away, leaving her grasping a box of

ribbed condoms and a fire-engine-red triangle of lace.

Condoms? Hah. In my dreams.

She tossed the box aside and hooked a finger beneath the scrap of lace, lifting it from the wrapping paper. Attached to the triangle were a couple of thin bands made out of some transparent, stretchy, silicon-like substance.

Oh. My. God. Heat crawled up her face. Hazarding a guess, right now her complexion exactly matched the color of the g-string. She hadn't worn a g-string since... since... well, ever. And if she wore *this* and dared sit down, the darned thing would have to be surgically removed from her butt crack.

Thank God for small mercies—namely that Lani had given Ruby the gift in advance and insisted it be opened on the morning of her birthday. If Ruby had opened this one at her party, in front of all her guests? She'd have curled up and died of embarrassment.

She checked the tag. Maybe—? Damn. It was even the right size. There went her only valid excuse to exchange it for granny knickers.

Ruby heaved a deep, bracing breath and fumbled to open the accompanying card.

A little something to give that special man in your life a big thrill! Love, Lani.

Geez. It was way worse than she'd imagined. Cue a full-body cringe.

Ruby rubbed the fine hairs on her nape, which had decided to sit bolt upright at the mere thought of their owner wearing that g-string to give a man a big thrill. A big nightmare for a week, more like. Ruby would much rather have dealt with one of Lani's phallic sculptures.

So she could face Lani with a credible outpouring of delight at the party tonight, Ruby rehearsed aloud what she was going to say. "Thank you so much, Lani! I'll save them for a... a... special occasion." Yeah. Like, if she ever had sex with something other than her vibrator again.

She eyed the last parcel—a large one—with growing trepidation. Because any gift from her mother was destined to wreak havoc on Ruby's self-image. Last year Pamela Roberts had presented Ruby with a gym membership. The year before, a Swiss ball and a manual of recommended exercises entitled *Core Strength*. Sadly, Ruby's "core" hadn't possessed the endurance to inflate the darn thing to anything resembling the correct dimensions with the stupid little pump enclosed with the ball and the manual. But hey, even a half-inflated Swiss ball had its uses. Like, for a spare seat whenever Ruby had a bunch of friends over.

She almost talked herself out of opening her mum's gift. Almost. But curiosity was a powerful thing.

She tore off the gift-wrap....

It was as bad as she'd predicted.

Her mum's gift was a set of Pilates DVDs that would—wait for it—allow Ruby to exercise to her heart's content without all the complicated equipment usually associated with Pilates.

Ruby fist-punched the air and hollered, "Yes, my friends, this entire workout regimen uses only an exercise mat—included as part of the gift, of course. Because when it comes to blatant hints, my mother leaves nothing to chance. Thanks, Mum. Woohoo. And various other expressions of faked joy."

At least Ruby always knew what to expect from her mother. *Her* gifts had lost the power to wound years ago. Unlike Mike's totally unexpected unpleasant surprise.

To take her mind off her brother's hurtful gift, Ruby opened the boxed set of Pilates DVDs and selected a couple.

Bun and thigh sculpting. Accelerated body sculpting. Ouch. Sounded painful.

The accompanying brochure described the basic exercises and showed photos of some lithe young thing demonstrating each exercise with a smile firmly fixed on her pretty face. Yeah. Right. Like any normal person could smile while doing *that*.

Ruby's mother was a born-again fitness freak—the worst

kind. Doubtless Pamela Roberts was fondly imagining her daughter huffing and puffing over hellish-sounding exercises named "The Hundred" and 'The Criss-Cross" at this very moment. What better way for a girl to spend her birthday morning than contorting herself into a pretzel, and rocking back and forth on her tailbone?

She should introduce her mother to Caroline—they'd get on like a house on fire because Ruby's workmate was another of those poor, demented souls who went to the gym and worked out on their birthday. *As if.* Ruby sooo would not be joining them. Instead, she succumbed to a wave of self-pity and heaved herself onto the couch, assuming her favorite lounge-lizard position. To add insult to injury, she had to extricate Mike's gift from beneath her bum.

The elephant in the room wasn't going away. Ruby couldn't ignore it any longer. *Bugger.*

Mike had always supported her. He'd never once put her down, or hassled her about her overly generous proportions. Until now.

In all honesty, she supposed it was bound to happen sooner or later, what with their mum's constant nagging at Mike to join The Dark Side for "Ruby's own good".

Her brother's birthday gift? The one that made her want to cry?

A cookbook. Specifically, a cookbook bursting with low fat, healthy recipes, cooked by a professional chef who used ingredients Ruby would never buy in a million years. That wasn't what upset her, though. No. It was the fact the cookbook was sponsored by a pharmaceutical firm to promote their latest wonder-pill for the long-term treatment of "significantly obese patients".

Ruby scrabbled about in the chip packet for another handful but there were none left—not that she recalled eating the entire packet but the empty bag sorta stated the obvious. Damn.

She wasn't obese.

Overweight, maybe— Oh, all right. Definitely.

Unfit? Well, yeah. But *not* obese.

She heaved the cookbook at the wall, and took no satisfaction whatsoever when it missed by a good couple of feet and smacked the carpet. Enough was enough. Either she was going to crawl under her duvet and refuse to come out for the rest of her life, or she had to do something to nip this constant nagging in the bud.

So what's a thirty-year-old girl to do when her beloved brother makes it clear as day he thinks she needs to lose weight?

Why, something utterly stupid, of course. Ruby rolled off the couch and marched into her bedroom. She would show Mike if it was the last thing she did.

RUBY CRITICALLY SURVEYED her reflection in the mirror. The cleverly draped dress disguised most of the wobbly bits she wanted to cover. The color suited her. She like the way the material swished, caressing her legs when she walked. It made her feel sexy... at least for a moment or two, until reality whispered in her ear, reminding her that she was anything but sexy.

Her broken doorbell squawked. Ruby quickly touched up her lipstick before swishing off to greet her first guest... who was a half hour early. Not that she minded. She'd been ready for the past hour, and having company meant she could quit rearranging canapés on their platters and obsessively checking her appearance.

Barring herself, everything was as perfect as Ruby knew how to make it. And, bravado being her specialty, she was determined to present a confident smiling face to her guests. She pasted on a wide, toothy smile and yanked open the door.

"Hey, Jules!" Ruby's forced smile morphed into a genuine one. She opened her arms to hug her best friend in the world.

Jules responded by planting a hand on Ruby's chest and backing her up a few paces so Jules could slam the door shut. And then Jules advanced, looking like doom personified.

Ruby danced clumsily backward, trying not to freak out at the sight of Jules' tight features and clenched jaw. Her stomach twisted into a huge knot. Something bad had happened—she knew it. "How come you're here so early?" she asked Jules. "Where's Alex? Is something wrong? Is he okay?"

"Chill. Everything's fine in Alex-land. He'll be here soon." Jules halted to toss her handbag on the couch. She grabbed Ruby by the wrists and peered into her face. "Are. You. Insane?"

Ruby blinked. "I—"

"That scrawny bitch put you up to this, didn't she? It's not enough for her to be a gym-junkie, she's got to suck you into her treadmill of pain and suffering too? Wait 'til I get my hands on her. I'll smack her into the next dimension. I'll—"

"Calm down, Jules."

"It's like that time she talked you into buying that bloody dress. She's pure evil!"

Ruby knew exactly who Jules was talking about. And "that bloody dress"—a testament to Caroline's scary-ass persuasive superpowers—still hung in Ruby's wardrobe. It'd been two sizes too small, but Ruby had let Caroline talk her into buying the dress because it was pretty and feminine, and Ruby had secretly coveted it. Not to mention been embarrassed as hell when the salesgirl loudly proclaimed to the whole store that the dress didn't come in a bigger size… and then ignored Ruby to bond with Caroline over personal trainer recommendations.

"You'll fit it if you do a little exercise," Caroline had said—insisted really—dismissing Ruby's protests with the supreme confidence of the terminally skinny. Yet despite Ruby's mammoth efforts, *and* eventual success in dropping a few kilos, when she'd finally dared to try the dress on it had still been far too tight. So tight, in fact, Ruby had busted the zipper and burst a couple of rather crucial seams trying to extricate herself from the damn thing. Nightmare. She still vividly remembered being sore and tired and red-faced from the exertion. And that at one stage, she'd seriously contemplated sleeping in the bloody thing, and wearing it to work the next day.

Her face flushed with heat at the humiliating memory—yet another one she'd rather forget. Alcohol. Yeah. That's what was required right now.

Ruby made a beeline for the drinks table and one of the many lethally alcoholic cocktails she'd premixed for the occasion. Mmm. What to choose?

She braved an experimental sip of Mai Tai mix before adding ice to the shaker. Not bad.

"Well?" Jules demanded.

Ruby shook the mix vigorously before pouring it into a glass. "Well, what?"

"Is Caroline showing her face tonight? I hope so. Because then I can strangle her. What was she thinking? She's supposed to be your *friend*, for fuck's sake!"

While Jules paced the floor and ranted, Ruby's fertile mind ran an entertaining little scenario featuring Jules and Caroline in a wrestling match. Tall, model-skinny, blonde Caroline, versus pocket-Venus, voluptuous, raven-haired Jules. The guys'd be thrilled to bits. They'd thank her forever. And if it came down to placing bets, Ruby would put her money on Jules, because Jules didn't take crap from anyone. Mind you, Caroline worked out regularly. She even sported some of those lumps in funny places that Ruby was reliably informed were called muscles....

She shook her head to clear the increasingly silly images from her mind, and downed a large swig of courage-boosting Mai Tai. "Much as I'd love to blame Caroline for forcing me to register in the triathlon, I can't. It was all my own idea." She hoped her expression didn't reveal even the slightest hint of the other reason—that her brother was so ashamed of his sister, he'd sent her a message she couldn't ignore rather than confronting her face-to-face. The bloody coward.

"It's time I got fit, and this triathlon seems like the perfect motivation," she said, as much to convince herself as Jules.

Jules simply stared, wide-eyed with horror. "This was *your* idea?"

"Yep."

"You came up with it all by yourself?"

"Yep."

"What the fuck possessed you to go and do something so incurably stupid?"

"Here." Ruby slopped the dregs of Mai Tai mix into another glass and handed it to her friend. "You look like you need it."

Jules obediently downed a hefty swallow. And choked. "Jeeesus, that's strong!" She sank into a chair, wiped her watering eyes, and braved another more cautious sip of the potent mix. "Okay, Rubes, time to cut the crap. What really happened?"

Damn. Jules knew her too well.

Ruby flopped into a battered easy chair and contemplated her toenails. Huh. All that effort to paint them and she'd already managed to chip the polish. "It's because of what Mike gave me for my birthday. I was so damned angry and hurt that I—"

Jules threw up a hand. "Hang on. Mike? Your can-do-no-wrong brother? The same guy you'd swear farts roses after listening to you sing his praises? I don't believe it."

Ruby carefully placed her cocktail on the carpet beside her chair. She levered herself from the grasp of the squishy cushions, and stalked to the cupboard where she kept her recipe books. She snatched Mike's gift from the pile and held it up for Jules to see.

Jules craned her neck, squinting. "A cookbook? So what?"

Ruby brought over the offending item and plonked it in Jules' lap. Then she grabbed her drink and downed the contents as she watched Jules' face. And waited.

Silence from Jules as she flicked through the cookbook. Then openmouthed dismay. Followed by pity, which was the worst of all. "Oh," Jules finally said. "Shit. I'm sooo sorry, Rubes. What was he thinking?"

"Duh. It's pretty obvious what he was thinking."

Jules muttered something nasty beneath her breath. "What are you going to say when he calls you for your birthday?"

Ruby didn't answer because she hadn't the faintest clue. Chances were she'd do what she always did: Pretend everything was fine and quickly change the subject.

"You can't take this lying down, Rubes. You have to say something. Tell him how much he hurt you. Scream at him. Tell him he's an arsehole. And for God's sake, toss this piece of crap. Or by God, I will." Jules held out the cookbook and waved it.

Ruby snatched it and replaced it in the kitchen cupboard. "I'll toss it in the recycling bin later." When she could look at it without wanting to cry. Or hit something. Preferably Mike.

She held it together 'til she resumed her seat and copped a glimpse of Jules' sympathetic expression. Tears stung her eyes. She rounded her eyes and blinked them back. Wouldn't do to ruin her carefully applied mascara. Sheesh. Wanting to bawl your eyes out was pretty shitful when you had guests arriving any moment.

"It's not the end of the world," Jules ventured, her tone soft. "You could always pull out and forfeit the registration fee."

Ruby straightened from her slump. "No way. There's a real possibility I might come last, but I don't care. I'm gonna do this triathlon if it kills me. I'll be buggered if I'll pull out so everyone can say 'I told you so' behind my back. Don't suppose you would register, too, Jules? Just 'cause I'm determined to do this, doesn't mean I'm not scared witless. Having you with me for moral support would mean a lot. It's a women's triathlon for beginners, so it's not like we'll be mowed down by testosterone-driven guys stampeding for the finish line. We can take our time. No one'll care how we do."

Jules screwed up her nose. "Shit. Sorry, Rubes, but I can't wear a swimsuit in public for at least six weeks. And the chafing from sitting on a bike would probably be the end of me."

Huh? "Come again?"

"God, it's awful," Jules mourned. "My regular girl was crook last week, so I let a trainee wax my legs and bikini line. Big mistake. It was the kid's first time with a real customer and she didn't have her technique sussed. Now I have ingrown hairs everywhere. And I mean, everywhere."

She shifted, wriggling like she had a nest of ants in her pants. "Sorry 'bout this." She straightened her legs, lifted her butt off the couch cushion, and proceeded to itch her crotch through her silky trousers. "God, that feels sooo much better." Next, she yanked up her trouser legs and raked the skin of both shins with her fingernails.

Her legs were covered with inflamed red bumps. Ruby winced in sympathy. "You poor thing."

"You should see my bikini line—it's heaps worse," Jules said cheerfully. "Only way to fix the problem is to regularly exfoliate the hell out of everything, and wait for the hairs to grow long enough to wax again. Upside is, because of the chafing you-know-where, Alex and me are doing it—" she paused to stick out her tongue and pant "—doggy style. The orgasms are faaabulous."

Ruby snorted a laugh. She always knew where she stood with Jules. And Jules had certainly stood by Ruby over the years. Like the time Jules had decked a guy who'd dared make a crude joke about fat chicks. Ahhh. Such fond memories. God knows what she would do without her best friend. She wouldn't have a social life, that's for damn sure.

"Ooops, almost forgot. Happy birthday, Rubes!" Jules grabbed her handbag to rummage through its copious depths. "Got a little something for you in here somewhere. Somewhere.... Aha! Here." She tossed an oddly-shaped package into Ruby's lap.

Ruby tore off the tissue paper to reveal a bluish-white hunk of stone shaped like a knife blade. "Thanks, sweetie. It's, ah, very nice. Um, what is it, exactly?"

"It's a crystal. Aligns your chakras or some spiritual bullshit like that. An old dude in this weird little shop recommended it as the best one for you. And after reading your triathlon email, I figured you need all the spiritual help you can get."

Ruby stroked the striated surface of the crystal with a fingertip. Vaguely, she heard Jules nattering about exchanging the crystal if she didn't like it. Ruby must have shaken her head, or made some satisfactory verbal response, because Jules rose from the couch to fix herself another drink.

Hesitantly, Ruby lifted the crystal from the nest of tissue paper and weighed it in her palm. That was when she saw him. And, somehow, forged a mental link with him. He invaded her mind. She experienced everything he felt, his suffering, his anguish. And the tidal wave of horror and despair engulfed her....

THE SORCERER'S VOID had sucked him into a blackness so absolute that it defied any rational explanation. He was powerless, deprived of sensation, sight and sound, imprisoned in a vast expanse of nothingness. All that he was, all that he could be— his very essence—was held in stasis. Not so his mind, however. And his thoughts were dark and twisted things, born of despair and self-loathing.

He understood at some elemental level that this place-that-was-no-place was his punishment. He had feared this place as a child, and then laughingly discounted it as a grown man. 'Twas merely a tale to frighten naughty children. Everyone knew it did not truly exist.

Now he realized how wrong he had been, for here he was. Condemned to suffer forever in Halja—*Hell.*

CHAPTER TWO

SOME UNNAMED FORCE pried open Ruby's fingers. The visions cut off the instant the crystal dropped to the carpet. She was on her feet, yet she didn't remember moving from her seat. Her finger joints throbbed, and she massaged her hand. Even her jaw ached, as though she'd been grinding her teeth together.

What the hell just happened?

A flash of color and movement caught her eye, drawing her to the window. She pressed her nose to the glass and spotted an elderly man strolling down the footpath. His clothes were rather trendy for an old guy—jeans and boots with a white shirt, and a bright golden splash of silky material wrapped around his throat and tucked into the open neck of his shirt.

Auckland weather was mild this time of year, so the scarf struck Ruby as odd. She watched him until he rounded the corner and disappeared from view.

"Bugger! It's broken in half."

Jules' dismayed voice reclaimed Ruby's attention. She turned to see her friend kneeling on the floor. "Sorry, what's broken?" she asked, dazed.

"The crystal I bought you. You would have thought the bloody carpet might have cushioned it. What a piece of crap. God. I'm so sorry, Rubes. I'll buy you another one."

"It's fine, Jules, really." Ruby shook herself—physically and mentally—trying to slough off a lurking uneasiness. "My fault for being so clumsy. Must have gotten a bit heavy-handed with the alcohol in that Mai Tai mix. Anyway, it's all good. Because now I've got *two* crystals, and double the chakra power."

Jules grinned, admiring Ruby's faked positive take on the incident. "Trust you to look on the bright side."

"What kind of crystal is it, anyway?" Ruby asked. Not that she was curious or anything.

Jules re-wrapped the crystal halves in the torn tissue paper and placed the bundle on the phone table. "Beats me. The old guy from the shop called it *ky*-something-or-other. But I'm sure I'll remember after a few more of these cocktails." She waggled her empty glass at Ruby.

"What am I? Your slave? Get your own bloody cocktail."

"Some hostess you are."

The doorbell gargled like some unfortunate small creature dying a slow, painful death. Jules hunched her shoulders and made a face. "God. When are you going to get that damn bell fixed?"

"Never. I'm used to it now. It's quirky. Like me."

Someone jabbed the bell again, and Ruby could hear cat-calls and loud chatter from outside.

Jules pinned her with a sharp, too-knowing glance. "Are you ready?"

Ruby had no trouble deciphering that glance, or the sub-text of the question for that matter. Was she ready for the disbelief and unwanted advice from her friends regarding this outrageous goal she'd set herself? Was she ready to face their well-meaning platitudes that she was perfectly okay just the way she was? Was she ready?

The answer was, "Shit, no!" No way in heck was she ready. And, in retrospect, maybe it hadn't been such a good idea to email her entire contacts list about registering for the triath-lon. But Ruby would bluff her way through this evening—as she had so many others.

She smoothed her dress over her hips, threw back her

shoulders and stuck out her chest. "Fix me another cocktail, Jules. It's show time."

Jules saluted her with an empty glass. "You got it, babe."

Ruby sashayed over to the entranceway with an exaggerated wiggle of her bum that made Jules snort with laughter. She opened the door... and the effusive welcome she'd planned stuck in her throat. All she could do was stare, openmouthed, at the most beautiful man she'd ever seen in her life.

No exaggeration. Because Ruby was a connoisseur of the male form. Other women her age bought gossipy fashion mags. Ruby splurged her wages on her secret vice. Really classy magazines that celebrated the male form in all its masculine splendor. Ooh la la!

So how did this guy stack up with those airbrushed fantasy men?

Oh, he was right up there with the best of them. Really up there. Cover boy material—the best of the best.

He was tall—at least six foot. He'd scraped his blond hair back from his face and secured it with a tie. The severe style highlighted intense blue-green eyes the exact shade of an aquamarine necklace stuffed in the bottom of Ruby's jewelry box. With his high cheekbones and full lips, his face was saved from being too pretty by a nose that was a tad too long. It suited him, though. Made him appear regal. And the icing on the cake? A honed, muscular physique that appeared to Ruby's discerning eye to have been formed by years of actual physical exertion, rather than merely pumping weights at some fancy gym.

He was a man to sigh over. With a physique to die for. And Ruby was positive she wasn't merely imagining his amazing body because, courtesy of the unlaced leather vest he wore instead of a shirt, there was such an awful lot of him on display. In fact, she was having such a wonderful time drooling over all that burnished bare skin and those rippling muscles, she barely noticed the other guests hovering behind him. Or their grins.

Having completed her voyage of discovery, she dared raise her gaze to his face again. His gaze locked with hers. The rest of the world blurred, relegated to a tiny corner of Ruby's brain. Unimportant. Meaningless. There was only him and her. And God, the way he was looking at her—like she was some delectable treat he couldn't wait to eat.

A bray of high-pitched feminine laughter broke the spell.

Ruby blinked. And saw herself reflected in his eyes—a chubby, thirty-year-old woman, wearing a scarlet "look-at-me" dress and matching lipstick, who'd squeezed her feet into high-heeled sandals in a vain attempt to look sexy.

Sexy? Her?

Huh. Fat chance.

Haha. Good joke. And, as usual, the joke was on Ruby. As if any guy who looked like *he* did, would ever be interested in someone like her. Unless... he was being paid. Classic light bulb moment. Now it all made sense—his intent gaze, the way he made her feel special simply by focusing his attention on her.

It was all a careful act, designed to please. One of her friends had booked a stripper.

Ruby flushed, hyper-aware she was still staring. By now, everyone would surely have noticed her making goo-goo eyes at the gorgeous himbo. She could imagine what they were thinking. And for once she couldn't summon the smart repartee she relied on whenever she was embarrassed. She had nothing. So she dropped her gaze to stare fixedly at his chest.

Ah, what the hell. Might as well make the embarrassment count. Best get her thrills before he figured out he'd been paid to entertain *her*, and ran screaming into the night.

Her gaze drifted lower.

A figure detached herself from Mr. Dreamy's side. "Whose idea was the stripper, Ruby?"

"Uh, hiya, Caroline." Ruby tore her gaze from the stripper's fabulous abs to greet her workmate. "Um, I don't know whose idea it was."

Caroline clutched Ruby's shoulders and air-kissed her cheek left and right. "Whoever it was should be congratulated on their excellent choice in men," she purred. "Come on, Hunkalicious." She ushered him inside by the simple expedient of squeezing his bum.

He jumped like a scalded cat and Ruby caught a perplexed kind of frown before he smoothed his expression and sauntered inside.

"Nice present, Rubes!" someone called out amidst a chorus of "Happy Birthday!" greetings from those standing outside. Around a dozen of Ruby's friends filed in after Caroline, and clustered around the stripper, leaving the Birthday Girl hanging onto her doorjamb and gaping at their backs.

Rude!

"Hiya, Rubes." Jules' boyfriend, Alex, strode down the pathway toward her, brandishing a bouquet of orchids. "Happy birthday, babe." He kissed her cheek and presented the bouquet with a flourish.

"Thanks, Alex. They're beautiful." Her favorite flower. He'd remembered—he always did. He was a sweet guy. And Jules was one lucky, lucky girl.

Alex linked arms with Ruby and escorted her inside. "I gather *he's* the planned entertainment?"

"I guess so," Ruby said.

"Don't think it was Jules who organized him—better not have been, anyway." Alex uttered a low, rumbling mock growl that turned into a disgusted snort. "Babe, you better get over there before that estrogen-starved twig decides she wants your stripper all for herself. Look at her, groping his arse again. Jesus. Girl's got no class. That poor bugger's gonna have some mighty fine bruises tomorrow."

Ruby snickered at the twig reference. Alex preferred his women "to look like real women"—doubtless why he adored

Jules' curves. And got a pained look in his eye whenever he was forced to socialize with Caroline. He'd once commented that having sex with a scrawny thing like her would be like screwing a bag of bones. *Eeeuw.*

"I'm glad you're here." Ruby wrapped her arm around his waist to give him a quick side-hug.

He planted an affectionate kiss atop her head. "Wouldn't have missed it for the world."

Something prompted Ruby to glance up and she surprised Mr. Dreamy glaring at her and Alex. His eyes suddenly seemed more green than blue—and a pissed-off kind of green into the bargain.

A little jealous, perhaps? Typical. The stripper someone had chosen for her was *gay*. That anonymous "someone" had a real warped sense of humor.

Alex stiffened. Ruby guessed he'd also spotted the green-eyed monster rearing its ugly head. Hmm. Might be a good idea to suggest Alex go find Jules before Mr. Dreamy got the wrong idea and tried to chat him up.

"Will you look at that?" Alex murmured. "A man after my own heart."

"What do you mean?"

"Nothing."

Liar. Ruby scanned Alex's face for clues. He sported one of those insufferably self-satisfied expressions—the kind that screamed he knew something important, but he was going to make her work it out herself. For her own good, of course.

Men.

Cocktail in hand, Jules sidled over to join them. "Hey, babe." She kissed Alex on the mouth, taking her time about it. When she came up for air she said, "What were you looking so smug about?"

He wound an arm about her hips and squeezed her bum, eliciting a squeak. "My secret."

"C'mon, Alex," Jules wheedled. "'Fess up."

"Nope."

"Awww, Aleeex!" She pursed her lips in a cutesy pout.

He snickered. "You'll have to do better than that, babe."

The grin Jules hit him with was pure evil. "Just you wait 'til tonight. You'll be sor-ry!" Her threat was issued in a horror-movie-worthy singsong tone.

"Bring it on," Alex drawled.

Jules grabbed his arm and shoved it up behind his back. "Tell me."

"Gee. Ouch. Is that all you got?"

She increased the pressure.

"All right already. Geez. I was smugly contemplating that old saying about beauty being more than skin deep."

"Huh?" Jules released him to glance at Ruby in askance.

Ruby shrugged. "Sorry. Clueless."

Alex heaved a longsuffering sigh and changed the subject. "Honey, do you know who organized the stripper for Rubes?"

Jules considered said stripper thoughtfully. "No idea. He's pretty hot though, huh?"

"Don't ask me. I don't swing that way." Alex scratched his chin. "Gotta be his first private do, I reckon."

"What makes you say that?" Ruby asked.

"He doesn't know what to do with himself. Hasn't even brought along his own music. Must be an amateur. Hey, Rubes, you should get over there before the girls talk him into a Full Monty."

Ruby flushed at the mere thought of Mr. Dreamy shucking his leather pants along with his vest. Gay or not, he was off-the-charts hot.

"Go on, Rubes. Let him know *you're* the Birthday Girl!" Alex gave her a push.

Ruby stumbled forward, teetering on her higher than usual heels. Please God, she didn't trip and end up sprawled on the floor, crowned with a mashed bouquet of orchids.

Like magic, the gaggle of women clustered around her

stripper parted and he was there, reaching out to steady her with a hand clasped about her forearm.

Her flush deepened and she fought the urge to fan her cheeks with the bunch of orchids. "Uh, thanks. I'm, uh, the Birthday Girl. Is there anything you need before you, um, start?"

His lips curved upward for a split second before his brow knit into an impressive frown. "This is *your* celebration?"

"Yep. My, uh, thirtieth birthday." She waved a limp hand at the guests. "Hence the flowers and guests and stuff."

He winced, and released her arm. "As the guest of honor, perhaps you would be so kind as to request these brazen females refrain from pinching my arse." His perfect white teeth flashed in a sardonic grin. "I find myself ill prepared for such a mob."

Uh oh. An unhappy stripper. This wasn't going at all well. Still, despite his obvious unhappiness, his voice rolled over Ruby like liquid silk and it took a few moments before she could formulate any sort of coherent speech. "Um, right. Okay. Hands off, you lot!" She scowled at the bunch of smirking women. "You, especially, Caroline. Quit bruising the goods. It's rude."

Caroline made a face and stuck out her tongue. "Party pooper. When's this show getting on the road? I'm dying for him to get his gear off." She giggled as she swigged the cocktail she'd somehow managed to grab in between grabbing the stripper's bum. Caroline always did know how to look after number one.

"Your wish is my command." Ruby shoved her flowers at Caroline, and bared her teeth in a weak attempt at a smile. "Be a sweetie and put these in a vase? And I'll see what I can do about getting the ball rolling, 'kay? Thanks!"

Caroline abruptly seemed to recall it was Ruby's birthday and guests were supposed to be nice to the Birthday Girl. She shut her mouth with a snap and flounced off.

"Cocktail table is over yonder." Ruby shooed the rest of the hovering women away. "A bit of privacy, please?"

They grumbled but obeyed. Thank goodness.

"Sorry 'bout that," Ruby said to Mr. Dreamy. "Caroline comes on a bit strong when she drinks. It's her lack of, uh, *padding*. There's nothing to soak up the alcohol and prevent it from going straight to her head. She doesn't mean to be offensive. And she wouldn't pinch any man's bum. I mean, he'd have to be really hot—like you. If you weren't, like, amazingly good-looking, even if she were drunk as a skunk she'd not give you a second glance."

Oh, God. She was babbling. "So it's a compliment, really," she finished lamely, wishing the lounge floor would open up and swallow her whole. "So, um, do you need some music or anything before you start the, uh, show?"

"Show?" That cute little crinkle appeared between his brows again.

Ruby's brain kicked up a gear. "You *are* the stripper, right?" Crap. What if he was attached to one of her male guests and she'd totally gotten the wrong idea?

She mentally ran through the guest list to try and figure out who he might be partnered with. Nope. She had nothing. Besides, surely only a stripper would wear that sort of get-up in public. She was panicking for nothing. Well, not nothing, exactly. She was panicking because of him. He unsettled her. And the thought of him shucking his clothes.... Yikes. A pity fans had gone out of fashion because she could sure do with one to flutter and hide behind right now.

Ruby didn't allow herself to fall desperately in lust with men anymore. That would be begging for disappointment. But this man.... The perfect planes of his face, the incredible physique. He might be gay, and therefore unobtainable, but he'd stepped right out of her fantasies, and she wanted to enjoy this particular fantasy a little while longer. Hell, what was wrong with that? It was her birthday, after all.

"I am a warrior," he said, his tone ringing with unmistakable pride.

She smiled. "The Warrior Stripper. Yeah, well you certainly look the part. Great outfit, by the way. Don't have a clue how you manage the pants, though. Do they have strips of Velcro at the sides or something?"

He blinked, staring at her like she'd morphed into some alien creature.

She took pity on him. "Look. Here's the deal. If you're not comfortable taking off your clothes and prancing 'round half naked to entertain a bunch of drooling women, I understand. Believe me, I get it. You don't have to do this if it's freaking you out. You can leave—no hard feelings, okay?"

His eyes widened and his beautiful lips parted.

Friggin' fantastic. She was about to be lumbered with paying off an inexperienced gay stripper suffering an attack of the shys. She forced a smile. "If you haven't been paid, I'll—"

"You wish me to remove my clothes and dance for these people?"

Ouch. When he said it like *that* it sounded awfully sleazy. Ruby cooled her burning cheeks with the palms of her hands. "I guess. That's sort of the idea, anyway. Um, yes?"

"And I will receive a stipend to do this?"

Huh? *Stipend*? Ruby's stomach did the whole sinking sensation thing. Fab-u-bloody-lous. On top of everything, she had to score the foreign import with no real clue what he'd gotten himself in for. What the hell had she done to deserve this?

She inhaled a deep breath and silently counted to five. "That's generally how it works. Or so I'm told. But if you don't want to, that's cool."

She patted his arm, hoping to project reassurance. And hoping she didn't succumb to the temptation of squeezing his muscled biceps and whimpering. "I won't force you to do something you're uncomfortable about. But if you don't want to strip, I'll have to ask you to go. I'm sorry, but the natives are getting restless and if you stick around much longer they might take matters into their own hands." She jerked her chin toward the bunch of women gathered by the drinks table, all whispering and staring avidly in his direction.

Mr. Dreamy's gaze drifted over her guests. Around forty people had arrived, and were either squeezed into Ruby's kitchen, living room and dining area, or milling around outside on the lawn. Most of her guests were women she knew from work or the frequent and varied night-school classes she'd taken over the years. But there were a few men, too—boyfriends and husbands who hadn't been quick enough with an excuse to beg off this party, and got stuck with helping Ruby celebrate her birthday.

"And the men?" Mr. Dreamy asked. "Do they, too, enjoy the spectacle of a naked man dancing?"

How to say this without giving offence? "Well, I think most of the guys here tonight would actually prefer a *female* stripper."

"What about you, Birthday Girl? Do you prefer a female stripper? Or would you prefer me?"

Geez. Stupid question, much? Of course she preferred him over some pneumatic-breasted female stripper. To be honest, flamboyant public displays weren't usually Ruby's style. She preferred to confine her perving to the men in the pages of her magazines. But she wasn't about to miss the chance of a live performance from this Adonis-like male. God only knew what Mr. Dreamy thought of her. And it was just as well he couldn't read her mind. The poor guy would be shocked out of his socks… if he was wearing any with those boots.

He'd cocked his head, obviously still awaiting a response. Uh…. "I'm a girl," she blurted. "At least I was last time I looked. And I happen to like men. So if I'm going to watch anyone take off their clothes, of course I'd prefer it was a man." *And of course I'd prefer a man who looked like you and wasn't* gay. *But hey, beggars can't be choosers.*

His gaze turned speculative, like he was weighing his options. And then the quality of that gaze morphed to something so obviously approving that it brought another wave of heat flooding to her cheeks.

"There is no question that you are indeed female," he said, and pivoted on his heel.

"Hang on." She grabbed his arm. "What're you planning on doing exactly?"

He smiled down at her. A lazy, self-satisfied, supremely confident smile that made her toes curl. "I am going to entertain you."

He was actually going to do it—take his clothes off.

In her lounge.

To *entertain* her.

Ruby's knees turned to putty.

KYAN GRINNED. Going by the dazed expression on this female's face, her heightened color and the hitching of her breath, she was so enamored by the prospect of him removing his clothes she was on the verge of swooning. Perhaps she had never seen an unclothed male before. He opened his mouth to ask, only to shut it with a snap before he could inadvertently give offence.

Sorcery had ensnared him in his namesake crystal, and doubtless sorcery was to blame for thrusting him into a world so alien, so unlike any other world he'd experienced, it made him question his ability to discern friend from foe. But amid the riot of strangeness clamoring at his senses, Kyan's innate sense of self-preservation was still very much intact.

The women he'd encountered at this gathering thus far were bold creatures. They looked him directly in the eye when they fondled him, and made it abundantly clear they found him attractive. Their menfolk appeared unconcerned by this behavior, but Kyan, for all his brash confidence when it came to pursuit of women, was not foolhardy enough to take what these females so blatantly offered. He possessed neither sword nor weapon of any kind. The gods only knew what alien weapons might be brought to bear on him if he crossed some line and gave mortal offence. The odds that he would prevail against so many were not in his favor.

His gods had not entirely forsaken him, however. 'Twas obvious as a sand-lizard's ruby-red eye that this gathering he'd been transported to was a matter of some import for this woman in the short red gown, who'd opened the door, taken one look at him, and melted into a puddle of desire. She was the guest of honor, the Birthday Girl. It behooved Kyan to go along with her request and curry her favor. And, in truth, it would be no hardship to entertain her by displaying himself before all these people. He'd done far worse on a drunken dare.

His troop's commander, Wulf, had once said, "If it possesses something resembling womanly parts, Kyan will bed it." That wasn't entirely true. Kyan couldn't abide females who neglected to bathe regularly, or those with rotten teeth, or pustule-ridden faces. Nor ones with limbs like twigs, such as the scrawny female who had thrown herself at him the instant she laid eyes on him. Other than that, Kyan had no particular preference when it came to women. Short or tall, slim or robust, dark or fair, it was of no consequence. Given the chance, he would dally with any comely female.

And *this* woman, the Birthday Girl, most certainly fit his criteria. She was a sweet little dumpling, all soft womanly curves displayed in a sensual package that made him long to sample the plentiful cleavage on display.

The prospect of coin, too, was a significant factor in his decision to act the entertainer. Coin would give him the means to purchase clothing more suited to this realm, so that he could blend in. His gaze followed the path of her hand as it crept up to rest over her heart. And he wondered if her skin would feel as soft as it looked. With an effort he refocused his thoughts.

"Am I to presume my decision pleases you then, Birthday Girl?"

"Well, duh," the Birthday Girl said. "You're a freaking Adonis. And I'm only human. Of *course* the thought of you ripping off your clothes pleases me." She blushed to the roots of her hair. "Uh, that kind of came out wrong. Uh, whatever you want to do is fine with me."

She blinked and dropped her gaze to the floor. When she next spoke it was the barest whisper and he almost missed her words. "Like have your wicked way with me, right now, right here on the floor in front of everyone—carpet burns be damned. God. It's such a crying shame you're gay."

Kyan understood enough of her declaration to find it flattering. His grin widened.

Sensing his regard, her gaze darted to his and she clapped both hands over her mouth. "Omigod. Did I say that aloud?"

"Not exactly. But I have exceptional hearing."

She groaned, and her fair complexion proclaimed her embarrassment with splotches of crimson.

Hunger gnawed, and he absently rubbed his belly. The gesture drew her gaze down his body... and her naked wanting licked him. His cock hardened. And then it was his turn to suffer the heat of embarrassment. Gods. Even he balked at removing his clothes and displaying himself to strangers in this condition.

His gaze darted glanced about the room and lit on the food-laden table. He couldn't help himself, he groaned aloud.

"Whoa," the Birthday Girl said. "That expression on your face is exactly like mine every time I pass a Baker's Delight store."

Before he could decipher her meaning, his stomach growled. Loudly.

She giggled. "You're pretty hungry, huh?"

He dragged his gaze from the table and fixed it on her face. "I cannot remember the last time I ate," he said, with unaccustomed bald-faced honesty.

Her forehead creased in sympathy. "Help yourself—there's plenty of food."

"Thank you."

"No, thank *you*."

There was a tiny catch in her voice that gave him pause when he would have headed straight for the food. "For what?" he asked. "I have done nothing to deserve your thanks."

"For not running screaming into the night the instant I introduced myself as the Birthday Girl. For not sneering at me, or trying to put me down because—" She ducked her head, hiding her expression.

"Because?"

"Because of the way I look." Again, it was barely a whisper.

Her vulnerability shocked him. Did she truly believe herself unattractive?

Each society he had encountered had differing ideas about what constituted an attractive female form. Kyan had no clue what *this* world's ideal female might conceivably be, but for a man not to find her attractive he would have to be blind. Or a neutered eunuch.

He swept his gaze over the room, taking note of all the female attendees. Most were younger women. All were on the slim side, and a few were what he would term unhealthily underweight.

Ah. His little chick fretted over her ripe, womanly body. A pity. In his world, she would have been a prize, indeed. He had seen women far more plump than she display themselves on the Choosing Block, and whip the bidders into a frenzy with their unabashed femininity.

He tipped her chin with his forefinger, forcing her to meet his gaze. And he paid homage to her rouge-glossed lips with a gentle kiss.

The instant he touched his lips to hers, his stones tightened and his cock swelled. Kyan had no idea how long he'd been consigned to the void, but it seemed as though countless eternities had passed since he'd enjoyed a woman, buried his face in fragrant hair and his cock in a warm, willing body. And before he could do something he would regret, before he could drag her somewhere private and use her to assuage the hunger that burned through him, he released her.

He would fill his belly with food. Then at least one of his hungers would be fed. And with a full belly, perhaps his current situation would begin to make sense. Because right now, when he should have been gathering information about how he'd escaped the crystal sorcerer's spell, taking steps to ensure he was not be-spelled again, and, most importantly, discovering how to get back to his homeland, all he could think about was the woman standing before him, gazing at him with such naked yearning that his heart ached.

Kyan had been the object of many a young girl's desires since attaining his majority. If a girl's looks pleased him, and she was available and willing, he took her. And when he tired of her, he moved on with nary a backward glance. Feminine pouts and pleas affected him not in the slightest.

This woman?

Something told him he might not be permitted to forget her so easily if he took her to his bed.

"I like the way you look," he murmured. "I like the way you look very much indeed." He had not meant to say the words aloud, but he could not be sorry that he had, for his reward was a tremulous smile that filled the emptiness in his soul.

OMG. HAPPY BIRTHDAY, Ruby! Mr. Dreamy was sooo *not* gay. Be still her wildly beating heart. Ohhh, that voice—pure liquid sensuality. He made even the most mundane statements sound sexy. And ohhh, those lips….

What was she supposed to be doing again? Oh, yeah. Getting the strip show underway.

Ruby gave herself a mental smack upside the head and

pulled herself together. The kiss meant nothing. Neither did the compliment. He was simply being kind—laying on the charm real thick to keep the client happy. "If you need music to dance to, talk to that guy over there," she told Mr. Dreamy. "He'll sort it for you." She pointed to Alex, who'd slung his arm around Jules' shoulder and was nibbling her neck while she pretended to fend him off.

Lucky Jules…. Ruby sighed, long and loud and heartfelt.

Mr. Dreamy left her to her pathetic little fantasies and sauntered off to sample the food. Ruby ogled the progress of his tight, leather-clad backside, and sighed again.

Caroline shimmied over to stand next to Ruby and do some ogling of her own. "So?" she demanded. "Is he going to strip now, or what?"

"I don't want him passing out from low blood-sugar or something, so he's going to have something to eat and then get his gear off. That okay with you, Caroline?"

Caroline clapped her hands and performed a sinuous little wiggle of delight. "Goody!"

"Yes. Goody."

"What's up, Ruby-doo?" Caroline giggled inanely. "You don't sound too pleased. Doesn't he, like, do it for you, or something? I thought you had a thing for blonds."

"Oh, he's certainly good-looking enough." And he really, really "did it" for her, all right But…. "He seems pretty new to this stripping business. Might even be his first time."

Caroline's giggle morphed to a snigger. Apparently she didn't have an empathetic bone in her body. "So? He's gotta lose his cherry sometime. Might as well be tonight so we get to enjoy the show."

It was unlike Caroline to be so crude. Ruby examined her face, noting her friend's slightly glazed eyes and the hectic color spotting her cheeks. Uh oh. "You okay, Caroline? Maybe you should ease up on the cocktails for a bit. I've got some juice in the fridge."

Caroline waved her glass carelessly in Ruby's direction. The luridly blue liquid contents slopped over her hand. She giggled again as she slurped it from her wrist. "I'm perfectly fine," she said, and, you guessed it, giggled.

"Of course you are. Why don't you sit down over here." Ruby relieved Caroline of the glass before the contents ended up all over the carpet, and steered her toward a stool. "I'll get you something else to drink."

Caroline plopped down atop the stool and stuck both legs out in an inelegant sprawl. "'Kay. So long as it's nice and full of alcohol."

"Right. I'll grab you some canapés, too." Maybe a whole platter, to soak up the alcohol.

"Those li'l fishy ones? With the creamy stuff, and the greeny squishy salty thingies?"

"Salmon with cream cheese and capers. No problem." Turning on her heel, Ruby headed for the fridge on her errand of mercy—so-called since it would be a freaking mercy if Caroline didn't wake up without the mother of all hangovers tomorrow.

She'd finished pouring a jumbo-sized tumbler of juice when the stereo boomed out. Above the racket she could make out yells and catcalls. And then the excited chatter of female voices escalated. Her stripper must be about to do his stuff. Doubtless Mr. Dreamy was even now preparing to divest himself of his leather pants and vest, and prance half-naked around her lounge while shaking his groove thang to the music.

Ruby's pulse rate spiked. Did she want to stand by and watch her friends drool over this incredible-looking guy as he got his kit off?

Did she want to have to smile like it meant nothing when Mr. Dreamy hooked up with one of the many attractive women here tonight and went home with her?

The sad fact was that even though he'd kissed *her*, it was

merely because he was obliged to be kind to the Birthday Girl. Ruby understood that. But she couldn't help wanting more.

Dammit. Quit being so needy Ruby. You're not angling for a Happy Ever After. You merely want to see him strip.

She'd just turned thirty. She had no boyfriend. She hadn't had sex in what felt like forever. And he was Mr. Dreamy—the man of her dreams, everything she'd ever fantasized about in the flesh. So, by crikey, she was going to watch him take off his clothes, and enjoy every hot second of the peepshow. No one would have to know that while she watched him, she was pretending they were the only two people in the room. And that maybe, just maybe, he might see past the big butt, flabby tummy and dimpled thighs, and want to get to know her better.

As Ruby made her way back into the lounge she heard Lani call out, "What's your name, dearie?" to the "entertainment".

Lani's grin was huge. Her eyes sparkled with anticipation. Lani obviously had no qualms about watching handsome young men take off their clothes. And Ruby thanked heavens for the distraction, otherwise Lani might well be publicly quizzing her about that fire-engine-red g-string she *wasn't* wearing right now. She shuddered. Didn't bear thinking about.

"I am Kyan." Mr. Dreamy's deep, honeyed voice cut through the noise to resound in Ruby's head as clearly as though he stood right beside her.

Kyan. Mmm. The name was as exotic as the man himself.

A bunch of female guests started up a chant. "Ky-an! Ky-an! Ky-an!"

Wow. Ten points for originality. *Not.*

While people backed up to give him some room, Ruby grabbed the opportunity to elbow her way to a prime viewing spot behind the couch Alex and Jules had scored.

Jules craned her neck to grin up at Ruby. "Come and sit here, Birthday Girl." She shuffled over to make room on the couch but before Ruby could move, Caroline appeared from nowhere and plonked her butt down next to Jules.

"Just enough room for a skinny one," Caroline said, blinking at Jules and blithely ignoring her fierce scowl. "Yay for me."

Ruby tapped Jules on the shoulder to snag her attention. *She's pissed!* she mouthed and mimed downing a drink.

Jules puffed out a sharp breath laced with disgust. "Bloody typical."

"Typical what?" Caroline wanted to know.

Jules opened her mouth, doubtless to deliver some scathing set-down, and Ruby quickly intervened. She wouldn't be able to enjoy her unexpected birthday gift to the full if Jules and Caroline started bickering. "Here, Caroline. Try this." She handed over the juice.

Caroline raised the glass to her lips, caught sight of Kyan, and tipped juice down her front.

Great. Just freaking great. "I'll go find a paper towel," Ruby said, while Jules made a grab for Caroline's glass before she upended the entire contents in her lap. Or over Jules, for that matter.

"Don't bother, Rubes," Alex said. "She's pissed as a chook—guarantee she won't notice either way. Stay here or you'll miss the fun—that's an order, by the way."

"Yes, ma'am."

Alex rolled his eyes. "Gee, Ruby. Don't you want to watch the big strong man take off all his clothes?"

"Duh. What do you think?"

"Ssshh!" Jules elbowed Alex in the ribs. "He's starting his routine."

Ruby's gaze shot to the "he" in question.

Kyan's routine wasn't much of a routine. It consisted of flexing his arm muscles for a bit, then shucking his leather vest and treating everyone to an uninterrupted view of his washboard abs. Ruby didn't mind. It turned out he could ripple them in *the* most amazing ways.

He gyrated his hips a couple of times. Mmmm. That was more like it.

His hands went to the fly of his trousers. Ruby sucked in a breath and held it while her body temperature flashed hot-cold-hot. She wished she'd thought to fix herself another drink so she could cool her face with a chilled glass.

He unlaced his fly.

Hoh boy. She distracted herself by wondering how in the hell he was getting out of those tight leather pants. Talk about a mystery. She still couldn't see any sign of lacing, Velcro, or convenient zips down the outside legs. Should be extremely interesting, to say the least.

Kyan collapsed gracefully to the carpet and stretched out on his back, cupping his hands behind his head—a picture of nonchalance. He resembled a fallen angel, lying there, waiting for some innocent to happen by and be tempted into sin.

In the sudden hush, he said, "Who would like to assist me with my boots and pants?"

Oh. Okay. *That* was how.

Caroline shoved her orange juice at Jules and launched herself from the couch. She wasn't the only one. Ruby had never seen anything like it. Opposing rugby teams engaged in an all-out stoush showed more restraint than the horde of women who accepted Kyan's invitation. They were on him in a matter of seconds. Bent eagerly over him, kneeling beside him—astride him, too.

Ruby glimpsed the occasional flash of battered black leather and tanned skin amidst a sea of bobbing heads, slightly parted lipsticked mouths, and grasping hands. Damned if the scene didn't look mildly obscene—like a seething mass of succubae feeding on their male victim. And each delighted peal of feminine laughter made Ruby want to grind her teeth and pull someone's hair.

When one of the women moved, Ruby caught a clear glimpse of Kyan's face. His expression showed faint amusement, as though these women were acting exactly as he'd foreseen. He didn't help or hinder his admirers as they struggled to tug off his pants, which were proving more difficult to remove than his boots. He didn't single out any of the women for special attention. He lay there, perfectly relaxed, staring at the ceiling as they stripped him.

Caroline was bold enough to press a kiss to his stomach, and even made a production out of swirling her tongue around his navel. But Kyan didn't so much as bat an eyelid at her provocative caress. Ruby decided his lack of reaction stemmed from the fact he was accustomed to female adoration—a man who was all looks and no substance, who got by on his looks alone, and only had to crook a finger to be swarmed by willing females.

A glimmer of guilt pricked her. Could he really be that shallow?

Perhaps she was being unfair. Ruby, of all people, knew not to judge a book by its cover. People had been judging her since the day the Plunket nurse had kindly informed her mother that baby Ruby was "a wee bit too bonny". In other words, well above the average weight centile for her age.

She nibbled her lower lip and wondered who Kyan truly was behind that handsome face and perfect body. Not that she'd ever get the chance to find out. She was damn sure the only way she would end up in a compromising position with a man as good-looking as Kyan would be if he were roaring drunk.

And hadn't had sex in a year.

And she was the only woman available. Like, if they were stranded a deserted island with no chance of rescue.

Sighing, she decided she might as well take advantage of Caroline's preoccupation and swipe her seat on the couch.

As Ruby got comfortable, Jules nudged her. "What do you reckon, Rubes? Pretty hot?"

"Hot," she agreed.

"If you like that kind of over-developed physique," Alex said. "And his routine's a bit basic. Not much dancing involved. Even I could do that. Not that I'd want to, of course."

"Aw, don't be jealous, darling," Jules cooed. "I'll take you over him any day of the week." She considered Kyan—or what she could see of him—through half-closed eyes. "Something's missing. He's—"

"Incomplete?" Alex said.

"Maybe. Reminds me of an artificial thing created to be the perfect man. I feel sorry for him."

"Harsh," Alex said. "Maybe he needs to find the right woman. Someone to humanize him a bit."

"Mmmm." Jules kissed her boyfriend on the cheek. "I knew there was a really sensitive guy somewhere under all the bull-shit."

"Right back at ya, babe." Alex draped an arm around her and she snuggled into his side.

Ruby sighed again. Jules and Alex were perfect for each other.

Kyan's willing posse had at last managed to peel off his trousers. The woman who'd scored the jackpot waved his pants around her head like a lasso before draping her trophy about her neck. From the way she kept stroking her palms over the leather, Ruby reckoned Kyan would be bloody lucky to get them back.

A couple of the women hauled him to his feet. He stood there, girls hanging off both arms, his only remaining clothing a pair of short pants with a drawstring waist. The underwear looked like it might be made of silk. The cloth was thin and the fit was snug. It sure didn't hide much.

Ruby's mouth went dry. Wow. Mr. Dreamy was completely magnificent….

And he knew it.

The thunderous, insistent beat of the music overwhelmed the appreciative yells from Ruby's guests. The booming bass beat resounded so strongly in her belly that she felt mildly queasy. Her head pounded. When she closed her eyes she saw tiny sparks, soaring and diving in a frenetic dance.

Thankfully, someone turned the music down. And awareness tingled up Ruby's spine. She slowly peeled open her eyelids and her gaze fixed on Kyan, who now stood directly in front of her, denuded of women save for Caroline clinging leechlike to his arm.

"Do you like what you see, Birthday Girl?" he said.

"Yes. Of course. Very nice. Thanks heaps." Flustered, Ruby scrambled to her feet and extended a hand. Instead of shaking it, as she'd expected, he turned her hand and planted a kiss on her palm.

Whoa. Weak knees. Puckered nipples. Tingling in unmentionable lower regions. Racing heart—talk about textbook reactions.

When he released her hand, Ruby sat down again. Rather quickly. Before she collapsed in a large puddle of neediness and embarrassed herself further.

Caroline reattached herself to Kyan the instant he straightened. She nuzzled his neck and gave him the blatant come-on by sticking her tongue in his ear. He ignored her, his gaze intent on Ruby. "What is your name?" he asked.

Points to him for not being easily distracted. "I'm Ruby."

He cocked his head to one side as he stared down at her. A frown furrowed his brow. "Ruby. That does not... sound right."

Stung, she shot one right back at him. "Well 'Kyan' is pretty funny, too, if you ask me. Is it short for something?"

"Of course. 'Tis short for Kyanite. And yours?"

"Well, not that it's any of your business, but the name on my birth certificate is Garnet Ruby Roberts." Despite herself she snorted. Talk about being disadvantaged at birth. Small wonder she'd turned out the way she had. With a screwball name like that she hadn't stood a chance.

"But I can't abide Garnet for a first name," she said, provoked—as always—to explain. "So I go by Ruby—the lesser of the two evils, so to speak." Not that her brilliant decision to change her name when she'd been younger had magically stopped the teasing, as she'd desperately hoped. Her gaze dropped to her toes as she shoved away the painful memories.

Kyan shifted, drawing Ruby's attention again. She glanced up to gauge the expression on his face. And then wished she hadn't. She wriggled beneath his intense stare but couldn't look away. He was too compelling. And, as she stared at him, her eyes widened at the shadows flitting across his face, the empathy that shone in his eyes—as though he knew exactly what she'd been thinking and understood it on some deep personal level.

Nah. Surely not. What on earth would a demigod like Kyan have been teased about? She would bet anything he'd been a really gorgeous little boy.

Discomfited, she sought to lighten the mood with more chatter. "Not that Ruby's much better than Garnet. But since my mum's favorite color is red, I suppose I should consider myself lucky she didn't call me Scarlet Crimson, or some other nightmarish combination."

"Like… like… Cherry Tomato!" Caroline laughed so hard at her own wit she released Kyan's arm, overbalanced, and ended sprawled across Alex's lap.

"Yours, I believe, Kyan?" Alex said, leaning back with his hands in the air as Jules shoved the still giggling Caroline off him.

To Ruby's surprise, Kyan completely ignored Alex's kind offer. "I am pleased to meet you, Garnet—" He grimaced in pain. "Ruby Roberts," he finished with a ragged whisper.

"Nice to meet you, too, Kyanite," Ruby said.

Kyan clutched his head, groaned, and then keeled over as if he'd been poleaxed.

Before Ruby had time to wonder what had happened to

him, a sharp pain bloomed in her skull....
    And everything went dark.

CHAPTER THREE

RUBY SLIT ONE eyelid and promptly shut it again. Uhhh. She felt like death warmed over. She gave it a couple of minutes and dared stretch her arms over her head. *Yeow.* Bad move. Muscles she hadn't known existed begged for mercy. The couch wasn't the most comfortable piece of furniture to snooze on but she didn't remember it being *this* bad.

Hang on. The couch? Why the heck had she been sleeping on the couch? There'd better bloody not be anyone sleeping in her *bed* or there was sooo gonna be trouble. She tossed aside the blanket that someone had tucked around her, and lurched to her feet.

"Jeeeeesus!" She moaned, clutching her head. One could be forgiven for thinking she'd drunk two whole *jugs* of cocktail mix instead of only two glasses or so. As she staggered across the room, she sent a prayer of thanks to the kind soul who had removed her shoes. If she'd had the misfortune to be wearing high heels right now, she'd wouldn't have managed more than a couple of steps without doing a face-plant.

Her bedroom door was shut. She flung it open with a little more force than strictly necessary, and winced when it kissed the wall. A shaft of bright sunlight pierced a gap in the curtains. Typically, it headed unerringly for her eyes.

A few whimpers later, she plucked up the courage to peel open her eyelids and try again. And when her hazy vision finally settled down, she focused on her bed. Or to be precise, the very large lump in her bed that was currently emitting snoring noises fit to wake the dead.

Great. One of her guests hadn't gone home last night and—

Guests.

Her birthday party.

Omigod. The *stripper*!

Ruby forced her brain to logical thought. The stripper had kissed her. Then he'd stripped. And she'd... she'd....

Obviously, she'd passed out at her own party. In front of all her guests.

Ah, crap. She was never going to live it down. Never. Her friends and workmates were going to dine out on this for the next decade. Her life was over—not that it'd been that shit hot to begin with.

She checked the lump again. It hadn't moved. Which meant she would have to exert herself to wake it up and request that it leave. Fabulous. It'd better not expect breakfast before it left, either, 'cause right now she was so *not* in the mood for being polite to uninvited guests.

She stomped across the room to stand beside the bed—all the better to give the unwelcome lump some superlative evils. From the size of the lump, and the deep timbre of the snoring, it was male. He'd pulled the duvet over his head until only a shock of dark hair could be seen.

Ruby yanked back the cover and bit back a shocked gasp.

Mike!

At some stage last night, her brother had turned up to join her birthday celebration. Talk about bad timing. With the Birthday Girl inconveniently KOed on the couch, Mike would have missed any actual partying because everyone would have taken off not long after Ruby crashed. That was the polite thing to do—make tracks when the guest of honor passed out. Then again, knowing her friends, they might well have shrugged and partied on until the copious amounts of booze

Ruby had provided ran out.

Her shoulders slumped. The carnage in her kitchen, lounge and dining area was bound to be dire.

She considered waking Mike so he could help with the cleanup, but decided to do the sisterly thing and let him sleep. He'd probably caught the late flight from Christchurch, and then had a forty-five minute drive from the airport to her North Shore home. He'd be knackered. When he woke, *then* she'd decide whether she was thrilled to see him or not speaking to him ever again.

Ruby headed for her wardrobe and confronted her panda eyes and lipstick-chapped mouth in the full-length mirror. Yikes. Not pretty. She grabbed her dressing gown from the wardrobe and left Mike to his beauty sleep.

In the bathroom, she downed two paracetamol tablets for her pounding head, cleansed off the smeared remains of her makeup, and brushed her teeth. Better. And once she'd wallowed under a hot shower for a while, and the painkillers had kicked in, she might even feel human.

The bathroom had a shower over the bathtub, but its saving grace was a decent-sized tub, long enough for Ruby to lie full-length and have a good soak when she felt the need for some pampering.

The shower curtain was already pulled around the bath. Strange. She never left it like that. She reached behind the curtain and turned the shower mixer on full blast—

And almost jumped out of her skin when someone let rip with an earsplitting bellow.

Omigod. This couldn't be happening. Ruby's heart pounded, and her hand shook as she reached out to yank back the curtain. Primed by years of watching horror movies with her brother, she loosed a shriek even before her brain registered what she was seeing.

The guy who'd dossed down in her bathtub overnight struggled to his feet and yelled, too. Not that Ruby could blame him. Being woken by a steaming hot face-full of water must have been more than a bit shocking.

They both stood there, goggling at each other like idiots, chests heaving as they sucked in air.

The bathroom door crashed open.

Ruby shrieked again, her racing pulse echoing like thunder in her ears. Who—?

Her brother crouched in the doorway, clad only in black satin boxers, and waving Ruby's old cricket bat like he meant business. His gaze skittered wildly about the room as he prepared to wallop the intruder who had scared the bejesus out of his sister.

The "intruder", in all his almost-as-good-as-naked glory, dripped water like a half-drowned cat. The pillow and duvet that he'd slept on in the bath were sodden.

Ruby thanked all the stars above that she hadn't taken off her dress before she'd yanked open the shower curtain. That would have been far more humiliating than mistaking Kyanite for some psycho killer.

"Sorry. Didn't realize it was only your stripper." Mike yawned and rubbed the sleep from his eyes. "Some birthday present, Rubes."

"Beats the one you gave me," she muttered, quickly averting her gaze when her brother stretched and scratched his unmentionables.

"What'd you say?" Mike asked.

"Nothing." Ruby shut off the shower mixer. "What are you still doing here, Kyanite?"

He blinked water from his eyes. "Kyanite is my true name, but I would prefer you call me *Kyan*. And I do not know how I came to be here in this... this...." He waved a hand at the bathtub.

"Bath?"

"Bath. The last thing I remember is saying your true name aloud. And then I awoke here. In your *bath*. When the stream of hot water gushed over me."

"Alex and I carted him in here last night," Mike told Ruby. "No one 'fessed up to booking him so we didn't have a clue which company to call. Could hardly turf him outside and leave him on your front lawn."

She glared at her brother. "Granted that would have been a bit mean. But didn't it occur to you two supposedly intelligent guys to, gee, I don't know, load him in a car and dump him off at North Shore Accident and Emergency? And maybe, since I'm your *sister* for God's sake, you might have called a doctor? To make sure I was okay? Since I fainted for no apparent reason?"

Mike shrugged. "I checked you both over pretty thoroughly. Kyan seemed fine—healthy as a bloody horse—and I was assured he'd had no alcohol whatsoever from the time he arrived. Jules told me you hardly had anything to drink, either, Rubes. So in my professional opinion, you were both a little overwhelmed by the heat and the, er, *emotion* of the evening. And as you both appear to have fully recovered from whatever it was that laid you out cold last night, you can thank me later for saving you a heap of money for an after-hours callout charge."

Since Mike was a St John's Ambulance medic, Ruby couldn't refute any of that. But— "You left a strange man sleeping in my bathtub. And then you left me on the couch while you slept in my bed. How come you didn't take the spare room?"

"You seemed quite comfortable snoring away there, so we decided to leave you. And your queen-sized is a whole lot more comfortable that that saggy old double in your spare room."

Sheesh. Ruby inwardly winced. And supposed she should be grateful Mike hadn't stated the obvious: It'd been easier to leave her on the couch rather than risk someone putting their back out trying to move her. She gritted her teeth, swallowing the torrent of hurt she was tempted to spew at her brother.

Her head hurt. Her back hurt. Hell, everything—including her brain—hurt. And to complicate things even more there was Kyan. She wished with all her heart he hadn't hung 'round to disturb her peace of mind. And other things.

Ruby scrubbed her face with her hands. "Just— God. Bugger off out of here. Both of you. Now. I need a shower. Followed by a very strong, very large dose of caffeine before I tackle cleaning up. You have been warned."

"I'll make us some breakfast and help Kyan locate his clothes," Mike said, taking charge.

Good. Thank God someone was.

When Ruby plucked up the courage to look again, Kyan had removed himself from the bathtub. He was now dripping on the bathmat. His long hair was plastered to his head, and he had the hangdog expression of a man completely out of his depth. He looked like a crestfallen angel.

Ruby handed him a towel, and he squelched over to the door to stand next to Mike. Male solidarity in the face of the wrathful female, and all that manly crap.

"Bacon and eggs?" Mike asked.

"Fine." She bent over the bathtub to wring out the wet pillow.

"Scrambled or poached?"

"Scrambled."

"Anything else? Toast?"

"Please." How many more monosyllabic answers was it going to take for Mike to get the message?

"Shall I undo the zip of your dress so you don't dislocate your shoulder trying to do it yourself?"

Ruby's temper flared. She twisted around and flung the sopping pillow at her brother's chest.

Score!

"*Oof!* What'd ya do that for, Rubes? Now we're both bloody dripping wet."

"Out."

"Make sure you wipe the floor properly or you'll slip over. Do you have any idea how many accidents are caused by people slipping on wet bathroom floors?"

"Out. Now!"

Both men prudently decided to make themselves scarce, leaving Ruby to wring out the pillow and the duvet, and mop up the mess as best she could.

After what turned out to be the complete opposite of a relaxing shower, she dried her hair and wound a towel turban-like around her head. She wriggled into her dressing gown, and then cautiously cracked open the bathroom door to peek out.

All clear.

She dashed to her bedroom and quickly yanked the door shut behind her. To be absolutely sure, she fished a jandal from her wardrobe and wedged it beneath the door. With two men around, no way she was risking either of them walking in unannounced to inform her breakfast was ready.

Sure, she'd read a few romance novels where the hero came across a half-naked heroine and sexy-times ensued. That whole copping-an-eyeful-of-the-woman-bending-over thing could really ramp up the sexual tension if done right. But if that half-naked woman happened to be *her*? Yeah. Not so much. Ruby couldn't think of anything remotely sexy about being surprised while stepping into granny-pants. And if you paired granny-pants with a majorly reinforced bra, and all her wobbly bits in between? Whoever "surprised" her would likely require therapy for the term of his natural life.

Mike had dumped his overnight bag, overflowing with clothes, beside her bed. If he hadn't already grabbed something to wear then tough. He'd have to be extremely careful not to splatter himself with hot bacon fat.

Ruby dragged on a pair of navy track pants, an old white t-shirt, and a pair of sports socks. As she yanked her hair back into a ponytail, she eyed herself in the mirror. Hmm. Not bad. She almost looked the part—a woman ready for a morning jog. Only one thing missing. Running shoes. If she wanted to begin training tomorrow as planned, she would have to go buy a pair today. And a bike, too.

How exciting! Well, not the actual riding a bike once she'd bought one part, because that was a teensy bit scary. But the buying stuff part. A valid excuse to increase what she already owed on her credit card—yay. Maybe she'd splurge on some running socks and new t-shirts, too. Come to think of it, she also needed a swimsuit….

Ick. She cringed as she contemplated the horror of a shopping expedition for that last item—so fraught with possibilities for humiliation. It was almost enough to put her off breakfast. Until her stomach rumbled, giving lie to that brief dietary flirtation.

She jerked the jandal from beneath the door and mentally ran through her plan of action.

First, send Kyan back to wherever he came from.

Second, eat breakfast.

Third, convince Mike to accompany her to the bike shop, so the sales guys wouldn't be tempted to fall over themselves laughing when Ruby announced she needed a bike suitable for a triathlon.

Fourth, ditch Mike for a couple of hours in order to purchase running shoes and—oh God!—a swimsuit.

Fifth, compose herself over a cappuccino. Or maybe a latté.

By "compose herself" she meant sniffle pathetically into her coffee due to humiliation suffered during the quest to buy the aforementioned swimsuit, before meeting up with Mike again. With any luck she'd be home in time for dinner.

Sweet.

Now for the first hurdle. Mr. Dreamy, aka Kyanite, who preferred to be called *Kyan*. Mmm. Kyan sounded softer and more approachable. Less sharp. She could totally understand why he preferred that to *Kyanite*.

She opened the bedroom door. Her nostrils flared as the aroma of frying bacon wafted down the hallway. Mmm. Might have to switch numbers one and two around and send Kyan on his way after breakfast.

As Ruby made a beeline toward the source of that mouth-watering aroma, she noted the lounge was neat and tidy. No half-empty glasses. No beer bottles. Not a single platter sporting shriveled remains of canapés. She continued through into her beautifully clean and tidy kitchen and halted. Seemed her guests had cleaned up *everything* before departing.

How thoughtful. And if it got her out of washing up heaps of dirty dishes, she'd consider fainting at parties more often—though maybe not quite so early on in the evening next time.

Mike and Kyan were perched on stools at the breakfast bar, scoffing massive servings of bacon, eggs and hash browns.

Ruby was mildly disappointed to see both of them were dressed. Well, not disappointed about Mike, of course. Even privately admitting that her brother had a great physique made her want to grab the Yellow Pages and search for a therapist. Kyan, on the other hand, was a whole different story. One in which rippling abs, delectable pecs and bulging biceps played a starring role.

"Do make yourselves at home," she said, her tone curt and snippy to cover the wave of insta-lust she'd experienced at the mere thought of Kyan sitting half naked in her kitchen. "Don't feel you have to hold back when it comes to raiding my freezer and eating all my food. By the way, how long are you planning on staying, Brother Dear?"

"A week," Mike mumbled over a mouthful of bacon. "If that's okay with you. Annie's in Melbourne visiting her parents at the mo' so I'm at a loose end. Needed a break from work, so here I am."

Annie was Mike's fiancée, and one of the sweetest women Ruby had ever met. "Of course it's fine. You know you can crash here anytime."

"Cheers, Rubes. Coffee's ready for plunging, and break-fast's in the warmer drawer."

"Thanks." She wandered over to the kitchen bench to deal with the coffee plunger. "Anyone else for a cup?"

Kyan paused with his bacon buttie halfway to his mouth.

A man after her own heart. Why use a knife and fork when you can slap crispy bacon rashers between two slices of bread 'n butter, and demolish it that way? Ruby liked to do the same with hot chips.

Kyan sniffed the air, and exhaled with a deep, appreciative sigh. "What do you call that beverage, Garnet Ruby?"

Mike choked on his mouthful of food. "*Garnet Ruby*?" he spluttered.

Sheesh. Kyan really did sound like a foreigner from a far off land. "Just Ruby will do," she told him. "And this is coffee. I'm sure you've heard of coffee before, haven't you?"

"Nay. I have not heard of such a beverage. The aroma is familiar to me, though."

She raised her eyebrows. "What would *you* call this stuff, then?"

"If I am not deceived by the aroma, then I would name it *gahvay*. And I would very much like a cup, thank you." He turned his attention back to his breakfast and took another bite of his bacon buttie.

"What language is that, Kyan?" Mike wanted to know. "Arabic or something?"

"I do not know this *Arabic*. Surely my language is the same as that we are now speaking? How else would I understand you? Or you, me?"

"He's got a point there, Mike." Ruby tried not to laugh out-right at her über-smart brother frowning over Kyan's impeccable logic. It wasn't often someone got the better of Mike.

She placed a mug of black coffee in front of Kyan, along

with a carton of milk, the sugar bowl and a teaspoon. "Help yourself."

Kyan eyed the milk doubtfully. He stuck his forefinger in the sugar, scooped a few granules, and raised them to his lips. His tongue darted out to lick them from his finger.

The gesture was so damned sexy Ruby's breath caught in her throat.

Mike threw her an odd glance that she made a point of ignoring. Now was not the time to discuss the lamentable fact that she was lusting after Kyan in the worst way.

"Sweetener!" Kyan dumped two heaped teaspoonfuls of sugar into his mug and stirred it vigorously.

"Sugar," Mike corrected. "Want some milk, too?"

Faced with Kyan's uncertain expression, he hastened to elaborate. "It's cow's milk. Many people think it makes the coffee more palatable. More—"

"Milky?" Ruby couldn't help smirking at her brother.

"Nay." Kyan shook his head. "I will drink this *coffee* as nature intended."

"You mean you'll take it *black*," Mike said.

"As you say then, black."

Mmm. It was tempting to quiz Kyan about his origins but Ruby resisted. What was the point? He was leaving straight after breakfast. And speaking of breakfast—

She removed hers from the warming drawer and, juggling both the plate and her own mug of coffee, clambered onto the stool next to Mike.

"Hey, where's mine?" her brother asked, jerking his chin at her coffee mug.

"Get your own coffee. Consider it punishment for helping yourself to my bed last night."

Grumbling, he climbed from his stool to pour himself a coffee. "With an attitude like that there's no bloody way you'll be getting a birthday present out of me."

She glared at him. "Haha. Already got your present. And to

be honest, it sucked. So forgive me if I don't fall all over you to convey my thanks, okay?"

Mike paused with his coffee cup halfway to his lips. "Whaddya mean you already got my present? I haven't given it to you, yet."

"Oh. Right. That would be the present the courier *didn't* deliver yesterday morning." Ruby slid from her stool to fish the cookbook from the cupboard. She waved it under his nose. "What's this then, huh? A figment of my imagination?"

He grabbed her hand and snagged the book. "Oh, *that*. Listen, numnit, it's not what you're thinking, okay? That's not a birthday present, it's a chance to do a little bit of boasting."

She gaped at him. "Boasting? What the hell, Mike?"

"Yeah. *Boasting.* If you turn to the inside cover, you'll see Annie's name listed with all those who collaborated with the publisher, the drug company, and the chef, to put this book together. I thought you'd get a kick out of seeing her name in print."

Ruby scanned the inside front cover, her gaze focusing on where he was pointing. And there it was in black and white: *Annie Michaels, Registered Dietician.*

"Um, I guess I didn't notice that bit." Oh, shit.

Mike threw her the kind of sympathy-drenched gaze that told her he got it—understood exactly how betrayed she'd felt when she opened the parcel. "Geez," he said, his tone gentle. "I'm really sorry, Rubes. I should have put a note with it or something. I didn't think."

She bit back a hiccupping sob of relief that her brother was still on her side. Still refusing to judge her. Still accepting her, and loving her for who she was. "'S all right. Only me being overly sensitive."

She snatched the cookbook from his hands and shoved it back into the cupboard. Only once she'd resumed her perch on the stool did it hit her. Mike still owed her a present. After a rocky start, the day was looking up. "So what *are* you getting me for my birthday?"

Her brother grinned at the avaricious gleam in her eyes. "Well, after I got your email about the triathlon, I figured we'd head down to the bike shop and I'll buy you a bike. Am I the best brother ever, or what?"

She leaned over to hug him. "You're the best brother ever."

"I know," he said, smirking and basking in the glory.

"So hurry up with breakfast and let's get going. Places to go, bikes and other assorted stuff to buy." Ruby was eager to get started. And all-too-conscious she needed every single bit of assistance she could wrangle to train for this triathlon. The sooner they bought the darn bike, the sooner Mike could start teaching her to ride the darn thing. Unfortunately, politeness dictated she couldn't simply ditch her "guest".

She gulped down her coffee and cleared her throat. "Um, Kyan, is there any place we can drop you? We're heading for Takapuna shops but I don't mind driving you... wherever. So where do you live?"

It was an innocent enough question but Kyan didn't react as she expected. A gamut of emotions skittered across his chiseled features. Anger. Confusion. And finally, panic. And not your normal everyday panic—like the kind Ruby felt whenever she realized she was going to be late for work again, or had forgotten to put on knickers beneath her pantyhose. Nope. This was serious panic.

She'd opened her mouth to ask what was spooking him, but Mike smoothly took charge. "I'll sort out Kyan," he said. "Why don't you head off now and buy the other things you need? I'll meet you," he glanced at his watch, "say, around one at the bike shop? I'll go move my rental so you can get out of the driveway."

"Oh. Okay, whatever." Ruby was both relieved and disappointed to have the disturbing problem of Kyan dealt with. Relieved, because the longer he lingered in her house, the more he seemed like he belonged there... and the more she wished she was the sort of woman who would make a man like him want to stick around. Her disappointment stemmed from knowing she wasn't that woman—could never be that woman. And once she walked out her front door she would never see him again.

Her hangover-like symptoms revisited with a vengeance. She had no idea her head could hurt so damn much. But if she was completely honest, her heart ached even more.

KYAN STOOD BY the window, watching Ruby—as he'd been watching her all morning. He knew she was attracted to him—those glances she shot beneath her lashes when she thought he was unaware of her regard licked him like silken whips, stoking his need to take her for his own. The naked hunger that darkened her eyes was akin to a soft feminine hand down his trousers, stroking his cock and squeezing his stones.

She was pure contradiction, this lush, full-bodied female who oozed sexuality. With little more than a hot, longing glance, she had the power to make his cock throb until, inevitably, her sweet face flushed rosy pink and her gaze skittered away from his, giving Kyan some small respite to compose himself before her heated gaze smote him anew.

He'd learned Ruby could be vocal as any Elder stating her case before the priests at a monthly gathering. But she would invariably follow with some self-deprecating comment that confirmed to Kyan she was unsure of herself, and expected to be jeered at and informed her opinions had little or no value. It irked him mightily. If he had his way....

Nay. His current position was too precarious. Until he could confirm absolutely that the old sorcerer had no means of imprisoning him in the crystal again, he must first look out for himself. Gods willing, Ruby's desire for him would make her amenable to providing a roof over his head. And, once he'd found his way in this world, Kyan would decide whether to remain a while and indulge in a pleasurable interlude with her, or move on. Use her, in other words—as he had used so many females in the past.

With an effort he banished the self-disgust that gripped his belly. He was a warrior. He could not afford to let a woman worm her way into his heart. Not even a woman as tempting as this one.

He was torn from his brooding introspection when Ruby and her brother climbed into a pair of strange contraptions that coughed and then roared mightily.

"Aiee!" Kyan reared back from the window. What manner of ungodly beasts were these? His heart pounded and his hand sought a phantom sword that had vanished along with his mount when he'd been taken by the sorcerer's spell. He stumbled backward, his mind reeling, his confidence that he could tame this world, and use it as he saw fit, plummeting.

When he raised his cup of *gahvay* to his lips his hand shook.

Harden up, boy, a familiar voice hissed in his mind. *The Crystal Warriors will not accept a sniveling coward into their ranks.*

'Twas his mother's voice—a voice that dogged his nightmares even now, after all this time.

He had been a sickly infant—the result of a difficult pregnancy—and slow to master the usual childhood milestones. His father had believed him too frail to become a warrior, and pledged him to the priesthood. With hard work and years of diligent study, he might become a scholar of magic—a worthy calling. But not a calling that would satisfy *her*. He had never been good enough for her. He had tried his best to please her, but he couldn't help that he was clumsy and uncoordinated, and preferred music and books and drawing to swordplay. And she had berated him day in and day out for his "womanly" ways.

His mother had been taken from a world where the females were fiercely independent. Those such as she, who had proven themselves worthy of joining the warrior caste, fought along-side their menfolk and were treated as equals. The shame of being captured, and taken from her homeland, had poisoned her soul. Neither the high-status man who'd won her on the Choosing Block, nor the son she bore him, could expunge that shame.

She had believed that if her son eschewed the warrior path, it would shame both herself and her ancestors. She had refused to accept her mate's decree that their son become a priest's acolyte. She had badgered Kyan's father day in, day out, plead-ing her case until he wearily gave permission for their son to begin preliminary warrior training.

The rigorous, year-long indoctrination into the warrior way of life had almost broken Kyan—body and soul. Somehow he had found the internal strength to bear the jeers and the hazing, to ignore the massive bruises when he failed to defend himself adequately, and the shrieking muscles that made even crawling from his sleeping roll at dawn each morning tor-turous. He'd learned to bury both physical and emotional pain deep—to never let a hint of what he truly felt show on his face. And after that first hellish year he'd hardened up, and life had gotten easier.

It had gotten easier still when he discovered the flaxen locks and blue eyes and too-handsome face that provoked scorn from his peers, attracted women like fire-ants to rotting fruit. And, by the time he completed the five years training, he'd earned the respect of his peers for his prowess with sword *and* shaft.

After the secret ceremony that had bonded one of the priests' coveted crystals to his life force, Kyan had been foolish enough to hope his mother would finally take pride in his accomplishments. She'd disabused him of such childish no-tions with a humiliating public diatribe listing all the reasons he would never measure up to the warriors of her home world.

The shame of that day, the pity he'd witnessed in the eyes

of the youths who'd been crystal-bonded alongside him, had cut him to the bone.

Harden up, boy.

Kyan shook himself to dispel the bitter memories, and rubbed a gnawing ache in his belly with a fist. These foodstuffs must contain something that disagreed with him. But at least the bellyache had torn him from memories he would rather forget. And this time his hand was steady as he emptied the cup.

By the time Mike entered the kitchen Kyan's mask was firmly back in place.

"You ready to head off?" Ruby's brother asked. "There's a couple of shops at the Takapuna shopping center I wouldn't mind checking out—I can drop you off somewhere along the way. Or you can tag along if you're up to it."

"Are we to journey to this *shopping center* in the conveyance that roars?" Kyan did not relish such a journey, but if Mike and Ruby could so casually master such alien contraptions then *he* would master them, too.

Mike's eyebrows all but disappeared beneath his hairline. "You're really not from around here, are you? Where the hell do you come from, Kyan?"

Kyan bared his teeth in a semblance of a smile. "I do not think you would believe me if I told you."

Ruby's brother leaned his hips against the kitchen bench and crossed his arms over his chest. "Try me."

Chapter Four

SHOPPING FOR SWIMSUITS sucked.

After only half an hour in the cramped, pocket-handkerchief-sized changing room, Ruby made a couple of not-so-wonderful discoveries. First, that certain materials claiming to be "stretchy", weren't designed to stretch to their ultimate limit both lengthwise *and* across-wise. If she hunched over, some of the swimsuits kind of fitted, but as soon as she straightened up again, her circulation cut off in places she'd rather not mention. Suffice it to say, super-duper wedgies were the least of her problems.

Her second awful discovery was that the range of available styles designed to hide the multitude of problem areas *she* happened to possess were extremely limited. She'd found swimsuits with reinforced areas to minimize "problem" tummies, extra bust support for D-plus cups, and even some with extra oomph to firm and uplift saggy bums. But the miracle swimsuit Ruby needed had not yet been manufactured. Or perhaps it'd not even been *conceived* yet.

She wanted the ultimate minimizing swimsuit. One that would minimize her boobs, tummy, bum, and everything else. And despite today's supposedly modern technology, the nearest thing that came close to doing all that, while still designed to cope with getting wet, was a wetsuit. Which was so *not* an option, considering how impossible those things were to get on. Or off, for that matter. And as for flattering? No way—not with those hideous fluorescent stripy bits the manufacturers insisted on putting right over the hips or inner legs, that made even slim girls appear bowlegged and bulky.

To compound matters, Ruby had her heart set on a boy-leg style swimsuit so she didn't have to worry about waxing her bikini-line. "Bikini-line". Hah. What a dumb name. Ruby had never worn a bikini in her life, and had no plans to do so in the future.

It wasn't easy convincing the not particularly tactful pre-pubescent shop assistant that it was a waste of time shoving two-piece swimsuits over the changing room door. Finally, Ruby had been forced to firmly—and loudly—state for the record that there was no way in hell she'd be seen in public with her tummy roll exposed to view.

In the end she settled for a plain one-piece in basic navy.

"That one's quite tasteful," the shop assistant conceded when Ruby brought the swimsuit to the counter. "Consider-ing."

Up until then the girl had been walking the line so far as good customer service went. But enough was enough.

Ruby smiled at the skinny little thing. It would be im-mensely satisfying to snap at the kid for being rude and walk out without purchasing a thing. Or to lay a complaint with the shop's manager. But neither of those would be quite so satisfy-ing as what Ruby planned to do next. Ah, revenge. It was going to be so terribly sweet.

"I agree," Ruby said. "It *is* quite tasteful. I'll take it."

The skinny little thing's vapidly pretty face formed an ex-pression of obvious relief.

Hah. Ruby would bet her most comfy knickers this kid had never had to work so hard to make a sale before. Obviously she was thinking the nightmare was over, and she could get back to texting her friends on her mobile, like she'd been doing when Ruby had first walked in. Boy, was she in for a shock.

Time to sock it to her. Ruby upped the wattage of her fake

smile. "I'll also need a bunch of t-shirts and shorts suitable for jogging in."

In retrospect, she probably ruined the kid's entire day. And likely would be responsible for a sudden desire to switch careers, too. Oh dear, what a shame, never mind.

Next stop, the specialist store for running shoes.

The guy who attended Ruby was a consummate professional. He didn't bat an eyelid at someone like her wanting to buy proper running shoes and socks. And from his lack of reaction when she mentioned "women's triathlon", one might have thought he attended plus-sized women espousing truly unrealistic exercise goals on a daily basis. All he cared about was the welfare of her feet.

Ruby left the shop feeling almost buoyant. She glanced at her watch. Just gone midday. Plenty of time for a quick bite and a coffee before she headed back to the car to meet up with Mike.

She headed for her favorite café and ordered her usual: Latté in a bowl, plus the roasted vegetable and pasta salad with toasted pine nuts. Yum.

The staff at this particular café were always friendly and the coffee consistently good. Unfortunately, Ruby's enjoyment was marred by a bunch of scantily clad teenagers, who kept shooting her glances in between loud whispers and bouts of uncontrolled giggling.

After five minutes of stoically ignoring them, Ruby found it increasingly difficult not to feel self-conscious each time she lifted her fork to her mouth. Sure, she was eating a healthy salad rather than gorging on buns and cakes but they were still judging her.

She was seriously considering leaving her salad and asking one of the staff to pour what remained of her latté into a takeaway cup, when a familiar voice cut through her misery. "Hey, Rubes!"

She swiveled and spotted Mike and another man walking

toward her.

Great. She had no problem with her brother guessing she'd be at her favorite café and turning up to join her, but did he have to bring along a mate? Making polite chitchat with a stranger was so *not* what she felt like doing right now.

Plastering another plastic smile on her face, Ruby steeled herself to act as though all was right and good in her pathetic little world.

Mike jogged up to her table. "Thought we'd find you here. We're a bit early, I know, but we worked up an appetite."

"No problem," Ruby lied. "Aren't you going to introduce me to—?"

She abruptly recognized Mike's companion and her stomach performed a lazy, swooping somersault. *Whoa.* Kyan looked incredibly hot—in a good way—in his leather pants paired with one of Mike's t-shirts.

His gaze locked onto hers. His lips curved upward in a smile of welcome.

"Wha—?" Ruby's brain had turned to mush. Her throat was so dry she could barely speak. She swallowed convulsively and moistened her lips with her tongue.

Kyan's glance strayed to her mouth and stayed there until, unnerved by the intentness of his gaze, Ruby blotted her lips with a paper serviette. He shook his head slightly and blinked a couple of times, as though coming out of a trance. "Hello, Ruby," he said.

Her name on his lips made it sound oh-so sexy. Heck, it made *her* feel sexy—not to mention thrilled to call that particular combination of letters her own. And it was all she could do not to melt into a little puddle of lust and lie there on the unyielding polished concrete floor of the café, happily fantasizing about the impossible.

"H-hey, Kyan," she managed to say, in a voice that was barely above a squeak.

He lowered himself to the bench-style seat next to her. His

leather-clad thigh brushed against her hip… and the wave of longing that swamped her made her heart skitter and her breathing hitch.

Embarrassed, she jerked away from him, nearly sloshing the remains of her latté over the table as she sought to distance herself so she could breathe and think. And, if she was lucky, form coherent words.

From the corner of her eye Ruby noted she wasn't the only female affected by Kyan's effortless, lust-evoking sex appeal. The gaggle of Paris Hilton wannabes who'd been sniggering at Ruby feasted their gazes on Kyan. One even took out her fancy mobile phone and snapped a photo of him to send to her friends.

Ruby wondered whether Kyan liked them *that* young and *that* obvious.

Mmm. Apparently not. He seemed oblivious to their in- creasingly blatant efforts to attract his attention. He appeared more interested in the various little paper tubes of sugar ar- ranged in the ceramic condiments jar on their table.

Mike uttered a gurgling noise that sounded suspiciously like a laugh.

Ruby slanted him a glance and caught him smirking. "What's your problem?" she asked.

"Nothing."

She tossed him one of her narrow-eyed "you've so got some explaining to do" glares, and then jerked her chin at Kyan.

Typically, Mike pretended not to understand what she was getting at. Ruby let her brother win this round. But only be- cause good manners dictated she not ream him in public about why Kyan was still hanging around.

"You hungry, Kyan?" Mike asked.

"Indeed I am." He selected a tube of raw sugar, ripped it open, and sniffed the contents before pouring it into the palm of his hand. He toyed with the granules for a moment. And then, apparently satisfied, raised his palm to his mouth and licked the sugar from it.

A chorus of sighs gushed from the next table.

Good grief. At this rate the teenagers would end up doing a Meg Ryan and start fake-orgasming all over their energy drinks.

Mike dug two twenties from his wallet and handed the notes to Kyan. "Choose whatever you want. And can you get me a soy flat white and a turkey roll, please?"

Panic flashed across Kyan's face. Ruby was about to jump in and offer to order for them both when Mike spoke again. "Head on up to the food display case and select something that looks appetizing. Point it out to the girl behind the counter, and tell her you want it, plus one turkey roll, one flat white with soymilk, and one long black. Hand her the money and she'll give you the change, and a card with a number on it to bring back to the table. Okay with that?"

Kyan's frown deepened.

Mike ticked each item off on his fingers. "Turkey roll. Flat white with soymilk. Long black. Don't worry, I'll be right here keeping an eye on things. Holler if you need me."

Kyan gnawed his lower lip and gave a sharp nod. Ruby could hear him chanting the order beneath his breath as he stood. He squared his shoulders and set his lips in a grim line, looking very much like a man about to undertake a mission with dire consequences for failure. After one deep breath and a long, slow exhalation, he headed for the counter, clutching the notes Mike had given him as though his life depended on it.

The eyes of every female in the café, young and old, were on him—or more specifically, his gorgeous backside, as he bent to examine the café food in the lower level display cabinets. He glanced back at Mike, who gave him the thumbs up. And then he focused his attention on the patient café staff and began to place his order.

Ruby tore her gaze from the glorious picture Kyan's rear

view presented, and swallowed a sigh. Finally, commonsense seeped back into her brain. "What the hell was all that about, Mike?"

"Keep your voice down, Rubes. I don't want anyone to overhear this conversation, okay?"

"Fine. What-the-freak-ever. Tell me what's going on. Why is Kyan still here?"

Mike rubbed his face with his palms. "You're not going to fucking believe this, Rubes."

Really. "How about you spit it out and let me be the judge of that?"

Mike tossed her a lopsided grin. "Don't say I didn't warn you. So I ask where Kyan lives, right? And he gives me this spiel about the desert and a bunch of marauding warrior-types, yadda yadda. I figure he's talking about Afghanistan, or somewhere in the Middle East, right? Next, I want to know where he's staying now—like, here in Auckland. And he can't give me an answer."

He paused, as though waiting for Ruby's reaction. She made a rolling gesture with her hand for him to continue.

"Okay. So I quiz him a bit, because this is starting to sound a bit suspicious, you know? Turns out he knows zilch about New Zealand. Can't tell me a single thing about our fair country."

"Well, that's weird," Ruby said. "His English is pretty good, don't you think? So even if he's only recently arrived from overseas he should recognize at least some of the things New Zealand is famous for."

"You'd sure think so, but nope."

"How 'bout kiwis? The birds—not the fruit."

"Nope."

Ruby nibbled her bottom lip, searching for inspiration. Got it. "The All Blacks?"

"Nope. He doesn't have a clue what rugby is, either."

"Pineapple lumps?"

Mike rolled his eyes. "Now you're being daft."

"All right, how about *Auckland*. That's scrawled on signs all over the place—especially the airport. He must at least recognize *that*."

Mike shook his head.

"Bizarre."

"Exactly what I thought," Mike said. "But he's never heard of Auckland. And he doesn't understand what an *airport* is, let alone a plane. So I have this brainwave. I boot up your computer and Google a plane, so I can show him a picture or two. And get this, Rubes, he bloody near craps himself with amazement. I'd swear on my life he's never seen a plane before, let alone flown in one."

"Ummm, he came by ship?"

"Way ahead of you, Rubes. And the answer's still no."

Ruby scrunched up her nose and gnawed on her thumbnail. "What do you reckon, then? Druggie? Amnesiac? Nutcase? How about *really* good liar?"

"None of the above."

"You sure?"

"I'd stake my life on it," Mike said. "Kyan's far too congruent to be lying. Now here's where it gets freaky." He leaned closer. "I ask him what he's done other than stripping—like, what he did before he got into that. And get this. He tells me he's not a stripper, he's a warrior. One of a *tehun*—that's a troop of ten men. And this *tehun* was commanded by a dude called *Wulfenite*, Lord Keeper of the Shifting Sands fief."

Ruby stared at her brother. Oh. Okay. Apparently he wasn't pulling her leg. "You're serious? That's what he said?"

"Yep."

She snorted a laugh. "Where'd he come up with that load of bollocks? You know what, Mike? I'm leaning toward the complete nutcase scenario. I reckon all this stuff Kyan's told you is him buying into his stripper persona. He's kinda lost his grip on reality—living the role, and all that. Which is why he comes across so sincere and stuff. Because he truly believes what he's telling you."

"I wouldn't be so sure about that," Mike said. "See, I had another brainwave."

Ruby couldn't resist. "Brain-fart more like."

Mike ignored her sally. "You know he's named after a crystal, right?"

"Huh?" Ruby shook her head and fought to keep up with the lightning-fast subject change. "What on earth do you mean?"

"You know, a *gem*, or a stone—one of those New Agey-type crystals that supposedly have healing properties, etcetera."

"Kyan is a *crystal*?"

"Not quite. *Kyanite* is a crystal. As are you, by the way—your name, I mean. Both of your names, in fact. Think about it. Ruby and garnet. Both crystals."

"Wrong," she said. "They're *gemstones*, not crystals."

"Gemstones *are* crystals." He squinted and screwed up his nose, looking so endearingly comical Ruby wanted to laugh.

"Lemme see if I can remember this stuff." He snapped his fingers. "Got it. Ruby is a crystal for energy and vigor. It encourages passion, and shields against psychic attacks. Um, what else? Oh yeah. It's supposed to help people retain wealth."

Good grief. What a crock. "How come I'm always so short of money then?"

"Duh. 'Cause even though you're *called* Ruby, you don't actually *own* a ruby, do you?"

She mentally catalogued the contents of her jewelry box and had to give him that one. "Fine. Okay, Brother Dearest, if you really want to help me out with my finances, instead of lecturing me about credit cards and investments, buy me a ruby for Christmas."

Mike scratched his chin and appeared to be seriously contemplating her suggestion. "Not a bad idea."

Ruby guffawed, not bothering to hide her reaction to the bizarre turn this conversation had taken. Mike was beginning to sound like a tree-hugger. Next thing, he'd be extolling the virtues of smoking weed to all and sundry. "And you know all this stuff about crystals because—?"

"I Googled it."

Ruby toyed with the soggy remains of her salad. Google had a lot to answer for. "So, Kyan and I are both named after crystals. So what?"

"How about this for a coincidence, then? Kyan told me his entire troop—in fact, all the warriors of his world—are named after crystals. When each warrior is initiated, a crystal is chosen for him by the priests, and that crystal becomes his 'true' name."

"Wait a minute. Kyan's *world*? Doesn't he mean *country*?

"Nope. World."

"Oh, please. Surely he doesn't think he's a bloody ali—?"

Mike flung up a hand to halt her tirade, and smiled in a smug sort of way. Ruby figured he was about to floor her with some *fait accompli* of deductive reasoning. Wait for it—

"So, on impulse I Googled 'crystal' and 'warrior.' And you know what I came up with?"

She rolled her eyes. "Gee. I can't possibly imagine."

"A website. Crystal Warriors dot com."

"The plot thickens. And this is important how, exactly?"

"Because—" Mike's tone indicated he should be nominated for sainthood due to excessive patience "—the website's owner is an American woman named Chalcedony Laureano. She and her husband are using it as a tool to track down a bunch of missing men. And when I Googled this woman's name, I found she's also named for a crystal."

"*Laureano* is a kind of crystal? Sounds more like a kind of party pill or energy drink to me."

Mike closed his eyes and appeared to be praying for guidance. "Sometimes I wonder about you, Rubes. *Chalcedony* is a crystal. And her husband's name is *Wulf*. So what d'ya think of that?" He leaned back, gazing at her with a triumphant "so there" expression.

"So?" Ruby wasn't trying to be difficult. Honest. She wasn't following this at all.

"Geez. Weren't you listening when I mentioned Kyan's commander's name?"

She shrugged. "Sort of?"

"His full name is *Wulfenite*—also a crystal. Wulf. Wulfenite. Get it?"

"Yeah. I get it. And he's married to this Chalcedony chick. So?"

"God, Rubes. You can be impossibly dense at times."

Ruby slanted a sideways glance at Kyan, who was now chatting with the smitten cashier. No doubt he was charming her right out of her knickers. Or, by the size of her, it was probably a g-string.

Mike rapped on the table with his knuckles, demanding Ruby's full attention again. "Guess whose name is on the list of men Ms Laureano is trying to track down?"

"Gee. I don't know. Kyan's?"

Mike rewarded her guess with an ear-to-ear grin. "Right on. So guess what we did next?"

"We?"

"Me and Kyan."

She huffed a sigh. "I dread to think."

"I got this Chalcedony woman's number from International Directory Services and rang her. When I mentioned Kyan's name, and described him to her, she got very excited. We were on the phone for about an hour, and she told me—"

"You made an hour-long toll call to America? On my landline?" Bloody hell. Next month's phone bill was going to be huge. "Have you any idea how much that's going to cost? Sheesh. You might have to consider that my Christmas present to you."

Mike waved away her concerns. "I'll pay for the call. Shut up and listen. You're never gonna believe this, but Chalcedony Laureano insisted on speaking to Kyan. So I showed him how the phone worked and—"

"Lemme guess. He's never seen or used a phone before."

"Right. So then she puts her husband, this Wulf guy, on the phone to Kyan. Turns out they both know each other. They're both *Styrian* warriors. *Styrian* means 'Storm Rider' by the way. And Chalcedony Laureano's husband is—*was*—Kyan's troop commander. You should have seen the expression on Kyan's face while he was talking to this guy. Seems Wulf is Kyan's kinsman. They're related somehow—I didn't really get how. And this Wulf dude is one scary-arse mother."

Ruby sipped the dregs of her latté. No help there. Her head was still spinning. She drained the cup, taking her time, and when she plonked it back on its saucer, the perfect solution popped into her head. "Our problem's solved. We stick Kyan on the first flight back to the good ole U-S-of-A for Chalcedony and her scary-arse husband to deal with."

"'Tis not that simple a matter, Ruby." Kyan handed Mike his change and took a seat next to Ruby again.

Gee. Why did that not surprise her? Nothing in her life was ever simple. "Look, Kyan. If you don't have enough money for a flight home, I'll book you a flight on my VISA, okay? You don't even have to pay me back." And she'd offer to cover some weekend shifts at work to pay it off.

"He can't go home," Mike said.

Ruby glanced from one man to the other. They were definitely hiding something from her. "Okay, you two. Spill. What are you not telling me?"

Mike eyed Kyan. "You want to tell her, or shall I?"

Kyan sighed. "I will tell her."

"Better you than me," Mike muttered.

Ruby glared at them. Odds on it was a pathetic attempt at a

glare, but it was all she could summon. She pressed a fist to her churning stomach, her brain leaping to conclusions—all of them dire. Omigod. What was wrong? She wished they'd get the bad news over with and put her out of her misery.

"Ruby."

Kyan's voice, the way he uttered her name, sent little shivery frissons up and down her spine. Lust warred with her instinctive need to worry. But it was Kyan. He was gorgeous. No surprise that lust won, and the churning in her stomach morphed to a coil of heated want and need. "Yes, Kyan?"

He dropped his gaze and played with another tube of sugar.

She suppressed a groan-cum-sigh. Looked like she'd have to coax whatever it was out of him.

"I won't bite you or anything." Mmm. Maybe a little nibble on his ear. Or a little bit lower down…. *Focus, Ruby!*

Kyan met her gaze with obvious reluctance. "You and I are potentially life-mates, Ruby. You have been chosen as my woman."

If she'd had a mouthful of coffee right then she'd have spat it all over him. "Oh, please. Pull the other one—it's got bells on."

"He's telling the truth," Mike said.

She slid her gaze to her brother and blinked at his über-serious expression. "Not you, too?"

"'Tis true, Ruby," Kyan said. "And within four of your weeks, you and I will be subjected to a Testing. If we do not pass this Test, the best I can hope for from the Crystal Guardian is that he will again condemn me to the eternal torture of my kyanite crystal prison."

He paused, looking so grim Ruby's skin prickled. She shrugged off the chill of foreboding, refusing to believe it. This was complete codswallop, right? Insane drivel. "And the worst?" she finally managed to ask.

"Begging your pardon?"

"You said 'the best you can hope for' is that the Crystal Guardian will condemn you to... to... torture and stuff. So what's the worst case scenario?"

"The Crystal Guardian will destroy my crystal. And me along with it."

CHAPTER FIVE

RUBY STUDIED KYAN, waiting for a teasing smile to tilt his tempting lips. But the smile never eventuated. His expression was graveside serious.

Holy shit. He truly believed what he was telling her.

She glanced at Mike. Surely this had to be some elaborate ruse her brother cooked up to have some fun at her expense. Mike enjoyed a good joke.

But he wasn't smiling, either. That, more than anything else, worried Ruby. Her desire to laugh strangled in her throat and died an unnatural death.

"It's true, Rubes," Mike said. "The Crystal Guardian tested Chalcedony Laureano four weeks to the day she first met Wulf. They'd been an item, but they split over a misunderstanding. At first she thought he'd died in the fire that destroyed her dance studio, but then she realized he'd been imprisoned in his crystal again. So she tracked down this Guardian dude, and found a way to rescue Wulf. She and Wulf have been together ever since."

"Really."

"Really. And turns out Chalcedony's *mother* went through the same sort of experience with a guy called Malach— Malachite. Only she chose not to bond with him, so Malach ended up back in his malachite crystal, at the mercy of this Guardian again. The Guardian's the one who cast the spell on Wulf and his men a few centuries ago, and imprisoned them all in their namesake crystals, by the way. She—Chalcedony's mother—believes the Guardian destroyed Malach's crystal. And him along with it."

"But… but…." Ruby's heart was leaping about as if it wanted to burst from her chest and find a place to cower. Excellent idea. She desperately wanted to run away and hide, too. Instead she was glued to her seat.

Kyan took her hand.

Desire zinged through Ruby's veins, softening her hard-edged determination to give no credence to this outlandish tale. She stared into his eyes, ensnared by what-ifs and maybes, losing herself in their earnest blue depths. And then, some-how, Ruby was given access to Kyan's mind. She drifted through his thoughts and memories, and she saw the truth—or at least, the truth as Kyan believed it to be. But a kernel of disbelief that remained unmoved by a handsome face and earnest eyes, had nestled in her heart. She couldn't bring herself to accept that such a tale could be true.

How could it be?

And the instant that thought formed, some unnamed force contrived to prove her wrong. Before she could blink, Ruby was transported backward in time to the instant she had first touched the kyanite crystal Jules had given her. And this time, there was more to the vision. This time, Ruby was a silent witness to the casting of the curse that trapped eleven men in their namesake crystals….

THE OLD MAN untied the linen and spread it on the ground. He placed the eleven large gemstones in a circle, and himself at the center point. He was the focus, a man named after a crys-tal, a man who'd dedicated his life to learning how to harness the power of such stones. He struggled to his feet to await his fate.

Wulf reined in his battle mount and raised a hand to halt his troop. He barked a laugh. "A graybeard who should be a-bed, nursing his aching joints. This is the best defense you offer."

A small figure hurtled toward the old man, and Kyan's heart tripped in his chest as he willed the child to halt and not draw further attention to herself.

"Amie, no!" A young female lunged for the child but was restrained by the other women. Kyan guessed her to be the child's mother—a pretty female, ripe for the taking. Mayhap it would not be a bad thing if her child was taken in this raid. At least then there was a chance mother and daughter might remain together.

The little girl skidded to a halt beside the old man. Hands on hips, she faced Wulf. "Don't speak to me grandda' like that, ye big bully! Go 'way and leave us be!"

Kyan snickered at the spectacle of this slip of a girl giving their troop commander a piece of her mind. A pity such courage would go unrewarded.

"Silence!" Wulf snarled. "The girl-child is comely," he informed the old man. "Too, she shows no fear. When she comes of age, I will honor her courage by bidding for her on the Choosing Block. You show courage also, old man, so to appease this child of your blood I will spare your life."

"My life is already forfeit," the old man said. "But not to you Lord Keeper Wulfenite."

Kyan stifled his shock. How could this graybeard know of Styrian true-names? And how might he use such knowledge?

Wulf kneed his mount forward but the beast shied, forcing him to haul back on the reins. "Much good knowing my true name will do you, old man," he said, his calm tone earning Kyan's respect. "If you insist on resisting us then so be it. The earth will drink your foolish old blood as readily as it does that of younger men."

The old man merely smiled. He bent and whispered something to the little girl, and she dashed back to her mother. Once she was safely out of the way, he raised his hands to the skies and began to chant. "Verily the crystal for which thee be named/ Shalt form the prison in which thee be bound/ To atone the sins for which thee be blamed/ 'Til thee be blessed and thy true love be found."

Kyan's sense of foreboding grew, but Wulf merely threw back his head and laughed. "Blessed? What nonsense is this, old man? Mayhap you are addle-brained, yes? Warriors such as we have no need of blessings. And as for true love? Bah. 'Tis naught but a woman's fantasy."

The crystals surrounding the old man began to glow. Black clouds scudded across a rapidly darkening sky. A crackle of lightning haloed beams of light—each a different, unearthly hue—shooting up from the gems.

"What sorcery is this?" Malach, the tehun's leader, demanded.

The old man raised his arms to the sky again. "Kyanite, Malachite, Shattuckite, Okenite, Danburite," he intoned. "The stone thee be named for shall bind thee. I, Pietersite, bind thee."

The heavens answered with a rumble. Fear stabbed at Kyan like a well-honed blade, and he saw his dread reflected in the faces of his fellow warriors. But it was too late to take action. In the blink of an eye, he was sucked into a blackness so absolute that it defied any rational explanation. He was powerless, deprived of sensation, sight and sound, imprisoned in a vast expanse of nothingness. All that he was, all that he could be— his very essence—was held in stasis. Not so his mind, however. And his thoughts were dark and twisted things, born of despair and self-loathing.

He understood at some elemental level that this place-that-was-no-place was his punishment. He had feared this place as a child, and then laughingly discounted it as a grown man. 'Twas merely a tale to frighten naughty children. Everyone knew it did not truly exist.

Now he realized how wrong he had been, for here he was.

Condemned to suffer forever in—

Hell. Ruby full-body shuddered, her heart pounding as the adrenaline surged through her, prodding her to launch herself from her seat and run—run until she escaped the horror of the vision. But she was not strong enough to break free, and so she remained rooted to the spot, fighting a rising terror that threatened to sweep her away. And then something pierced the haze of fear and despair, calling her back to here and now.

There it was again—a fleeting caress. She blinked, and abruptly she was sitting in the busy cafeteria, with Kyan's hand clasping hers.

"Ruby!" His worried gaze searched her face.

She stared at him, dazed by the anguish etching his features, the remembered terror clouding his eyes.

He thumbed moisture from her cheek. She blinked, and realized her face was wet with tears.

Clarity smacked her upside the head. She knew the name of the crystal that was wrapped in tissue paper, sitting all but forgotten on her phone table. She would bet her life it was a *kyanite* crystal. And that both it, and Kyan, had to be linked somehow. It couldn't be coincidence that he was named after the very stone Jules had given her. Or that he'd appeared on her doorstep immediately after she'd had the first vision and the crystal had broken in two.

God. Everything he'd told Mike, everything he'd told her, was true. "How could you stand it, Kyan?" Her voice was little more than a whisper. "That endless darkness?"

"I do not know how I survived it. Nor do I care overly much. What matters is that for now, for however long the gods allow it, I am free."

Ruby chanted words that formed in her mind. "Verily the crystal for which thee be named/ Shalt form the prison in which thee be bound/ To atone the sins for which thee be blamed/ 'Til thee be blessed and thy true love be found."

It was a curse. *The* curse. The one that old man—the Crystal Guardian—had cast. Unthinking, she completed the spell, uttering the fateful words that had condemned the man beside her to a centuries-long torment. "Kyanite, the stone thee be named for shall bind thee. I, Pietersite, bind thee."

Kyan flinched as though she'd struck him. He bowed his head, covering his face with his hands, remembering or perhaps reliving the past. And Ruby knew the words of that curse would be forever etched into her memory.

Mike uttered a strangled sound and Ruby glanced up to see him gaping at her. "How—? How'n the hell could you know that spell, Ruby? Chalcedony Laureano only recited it over the phone to me less than an hour ago."

"I-I don't know. I saw a... a... *vision* of how it went down. I guess."

"I know how." Kyan's hands muffled his words. He lifted his head, slowly, pinning Ruby with his electric blue gaze. "The words are still engraved in my mind centuries after hearing them uttered. Ruby and I, we are bound now, connected in some profound way. That is how she knows."

Ruby inwardly shuddered at the suffering carved in the lines bracketing his mouth. She found it difficult to bear the intensity of his gaze, but the hope dawning in his eyes held her transfixed. He'd been thrown a lifeline: Her. She was his permanent ticket out of the crystalline hell he'd somehow been sprung from.

How ironic. All her life she'd dreamed of a boyfriend who was handsome and built like... well... *Kyan*. Someone who loved her for who she was, not how she looked. Someone who wouldn't have his head turned by some big-boobed stick insect swaying down the street in a short skirt and crop-top. Someone who was happy to have Ruby exactly how she was right now. Someone who wouldn't pretend to be happy with her, and then insist on trying to change her. And here he was. Kyan. The man of her dreams....

A man who needed her to save him from a fate worse than

death.

How was that for a cliché? As R.N.Z.A.F. pilots were fond of saying: What a cluster-fuck.

If Kyan had come to her willingly, somehow managed to convince her he wasn't playing a cruel joke and that he truly wanted to be with her, it would be different. But this?

He *needed* her. That was the only reason he was sticking around. Otherwise he'd have settled for giving the Birthday Girl a kiss, getting his kit off and some cheap thrills into the bargain, and leaving Ruby with nothing but the memory of that kiss.

"How about it, Rubes?" Mike's question interrupted her little pity party.

"How about what?"

"Are you going to help him?"

God. This so wasn't fair. Why couldn't fate have dealt her a normal man—one she had at least a chance in hell of a happy ever after with?

Tears stung her eyes and misery lodged in her heart. She'd be damned if she would cry though, not in front of Kyan and her brother. Not now. She pushed back the tears and turned misery into anger-spiked sarcasm. "You, my rational, too-smart-for-his-own-good brother, believe all this stuff? This Chalcedony woman could be a bloody psycho for all we know."

"I believe her. She sounded totally sincere, Rubes."

"Yeah. So do most psychos."

"Valid point, Rubes." Mike's serious expression turned sheepish, but only for a moment. He wasn't going to give up trying to convince her without a fight. "But when I spoke to Wulf, that sealed it for me. He described being imprisoned, and what he described exactly matches Kyan's experience. Plus, Chalcedony was given a wulfenite crystal by the Crystal Guardian. And from what they can figure out, Wulf appeared immediately after she dropped the crystal and it broke in two.

Kyan and I found the crystal you'd been given, Ruby and—"

"And it's broken, too. Yeah. I'm well aware of that."

"Can you remember what happened immediately after-ward?"

"Oh come on, Mike. I dropped it. It broke. I opened the front door and Kyan was there. But that doesn't prove any-thing." She didn't believe the evidence. She couldn't. But she wasn't prepared to let Mike know that. Or at least, not yet.

"Doesn't it?" he countered.

"I can't believe you're so ready to embrace all this hocus-pocus, Mike. You're a trained medic for chrissakes! How can you believe these wild tales of warriors from another world, surviving for centuries magically imprisoned in crystals? It's absurd."

"I believe in magic," her brother said. "Every time I witness someone recover from an accident that by all rights should have killed them, I believe. And when I bring back someone who's not been breathing on their own for far too long, and I know they should be brain damaged but they completely recover, it only reinforces my belief. I've seen too many mira-cles, too many things I can't explain. How could I not believe in magic?"

"But this—?" Ruby shook her head. "This is… fucking un-believable."

Kyan finally broke his silence. "Yet here I am, Ruby—a Styrian warrior not of your world, and I am as real as you. You have seen my prison—witnessed, too, the spell that captured me being cast. You have heard the sorcerer speak the words that bound me."

She nodded.

"Then how can you not believe? Help me, Ruby. Please. I need you."

She blew out a long sigh and slumped in her seat. He need-ed her. She understood that. But what about what *she* needed? What about afterward, when they'd passed this testing shit, and Kyan had his life back to live however he chose? She'd have to be thick as two short planks to think he'd stick around. This was real life, not a fairytale.

She examined every inch of Kyan's strikingly handsome face. He was a babe, all right. The sort of man that women conjured up in their wildest dreams. But Kyan wasn't a dream. He was real. And he was here, now, begging her to save him from the big, bad Crystal Guardian's clutches.

Ruby folded. Even though she knew that she would be badly hurt, she gave in. She would play this thing through to the end. And for now, having Kyan need her was enough. It would have to be.

"Don't have much of a choice, do I?" she muttered.

Kyan and Mike exchanged relieved glances.

She snorted. Loudly. And ignored the whispers and giggles from Kyan's teen fan club at the next table. "Yeah, yeah, Mike. Like you didn't know I'd be a sucker for a handsome man begging for my help. God, I despise being a sure thing."

Not even her brother had an answer to that.

The orders arrived and the guys chowed down. Ruby waited 'til Kyan finished his large slice of chicken pie and pasta salad. "There's one thing I'd like to know, Kyan."

"Anything, Ruby."

"What on earth did you and Wulf and the rest of your troop do to make that old guy hate you so much? Must've been pretty bad for him to condemn you for, like, an eternity."

Mike choked on his coffee.

Kyan stiffened. His face blanked until he looked inhuman, like a perfectly rendered replica of a human being—just as Jules had commented last night. Hard. Emotionless. Capable of anything.

Ruby shivered and rubbed her arms. He claimed to be a warrior, and she could well imagine how that vocation would fit him. She wondered how many men he had killed.

"Let's talk about that later, Rubes." Mike stood. He crumpled his serviette and tossed it on the tabletop. "Better go buy that bike, eh? Especially since you want to start your training bright and early tomorrow. C'mon, you two. Let's make tracks."

Ruby played along by groaning and dragging her feet. "Can't believe I'm gonna voluntarily torture myself like this. Bike ride before breakfast, swimming at lunchtime, and a run after work? I'm going to kill myself."

She knew Mike had deliberately tried to divert her attention. He must have discovered something important, something he and Kyan didn't want her to know. She let it slide for now. She'd bale them up about The Big Secret later. And one of them would tell her the truth or she'd refuse to play the game. Simple. All it'd take would be the threat of not making any effort whatsoever to pass the testing, meaning Kyan would have to stew in his heinous crystal for another few centuries....

She shot Kyan a glance. Yeah. Like she would ever be able to look at herself in the mirror if she let that happen. *Face it, Ruby. You're a sucker for punishment.*

AFTER THE EMOTION-LADEN lunchtime experience, the relative normality of the bike shop came as a welcome relief. Then again, what the hell was normal about Mike buying her a bike so she could take part in a *triathlon*? And there was nothing at all normal about Kyan, the gorgeous blond warrior who'd abruptly turned her life upside down.

At least she didn't have to attempt to squeeze into bike pants because they had run out of stock in her size. Ruby knew that because Mike insisted she ask. Damn him.

They left the shop wheeling not one, but two bikes: One for her and one for Kyan. Apparently Mike's brilliant plan was to have Kyan accompany Ruby on her bike rides to help her stay on track with her training schedule. With Kyan being an über-fit warrior and all, Mike had talked him into being Ruby's personal trainer.

Hah. A personal witness to her heaving, panting, incredible unfitness, more like.

Ruby groaned inwardly. Having a hot man cycle down the street directly behind her, ogling her huge bum? She couldn't imagine anything more fun. Bloody Mike. Doubtless her beloved brother thought he was doing her a favor but frankly, he was clueless.

Ruby parked her old Lancer in the carport. She was about to unlock the front door when Mike pulled up in the driveway. He wound down the window of his fancy Toyota SUV rental. "Don't bother unlocking the door, Rubes. Hop in."

"Where're we going?"

"Time for a lesson on how to ride your new bike," he said. "No time like the present."

Oh no. No. No. No. She was so not ready for this. "What? Now?"

"Now. Unless you're not really serious about this whole tri-athlon thing."

Crap. "Of course I'm serious. But no way am I getting on that bike in jeans. Give me a moment to change into something more comfortable." She unlocked the front door and headed for her bedroom. Looked like the humiliation was going to begin sooner rather than later. Yay.

CHAPTER SIX

YAN NOTED RUBY'S downturned lips and slumped shoulders as she emerged from the house. "She seems unhappy."

Mike tapped his fingers on the wheel that somehow directed the conveyance—the *car*. "She'll get over it," he said. "If we don't do this now, she'll get caught up with work and lose a week of cycling training. Best to get it over with before she chickens out altogether. "

"Chickens out?" Kyan thought he might have seen a chicken or two during the last raid. He recalled hearing that they tasted delicious... but he had no clue what Mike meant with his mention of chickens in this context.

Mike must have noticed his confusion—or perhaps automatically decided to elaborate for Kyan's benefit. Ruby's brother did his best to assist Kyan's comprehension where appropriate. "Chickening out means reneging on something," Mike said. "In Ruby's case, it means finding excuses not to learn to ride the bike because the mere thought of it scares her silly."

Ah. Kyan nodded. Gods knew there had been plenty of occasions in his past life when he would have "chickened out" given a choice. "She puts on a brave face that fools many."

Mike's fingertips ceased their rapid tattoo. "But not you. You see deeper, don't you, Kyan? You're not fooled by outward appearances."

"I, too, am guilty of pandering to the expectations of others—especially with regard to my choice in women."

Mike opened his mouth as if to speak, and then closed it again.

'Twas no surprise to Kyan that Ruby's brother was fiercely protective of her. He suspected he knew what Mike wanted to ask. "This face has been both a curse and a blessing," he said. "Suffice it to say, the many women it attracts have been the blessing. I freely admit to seeking solace with numerous women to escape the harsh realities of my life. And, as the women were willing, I see no need to apologize for it."

"And Ruby?"

Kyan shifted restlessly as he watched Ruby sit on the front step to lace up her shoes. Given the high stakes, it would be the height of foolishness to be completely candid with Mike.

After the initial shock at hearing what the future held for him, Kyan had formed a plan to ensure Ruby's full cooperation until the Crystal Guardian's testing took place, and he was free of the crystal's curse. His plan was simple. He would use all his wiles upon Ruby. Seduce her, and yes, even tell her that he loved her with all his heart. *Her* heart would be torn to shreds because, however gently he let her down, in the end she would hate him for his deceit. Too, he would hate himself for hurting her. But that would not stop him doing what needed to be done. He could ill afford compassion. Not when his sanity, and very likely his life, were at stake. Failing the Crystal Guardian's Test, and being condemned to his kyanite crystal to await death, was not an option Kyan was willing to dwell upon.

He was saved from having to lie convincingly when Mike drew his own conclusions. "I've seen the way she looks at you," Mike said. "She cares what happens to you, Kyan. She won't let you down—disappoint you, I mean."

"I know." Ironic given that Kyan knew *he* would ultimately disappoint *her*.

"If you hurt her, though, I'll have to kick your arse six ways to Sunday."

Kyan nodded. If—when—he hurt Ruby, he would *invite* Mike to kick his arse. And beat him to within an inch of his sorry, selfish life if Mike desired it. A beating would be no more than he deserved.

Nor was Kyan a stranger to beatings. His mother had favored a stick or whatever was close at hand. His fellow trainees, who hadn't appreciated the inclusion of a pretty-faced weakling in their ranks, had preferred to lay into him with fists and boots. Too, Kyan had been beaten by the warrior in charge of his training. That beating had been particularly vicious. Kyan's kinsman, Wulf, had put a stop to it with a single punch that had toppled the old bastard like a felled tree, and earned both Wulf and Kyan a severe reprimand from the training commander.

Strange. He'd never thought to thank Wulf for saving him from far worse injury than a few cracked ribs and severe bruising. Or for treating him with scrupulous fairness after Kyan had joined Wulf's troop. When this was over, he would contact Wulf and make amends. Kyan knew he had much to apologize for. He'd been bitter, resenting Wulf's success, coveting his accolades. He hadn't been the easiest man to command.

Mike cleared his throat, prompting Kyan to drag his thoughts from the past and his old life... the one Wulf had curtly informed him that he must cast aside because he could never return to it.

He glanced up and found Mike staring at him through narrowed, perceptive eyes that saw far too much for Kyan's comfort. But this time, Kyan did not attempt to disguise his inner turmoil. "I cannot promise that I will not cause her hurt when this comes to an end. I am be-spelled, Mike. What I feel for your sister—" He scrubbed his fingers through his hair. "Only the sorcerer who cursed me knows whether my feelings for your sister are true and real."

His feelings for Ruby…. What did he feel?

He admired her. He appreciated her acerbic wit. He liked her mass of dark hair that shone with cinnamon-colored highlights when the sun hit it just so. He thought her features were exquisite, especially her soulful brown eyes with their hints of gold flecking the irises—eyes that truly were windows to her soul. Her smooth, pale skin intrigued him. Her generous curves made him want to press his body against hers and luxuriate in her femininity. He appreciated those curves in ways that only a connoisseur of women could. The insecurities and vulnerability he glimpsed whenever she dropped her defenses cut him like a blade, and made him yearn to seek out those who had caused them and punish them. Harshly. Regardless of the bonding spell, Kyan believed all of those qualities would have attracted him to Ruby.

There were physical symptoms to consider, too. Namely the pain that had twisted his gut and throbbed through his veins when Ruby had left the house to go shopping—a pain that had escalated to a searing agony that had only eased once he encountered her again at the café. That pain had recurred when Ruby drove home in her own car, but it had been far less intense, merely a dull ache, almost as though Kyan's body recognized that he was trailing her to her abode.

He was tempted to ignore the gods-sent portent of Ruby's crystal-names and embrace his kinsman's explanation for those bizarre physical symptoms. The pain, Wulf insisted, was a physical manifestation of the sorcerer's bonding spell—an unpleasant side effect of the bond that had been initiated after their exchange of true-names. Whenever Kyan was parted from Ruby, he would feel physical pain. The more distance between them, the more intense the pain.

Thus, was it not reasonable to suspect the sorcerer's magic was the root of *all* Kyan's feelings for Garnet Ruby Roberts? The Crystal Guardian was a powerful man, obviously highly favored by his gods. Kyan could well believe such a man would manipulate even a woman's true-names to his own ends.

But what of feelings that ran deeper than mere "like" and desire? The ones Kyan feared would tie him to a woman with the power to destroy the protective walls he'd so painstakingly constructed, and lay bare his soul?

Nay. Kyan could not allow himself to love Ruby—a woman named not for one precious stone, but *two*. He'd vowed to never give a woman such power over him. He refused to be dependent upon a woman for his physical and mental wellbeing. He must bury his turbulent, disturbing feelings for Ruby. He could not afford to give them rein.

It was for the best. Because in truth, he did not deserve her.

"Fair enough," Mike finally said. "I appreciate your honesty. But I'll still have to kick your arse if you hurt her." He whacked the steering wheel with the heel of his hand and a shrill honk rang out.

Ruby hurried over to the car and opened the rear door to clamber into the backseat. "Impatient sod," she muttered.

"Day's not getting any younger," Mike said. "Buckle up."

Kyan glanced over his shoulder in time to see Ruby stick out her tongue at her brother's back. He grinned, charmed by the childlike reaction. Charmed by so many things about this complex, fascinating woman, who didn't comprehend the power she could have over men—over *him*—if only she believed in herself. If only she could see herself as he saw her.

AFTER WOBBLING 'ROUND the grounds of Mairangi Bay Primary—her old school—for two hours, Ruby decided she was getting the hang of this riding lark. As a bonus, she suspected that despite her lack of bike pants, she was far more comfortable on her bike than Kyan was on his. If his frequent grimaces and the occasional squirming were anything to go by, tight leather pants and a hard bike seat didn't go well together. Poor guy really should have gotten changed first. At least Ruby's unsculpted bum had plenty of padding.

Sore backside and other masculine dangly bits aside, Kyan appeared very competent on his bike. In fact, if there was a god of cyclists, then Kyan might have been created in his image. Even the racy silver helmet Mike had bought suited him. Ruby sighed, wishing she had even half his skill at handling what must have been a strange and totally alien piece of machinery.

Still, she shouldn't be so hard on herself. Kyan would have spent years honing his body-awareness. Little wonder balancing on two wheels was a breeze for him. He was obviously extremely fit, too. And doubtless damn good at fighting, because he'd gotten through a couple of decades of warrior-ing without a scar to mar his pretty face. Either that or he was a coward who scarpered when things got dicey. Unlikely. Somehow she couldn't picture Kyan fleeing a battle.

"Righto!" Mike called from his makeshift throne on the jungle gym. "Time for a bit of a challenge."

Uh oh. Ruby braked hard, skidding to a slightly wonky stop. "What do you mean by challenge, exactly?"

"Follow me." Her brother swung down from the wooden platform and jogged over to front entrance of the school. He pointed down the road, beyond where he'd parked the car. "Remember that pedestrian path we used when we walked to school, Rubes?"

She nodded. "Yeah, why?" She was getting a bad feeling about this.

"You're going to cycle along the road until you get to that path. Then you're going to cycle down it, and continue up Maxwelton Drive until you get to our old house on Nereus Place. I'll take the car 'round and meet you there."

Chills skittered down Ruby's spine, making her sweaty, overheated skin clammy. "You have got to be bloody kidding me. Have you forgotten how steep that path is?"

"Nope. Perfect opportunity for you to practice applying the brakes to control your speed when you're riding downhill."

Mike paused, doubtless to absorb the unmitigated horror Ruby knew was plastered all over her face.

Her brother's no-nonsense tone softened. "Look, Rubes, this is the safest way to learn. It's a pedestrian track, so there'll be no cars to worry about until you hit the road. Plus, it's a weekend, so there are no school kids using the path, and the road traffic will be light. No way will you be able to avoid all slopes and find a completely flat route around where you live. You've got to learn how to negotiate hills sometime."

"But I was going to ride on the footpath around home— until I'd been riding a while, anyway."

"Do you really think the triathlon course is going to be on a footpath?" Mike snorted. "Not likely. Besides, technically it's illegal to cycle on the footpath."

"I will follow you and see you come to no harm," Kyan said. "Be brave, Ruby. You can do this. I know you can."

Yeah. Like Kyan would be able to stop her arsing over when he was riding *behind* her. He'd only be good for picking up the pieces after she'd come a cropper.

Two novice cyclists, and a really steep hill. Lovely. What the hell was Mike thinking?

Her brother gave her his sternest "I believe in you, I know you can do this" eyes.

Epic fail.

"If you don't at least try," he said, "there's no way you'll be confident enough to handle riding on your own early in the morning. You won't be able to rely on Kyan to keep you safe, either—he'll be too busy keeping himself out of trouble. Look, I have to know you can look out for yourself or I'm trading in the bike."

She sucked in a deep breath. "All right. I'll give it a go."

"That's my girl. And remember, Kyan will be right behind you." Mike slapped Kyan on the back and grinned like a proud parent.

Fine and dandy for him. He'd be safe in his car—not careening down the effing mother of all hills, gripping the handlebars so tightly his skin was likely to become permanently bonded to the handles.

Ruby tugged her helmet's straps, tightening them still more beneath her chin. Then, trying not to think too hard about the vast amount of exposed skin she would graze if she fell, she pedaled off.

It was fun for about five minutes. The road leading away from the school sloped gently downward, making the going easy. She'd just begun to relax when she spotted the walkway entrance. She cycled up to it, signaling a stop well before she reached it so Kyan didn't smack into her. Biting her lips, she positioned her bike at the top of the narrow concrete path, and looked down.

God it was steep.

She vividly remembered struggling up it as a youngster, dragging her feet and her schoolbag, falling ever further behind Mike with each step she took. Often when Ruby revisited places that had seemed incredibly vast or large to her as a kid, they didn't seem anywhere near so imposing as an adult. Not this time. The walkway appeared twice as steep as she remembered. Either that or sheer terror was playing tricks on her.

She must have uttered some sound—a whimper of dread most likely—because Kyan reached out to gently squeeze her forearm. "You do not have to do this if you are afraid, Ruby. You have nothing to prove."

"That's where you're wrong." She managed a tremulous smile. "I *have* to prove I can do this—to myself if to no one else." Before he could respond, she launched herself down the hill.

Despite her rigid grip on the handbrake and heavy pressure on the back brake, the bike continued to gain speed. When she dared ease off the pressure slightly, and didn't start to wobble, she started to enjoy herself.

The breeze whipped back her hair and plastered her sweat-sodden t-shirt against her front, but for once she didn't care what she looked like. Damned if it wasn't exhilarating as hell. And before she knew what was what, Ruby had reached the flat portion of the path.

As she juddered off the footpath, instinct kicked in and suddenly she was zipping along the side of the road like she'd done this umpteen times before.

Kyan whizzed past her, hunched over the handlebars and pedaling for all he was worth.

"Hang a left at the corner," she yelled after him. "Then head straight ahead up the hill until you see the signpost for the first street on the left!"

She hoped he'd heard her, otherwise he might lose himself in one of the other side streets veering off from the main road. Not that it was her problem if he got lost. Mike would just have to cruise the streets until they found him—or until Kyan found *her*. If this mythical bond was all it was cracked up to be, then Kyan should simply be able to follow his nose until he located her.

By the time Ruby reached the intersection and turned left to pedal up the hill, she was losing the momentum she'd gained from the walkway. Pedaling became a chore. Her non-existent muscles screamed protests. The only thing that kept her going was the thought of flopping into the backseat of Mike's comfortable rental while he drove her home.

She grit her teeth. Her world narrowed to her bike and the increasing effort it took to push down the pedals and propel it forward. Through the haze of exertion she heard Kyan urging her onward. And, after what seemed like an hour but was probably merely minutes, Ruby crested the side street intersection and found herself cycling on the flat again.

Success. She'd done it.

Mike was there, waiting as promised. Kyan, too. As they approached, both men beamed at Ruby like she'd achieved a really huge milestone. Ruby grinned back. Anyone who knew her well would know the effort it'd taken for her to do this was pretty remarkable.

She brought the bike to a halt and attempted to dismount. Bad move. Her knees wobbled and then folded like limp noodles. She crashed to the footpath and lay on the concrete with the bike on top of her, shaking with shock from both the unexpected fall, and sheer relief it was all over.

Kyan dropped his bike to the curb and raced to her side. He tossed her bike onto the grass verge and lifted her as though she barely weighed anything at all to cradle her in his lap. "What is wrong, Ruby? Are you hurt?"

She stared up at him, marveling at his anxious expression. And the way he held her—so tenderly, like she was fragile. The first tear dripped down her cheek. And before she could figure out why she felt so heartbroken, it was too late to hold it all inside and she began to cry in earnest.

Kyan pulled her close, tucking her against his chest while he rubbed her back.

It wasn't fair. This completely gorgeous man was holding her as though he cared. Looking at her as though he cared. But she knew he couldn't possibly care about her. He was simply being kind. She could never have a man like Kyan for her own—not without benefit of a magic spell.

As though he'd read her thoughts, he lifted her chin in his hand, forcing her to meet his gaze. He unclasped her helmet and placed it on the ground, smoothed back the tangled hair from her face... and then he kissed her.

It was a gentle kiss. His lips barely brushed hers before he climbed to his feet, yanking her upright with him. He stared down at her, puzzled, as though he couldn't comprehend what had just occurred. The moment lengthened, and then his face blanked into that perfect emptiness of expression again, and he released her hands. He picked up her bike and wheeled it to Mike's car.

Ruby stood there, still dazed from the emotions his kiss

had aroused. How could a mere brush of a man's lips have such a devastating effect?

Her limbs felt languid. Her skin tingled as though she'd been wallowing in a hot bubble bath. She flexed her toes experimentally. Yep. The pudgy little digits had curled. She'd read about that phenomenon in books but believed it an exaggeration—authors getting a little carried away when the hero plants one on the heroine and all that.

Evidently not.

"You okay, Rubes?" Mike waved a hand in front of her face. "Earth to Ruby. Anyone home?"

She snapped back to the present. "Oh. Mike. Hi. I'm okay, I guess. Maybe a scrape or two on my legs."

He cupped her elbow, escorting her to the car.

"What the hell just happened?" she asked.

He shrugged. "It's been a long day."

"Yeah. It has." She risked a glance at her brother before she climbed into the backseat. He sported another one of those secretive smirks on his face. Great.

She slumped against the seat, tipped her head back and closed her eyes, wishing she knew what the hell Mike was so pleased about. And why Kyan had suddenly distanced himself from her.

KYAN CLIMBED INTO Mike's vehicle—a wondrous conveyance. And one that should have commanded his full attention. He should have been eager to quiz Mike about its intricacies. He should have been determined to gather as much information as possible about this strange new world. Instead, he could only focus on a woman.

Garnet Ruby Roberts.

What was it about *this* woman that so disturbed him?

No female he'd previously encountered had bedeviled both his cock *and* his mind. Rationally, Kyan knew the Crystal Guardian's sorcery must play a substantial role in the attraction Ruby held for him. But no matter how often he reminded himself of that very pertinent fact he could not stop thinking about her. Wanting her. Caring about her. He'd known her scant hours. And yet she'd burrowed into his heart and become dear to him just the same.

Witnessing the terror in her eyes when Mike had told her of the steep track he expected her to negotiate, and the grim determination to attempt it regardless…. Kyan had felt a burgeoning pride for Ruby's achievement. Even his mother, who had filled his ears with tales of her physical prowess, might have balked at such a feat. The potential mate the old sorcerer had chosen for him was no fragile female who wilted when confronted with a challenge. She possessed a warrior's spirit. She'd confronted her fears, crowed with joy as she conquered them. And even though her physical fitness had proven less than equal to the task she'd been set, she'd soldiered on to the point of exhaustion, refusing to give in.

Kyan recognized that brand of gutsy determination, and sensed a kindred spirit. He, too, knew what it was like to push himself beyond his physical capabilities to the point of collapse, only stubborn determination not to quit driving him onward.

When Ruby had faltered at the end of the ride, Kyan's heart had clenched so tightly he could barely breathe. And then, as he'd held her tight, tried to soothe her hurts, *kissed* her, all his carefully laid plans had gone awry.

Afterward, when he'd gotten his life back and a crystalline prison was no longer held over his head like some sword wielded by a vengeful god, Kyan had *planned* on treating Ruby as he treated any other woman. He'd *planned* to stay only as long as the relationship remained amiable and uncomplicated. When she became too needy, too demanding—wanting more than he was prepared to give—he had planned to leave. Alluring as his past bed-partners had been, the longest any woman had warmed his bed had been a se'nnight. So he'd reasoned that not even a woman of Ruby's caliber—beguiling as she was—would convince him to stay.

But the instant he'd pressed his lips to hers, felt her respond to him, experienced the depth of his own response—a visceral response that had shaken him to his core—he knew he was in trouble. And as he'd held Ruby in his arms, comforting her the only way he knew how, Kyan could not overlook the sobering fact that if *his* longing for Ruby was indeed rooted in a sorcerer's spell, then *her* longing for him, too, might well be false. And the thought that she might not truly desire him, that the naked yearning in her eyes was not true and honest and real? It gutted him as efficiently as any skilled sword thrust to an unprotected belly.

Damn that godless bastard of a sorcerer to *Halja* for eternity for putting him through this—for putting Ruby through this!

Little wonder, Kyan mused, that he had reacted in the only way he knew how—by pulling back, slipping a mask over his face and distancing himself. And in so doing, he knew he had hurt Ruby deeply. Apparently Mike would be kicking his arse "six ways to Sunday" sooner rather than later.

CHAPTER SEVEN

RUBY WANDERED INTO the lounge and spotted her answer phone message light blinking. The message was from Jules... and her tone screamed worry and concern. Turned out Jules had left another voice message on Ruby's mobile, too. And finished with a *Don't make me come over there. Ring me!* text message.

The sheer absurdity of her situation with Kyan abruptly crashed over Ruby, rocking her back on her heels. Talk about cold hard reality check. What the heck was she going to tell her best friend?

For all of ten seconds she debated not calling Jules back until tomorrow. But that was tantamount to an invitation for Jules to front up in person. And much as she loved Jules, Ruby couldn't face her best friend right now. Everything was happening too fast. She needed time to come up with a plausible excuse for Kyan to hang around for a while. And, looking at the time Jules had sent that text, Ruby reckoned she had about thirty minutes, tops, before Jules started bugging her in earnest.

Mike and Kyan were in the garage, making room to stow the bikes. Ruby stalked to the nearest window and flipped the latch. "I'm grabbing a quick shower," she yelled at Mike. Hopefully the hot water might unclog her brain so she could come up with something solid to tell Jules. "And I'm thinking takeaways for dinner?"

"Sounds good," came the shouted response.

"It's either that or toasted sandwiches." Cooking up a storm for two large ravenous men on a Sunday night was not her idea of a relaxing evening. The canapés and snacks for last night's party had taken hours to prepare. She reckoned she deserved a night off.

"Whatever," Mike yelled back. "I'm not fussed."

Takeaways, it was.

Ruby showered as quickly as humanly possible, and scuttled back to her bedroom to throw on some clean clothes.

The phone's ringer blared from the lounge. Dammit! Her sluggish brain was still struggling to concoct a story that would satisfy her inquisitive best friend. She had nothing.

She skidded to a halt in the doorway as the reason Ruby had to lie to her best friend in the first place picked up the phone receiver and said, "Hello, this is Kyan."

Please, God, cut me a break and let it not be Jules calling?

"Yes," Kyan said. "I am the man who took his clothes off at the party last night."

Oh, crap. Ruby clutched the doorframe. She was in trouble now—deep, deep, trouble.

"Yes," Kyan said, "I stayed here last night." An excruciating long pause, and then, "I will get Ruby for you now." He glanced up, spotted her cowering in the doorway, and held out the phone. "'Tis your friend, Jules."

Ruby gulped, and walked over to take the call. "Hi, Jules."

"He's still there? How come, Rubes?"

This was going to take a while. And if she was going to be subjected to a bollocking from her best friend, she might as well make herself comfortable. Ruby stretched out on the couch and tried to ignore the way Kyan was eyeing her. He had that whole staring at her like she was something yummy thing going on again. "Oh, yes I'm fine, Jules. Fully recovered from my fainting episode last night. Thanks *so* much for asking."

"Yeah, yeah. Mike already told us it was nothing serious. Probably some mild bug or the heat. So spill, Rubes. What's the hot stripper still doing at your place, huh? And answering the phone like he lives there?"

"Um… he's going to be staying for a month."

"Oh, really." Jules managed to imbue those two words with so much hot and heavy naughtiness that Ruby's face and neck flushed with damning heat.

Her brain finally emerged from hibernation to help her out with a halfway decent lie. "Turns out Kyan and I go way back. We're friends from… primary school, actually." Yeah. That'd work because Jules had moved into the neighborhood a few months after Ruby had started intermediate school. "He was in my class three years running before his family upped and moved overseas," she elaborated. "We didn't recognize each other at first. I've changed quite a lot and he's, er, grown up a bit since then."

"I'll say." Jules snickered. "How come you didn't recognize his name? 'Kyan' isn't that common."

Bugger. Jules was too damn smart. Some embellishment was needed. Fast. Ruby uttered what she hoped was a passable wry snort. "Oh, you're gonna love this, Jules. He's going by his middle name now—just like I do. Back in primary school he was, uh, *Augustus*. He got sick of being teased about it and decided 'Kyan' was the lesser of the two evils."

"Augustus? Sheesh." Ruby could picture Jules shuddering in sympathy. "Poor bugger. What were his parents thinking?"

"Yeah. Pretty dorky, huh? Not even shortening it to 'Gus' could save that one."

"I'll say. What a hoot! So you two have been doing some catching up, huh?" Again with the insinuating undertone.

"Yep." Ruby attempted to infuse airy lightness into her voice. "Been great, actually. When he first, uh, *left*, we wrote to each other for a while—did the pen-friend thing. But eventually we lost touch. You know how it is."

"Betcha didn't think he'd turn out such a hottie."

"I had absolutely no idea." Ruby crossed her fingers.

"So you two are just good friends, then?"

Don't blow this. Deep breath.... "Yep. We're just good friends. What else could we be?"

"Mmmm."

"Oh, come on, Jules. Don't read anything into this, okay? Kyan needs a place to crash for a bit and I've offered my couch. He and I are friends. Period. Nothing more." Ruby shot Kyan a wary glance from beneath her lashes. His brows were creased, gorgeous mouth thinned to a tight line, and the way his arms were crossed over his chest? Ah, crap. Majorly unimpressed male.

"Riiight," Jules said. "Just friends."

"That's right." Ruby's heart sank to her toes. "Just friends."

Kyan pivoted on his heel and stalked toward the kitchen. His rigid spine proclaimed his outrage, and it took every ounce of self-control Ruby could muster to remain lying on the couch and not run after him to plead for forgiveness.

She closed her eyes, hating herself. But it was for the best. And so she rallied enough to burble into the phone, "He's going to help me out with my triathlon training." At least, she hoped he would. If he wasn't too pissed off with her.

"So you're still going through with the triathlon?"

"Yep." She needed something to take her mind off this mess.

"Good."

"Good? " Ruby blinked and fought the impulse to bang the phone receiver on the arm of the chair. "That's a turn around. I thought you weren't keen for me to do this?"

"I wasn't—when I thought you'd been pressured into it by the Stick Insect With No Soul. But because it's your own idea, and you're determined to see it through, then all power to ya, babe. I'll be backing you all the way."

"Thanks, Jules." At least Ruby would have one person

cheering her on from the sidelines if Mike couldn't make it up for the event.

"Hey, you still on for this Saturday night, or you want to flag it until Kyan's gone?"

"Of course I'm still on. Wouldn't miss our monthly movie night for the world." A girls' night out was exactly what she needed after having all this supernatural woo-woo crap dumped in her lap.

"Mike's here 'til next Sunday, so he and Kyan will probably watch the cricket on TV and drink beer. They don't need me for that. What movie do you feel like seeing?"

"Play it by ear, huh?" Jules said.

"Cool. See you then."

"Bye, Rubes."

The tight knot twisting and turning in Ruby's stomach unraveled a tiny bit. She hated lying to Jules but she didn't have much choice. Unloading the whole story over a latté, and trying to convince Jules that she wasn't completely delusional wasn't an option. Now all Ruby had to do was keep her mouth shut at work so none of her workmates realized she had an incredibly hot, all-too-*available* man staying for the next four weeks.

Hmmm. Now there was an idea. A certain man-hungry workmate had seemed *very* keen on Kyan. Maybe Ruby could invite Caroline over, and *she* could bond with Kyan.

The more Ruby thought it over, the more it seemed like an excellent idea... and the best way to get her life back on track. She scrambled off the couch and scurried over to the lounge window. "Hey, Mike! Where are you, bro?"

"In the garage," came the faint reply. "What's up?"

On her way out the door, Ruby glanced into the kitchen and spied Kyan leaning against the bench. He'd placed three mugs, the container of ground coffee and the plunger on the bench, and was frowning moodily at the electric jug.

She pointed to the wall-mounted power outlet above the

bench. "You need to push that switch down to turn the power on. Otherwise the jug won't be able to use the electricity to boil the water."

He flicked the switch down. "Thank you."

"You okay with how everything else works?"

"I believe so. Mike showed me this morning."

"Cool." She trundled out the back door and headed for the garage.

Mike was moving a pile of cartons to make enough room to store the bikes, while still allowing Ruby to park her car in the garage. "What the hell is all this junk, Rubes?" he grumbled. "Don't you ever throw anything away?"

"Considering the majority of these cartons contain *your* junk, I'm sure you'd be thrilled to bits if I tossed them."

He sat on a carton and swiped his brow with the back of his hand. "My junk?"

"You know, the stuff you didn't want to take to Christchurch with you five years ago, and begged me to store for 'a couple of months' until you got sorted."

"Oh. That junk. I'll have a good look through it tomorrow while you're at work and let you know what I want to keep and what you can toss."

"Gee, how kind of you. A trip to the dump is right up there with my very favorite things to do in my spare time." She dialed down the snark. "Look, Mike, I've got this great idea that would solve my big blond warrior-from-another-world problem. How about we throw Kyan at some attractive single female? Like, Caroline, for instance. And let them... bond. If they hit it off and live happily ever after, we're sweet. And if they don't make it, and Kyan ends up back where he started, the Crystal Guardian can find him some other woman."

Mike's gaze turned frosty. No, frosty wasn't the right word. He stared at Ruby like she'd turned into something gross that he wanted to scrape from the bottom of his shoe. "You'd seriously palm him off on that scrawny bitch and send him back to that place he was trapped in? Shit. I thought better of you, Rubes."

Ouch. "Hey, that's hardly fair. I didn't ask to be bonded to this guy, all right? What's wrong with passing on the bond? Caroline seems to like him. And she's more his type than I am." Wasn't that the truth? Slim, polished to perfection Caroline, and movie-star handsome Kyan. A match made in heaven.

Mike shoved a lock of hair from his eyes and stood to stretch the kinks from his spine. "It's not that simple, Rubes. Chalcedony told me once the bond is initiated, it's irrevocable. And according to her mother, Crystal Warriors who don't complete the bonding process return to their crystal and are destroyed by the Guardian. In other words, he murders them. Chalcedony has some doubts about that last bit, though no hard proof either way. But if it turns out to be true, do you want to be responsible for this Guardian having a shot at killing Kyan?"

Geez. Way to lay on the guilt. Ruby ducked her head. "No, of course not. But—"

"You're it, Rubes. You're Kyan's only chance of getting out of this mess. And I'm sure the Crystal Guardian had his reasons for choosing *you* as Kyan's potential life-mate. So suck it up and deal."

She raised her chin to glare at him. "Yeah, right. And maybe this old guy's a few sausages short of a barbecue. I wouldn't be surprised if having nothing to do but watch a bunch of crystals for centuries on end has screwed his brain."

"Maybe." Mike's gaze turned über-serious. You've shared a little of what Kyan suffered when he was imprisoned in the crystal, right?"

She shuddered, reluctant to dwell on that nightmarish experience.

Mike took that as an affirmative. "Bottom line? Are you prepared to condemn a human being to an existence like that without at least *trying* your utmost to prevent it? I know I couldn't."

Dammit, Mike had her there. And he knew it.

"Sorry, Rubes." He patted her shoulder as he brushed past her. "Hey, listen. I'm gonna take Kyan out and buy him some clothes and a pair of sneakers. The stuff I can spare isn't going to do him for an entire month, and he can't kick around much longer in those heavy boots and leathers. We'll grab something to eat while we're out, too. Give you some space to think. But try not to come up with any more wild schemes, okay?"

"Yeah. Okay. And I'll pay you back for the clothes and stuff."

"No worries." Her brother waved away her offer. "It's the least I can do."

Ruby followed Mike from the garage, scuffing her feet as she worked through what he'd said. And what it meant for her. She wasn't watching where she was going and she nearly bumped into Kyan, who was juggling three cups of coffee. Mike got his mug handed to him with a smile. Ruby got hers with a scowl that made her stomach swoop—and not in a good way.

"Thanks." She took a sip. It was strong but drinkable. The man learned quickly.

"Why are you so eager to be rid of me, Ruby?" Kyan's generous mouth was still tight with displeasure.

Ah, shit. He'd obviously overheard her cunning little plan. Worse, he wasn't at all enthused by it. "Um—"

"Does my appearance displease you, Ruby?"

"I… um…. No? I mean, you're *very* good looking, Kyan. As I'm sure you know. But that's not the point. I—"

"Then why do you want to give me to this *Caroline*?"

He practically spat the name. Yikes. He was really pissed off. His eyes were little slits, and a deep angry-looking flush was crawling up his neck.

Ruby couldn't figure out his deal. Surely he'd be pleased to get rid of her? He only had to crook his little finger and he could have women flocking to him. He could have any woman he wanted. So why fixate on *her*?

Aha. Clarity smacked her upside the head. Now she got it. And boy, wasn't clarity a heinous bitch? "You're pissed off because you're stuck with me 'coz of this life-mate thing, and you think I don't want you. That's it, isn't it, Kyan? You're used to having women fall all over you, eager to do anything at all to get you to notice them. But I'm not your typical groupie. I'm right, aren't I?"

Crimson slashed his cheeks. "Nay. I—"

She rounded on him, prodding him in the chest with her finger. "You're having a tantrum because you think I should be gagging for you, thrilled to bits to have someone as gorgeous-looking and built as you are paying me some attention."

His Adam's apple bobbed as he swallowed. "That is not true. I—"

"I've got news for you, buster, and it's all bad. I've spent my whole life being jeered at by the so-called beautiful people. And you know what, Kyan? Looks don't matter to me any-more. God knows, if I dwelled too much on how *I* looked, I'd fucking slit my wrists and put myself out of my misery tomor-row. So if you think I should throw myself at your feet and whimper with gratitude because I'm lucky enough to have been chosen as your life-mate, you can think again. I have more class than that. And I deserve more, too. A whole lot more!"

He stood there, no doubt rendered speechless by her mas-terful tirade.

She'd expressed herself rather well, Ruby thought—really gotten her point across. Pity most of it was complete bollocks. Because in truth, she was lusting after Kyan in the worst way. And to be brutally honest, she would give her right arm to be a tiny bit thinner. But he didn't have to know that. She jutted her chin in challenge. "So, you vain bastard, what do you think about that?"

He inhaled long and deep, and she tried not to ogle his chest.

"I, too, have been teased for my looks," he said. "As a child and a trainee warrior. And by members of my *tehun*, my troop. 'Tis not a pleasant experience." He paused, cocking his head to one side. "Do you truly not believe you are pretty, Ruby?"

"Huh?"

"Your face is exquisite. And your eyes are so beautiful they haunt me."

She glared at him, prickling all over with suspicion. "You're pulling my leg, right?"

He scratched his head, frowning.

"It means you're joking at my expense," she said. Geez. It was impossible to have a decent argument with someone who didn't understand a lot of what she was saying.

"I am not joking."

Oh. He didn't sound like he was joking. And from the intent, serious expression on his face, he didn't look like he was joking, either. "Oh," she said. "Um…. Gee, thanks." And then, dammit, she blushed.

She stared at him. He stared back. The silence deepened, and so did Ruby's blush.

Mike chugged his coffee, and she could have kissed him when he spoke and broke the tension. "C'mon, Kyan," he said. "Let's go buy you some comfortable clothes. And afterward I'll take you out for a beer."

"My clothes are very comfortable, Mike."

"Not as comfortable as the ones I'm gonna buy you. Trust me." Mike relieved Kyan of his mug and handed it, along with his own, to Ruby. Then he grabbed Kyan's arm and towed him toward the car.

Ruby waved the mugs at her brother. "Hey, thanks! Why don't I wash these up for you? Because obviously I've got nothing better to do!"

Mike backed the car out of the driveway and took off down the road in a helluva hurry. But not before she glimpsed an all-too-familiar smug smirk on his face.

Bastard. Her life was a soap-opera-worthy disaster right now. What'n the hell was there to smirk about? Ruby headed back inside to phone in an order for delivery pizza.

BY NINE O'CLOCK Kyan and Mike still hadn't arrived home. Ruby shoved the leftover pizza in the fridge and went to bed. She was tired, stressed, and very, *very* confused. And if she was going to get in a bike ride before work tomorrow she needed an early night.

Mike and Kyan were grown men. They could sort out their own sleeping arrangements. Plus, there was the added bonus that if she was already in bed when they got home, she wouldn't have to put up with her brother's smirks. Or face Kyan again. Because that would be a sleepless night waiting to happen. And the last thing she needed was to be obsessing over Kyan. Or what he'd said. And the way he'd said it.

Of course the instant her head hit the pillow and she closed her eyes, she obsessed over Kyan. It was sort of okay having him around while Mike was here. But what about next week, when she was alone with him without her brother to run interference? And had Kyan really meant what he said? Did he truly think she was pretty?

Gah. This was freaking ridiculous. Ruby yawned and assumed the sleeping position. But no matter what she forced herself to think about, images of Kyan intruded.

She tried counting sheep. New Zealand had about fifty million of the woolly jumpers, so it should have occupied her mind for quite some time. Except by the time she reached a hundred she was no longer counting sheep. Instead, she was counting the number of Kyans hurdling the fence. And admiring each Kyan's athleticism, and the marvelous play of his muscles when he jumped. And the way his cock bobbed when he—

Oh, God. She was imagining him naked.

She groaned, grabbed a pillow, and pulled it over her face. And maybe the lack of oxygen helped because the next thing she knew, she was yanked from sleep by something prodding her back.

She wriggled.

It sort of pulsated.

She tried to edge away but the arms that were wrapped around her tightened, and refused to budge. Her sleep-fuddled brain made a halfhearted attempt to form a coherent thought, but gave up. It was too much effort. Especially when she was warm and comfortable and content.

Something throbbed against her spine again. *It* sure was awake—whatever it was.

Ruby yawned and tried to roll over onto her back. No joy there. Those strong arms cuddled her closer. Mmmm. They were nice arms. It was nice to be held like this—

Bloody buggering hell!

She choked on a gasp, shocked to full consciousness by the realization someone had crawled into bed with her. Her t-shirt had ridden halfway up her back sometime in the night, and given the hard rod of flesh currently prodding her spine, that someone was definitely male, definitely naked, and definitely well endowed. In fact, it was a wonder he had any blood left to circulate in his brain.

She inhaled deeply, her senses awash with the heady scent of warm male skin.

Kyan's skin.

Her heart thudded in her chest. Surely he had to feel it racing. What should she do? Pretend to be asleep? Ignore that he was naked and obviously aroused?

And that was the other puzzling thing. In bed with her, and aroused? Was this guy desperate or what?

The tense darkness of the room throbbed with Kyan's whispered, "Are you awake, Ruby?"

She managed to disguise her reaction to the oh-so-sexy huskiness of his lowered voice by turning her squeak into a loud, unladylike snort. And if anything should have put him off and sent him slinking back to the couch where he belonged, that should have done it.

Sure enough, the mattress dipped as his weight shifted and he pulled away from her.

Ruby locked her pain away so she wouldn't embarrass herself further by burying her face in her pillow and sobbing. How typical of a man to seek the most comfortable bed. And how typical that now he was confronted with the stark reality of waking up to *her*, he was making tracks. Honestly, what else had she expected?

She shouldn't feel this hurt, this devastated, that he'd snuck into her bed, snuggled up to her, then skulked off the moment his brain won dominion over his dick. She shouldn't have felt anything at all because she'd learned better. She'd learned to stick to the rules of the dating game for not-so-slim women.

Rule Number One: Don't approach a man. Always let him come to you. And even then be wary, because he might be trying to win a bet with his mates.

Which led to Rule Number Two: Don't expect anything, then you won't be disappointed. Don't be surprised when he never calls like he promised. Don't be hurt when he dumps you because his mates tease him unmercifully, and the shallow bastard cares more about what his friends think than being true to himself.

And lastly, the most important rule of all. Rule Number Three: Perfect the "just friends" vibe, and never, ever, let on that you're really attracted to him.

Ruby had the rules sussed. The incredible invulnerable woman, that was her. But not this time. This time, she was sooo kidding herself if she believed she wasn't hurt by Kyan's rejection.

Why this time, with this particular guy? Was she insane? He was a walking fantasy, the epitome of unattainable. What was it about Kyan that piqued her hopes and forced her to dream about the impossible coming true? Laid waste to all her carefully erected defenses and left her so achingly vulnerable?

A feather-light caress stroked her spine. Huh. Could be he got his jollies from tickling sleeping women until they woke. But Ruby wasn't in the mood to play his silly game. She'd had enough. She rolled onto her back, her eyelids still squeezed shut in faked sleep. She wished he would just go away and—

"Eep!" Her eyelids flew open. Seemed Kyan hadn't left the bed after all—merely moved right to the edge of the mattress. And now he was shimmying down the mattress beneath the sheet. His hair brushed her thighs. His lips on her skin sent waves of heat and longing rushing towards certain girly parts that had been neglected for far too long.

Humiliating, much?

She yanked up the sheet to peer down at him. "What the hell do you think you're doing down there?"

"Aha." His voice was a deep, sexy vibration against her thigh. "I knew you were awake."

"Yeah. So it's—" She craned her neck until she glimpsed the alarm clock on her bedside table. "Three a.m. The middle of the night. And yes, I'm awake. Thanks for that, by the way. Especially when I've got to get up early to fit in a bike ride before work."

His response to her pointed sarcasm was to run one hand down her inner thigh while the other delved beneath the waistband of her undies. He combed his fingers through her pubic hair… and then cupped her mons.

Ruby caught her breath, rendered speechless by the blatant sexual intention of that caress. Her flesh flared white-hot where he touched.

His fingers parted her folds, stroking, probing gently, and

she yearned to open to him, to grind herself against his hand. Somehow she resisted that almost overpowering urge. To react, to show him how much she wanted this—wanted *him*— would unleash her carefully suppressed dreams and desires. Her longing for Kyan would romp roughshod over rationality. And that would be bad. Really, really bad. Because she knew how this little tryst would ultimately end and she didn't want to open herself up to that much hurt and humiliation.

One finger pushed inside her, then two. His thumb stroked her clitoris—knowing, uneven strokes, sometimes firm, some- times barely a tickle with his thumbnail—and despite her resolve, her body tensed in anticipation of each caress. She wanted Kyan's cock inside her. She wanted him to make love to her. She wanted him to—

Love her.

Kyan as her life-mate. Loving her.... For a lifetime....

The sheer impossibility of that thought was enough to snap Ruby from her dreamlike state. Kyan might have been cooped up in some mother of all hells for the past couple of centuries, and was now desperate to get his rocks off, and *she* might have been secretly wishing for an end to her man-drought, but that didn't mean she would be an easy lay. Not when she had a vibrator in her drawer, and he possessed a perfectly good hand.

She reached down and grabbed that oh-so-clever hand be- fore it worked any more of its magic and her resolve dissolved. "Kyan, I don't think—"

"Now is not the time for thinking, Ruby. Now is the time for feeling."

He shook off her hand and made quick work of her undies by yanking them down her thighs.

"Hey!" Heat flooded her face and she thanked God the on- ly illumination in the room was a wafer-thin shaft of moonlight peeking through a small gap in the curtains. She squirmed, trying to sit up, but he pushed her thighs apart. His tongue replaced his thumb, flicking and swirling the now swollen bud of her clit. And when his fingers began a rhythmic thrusting deep inside her, all thought of getting away from him fled. Her inner muscles clenched around his fingers and she sank back against the pillows as the deliciously heavy, unfamiliar pressure inside her built.

So this is what it's like to have someone else bring you to orgasm. None of her previous partners had succeeded—or perhaps they simply hadn't cared enough to learn the ways of her body and understand what she wanted. Not that she blamed them.

Kyan, though, was different. He instinctively knew what she wanted—needed. And what he was currently doing aroused her to fever pitch. She writhed and bit her lips, but she could not suppress a moan as the intensely pleasurable tension built and built, until she hung poised on the edge of something wondrous. The teasing flicks of his wicked tongue were replaced by his mouth and lips, devouring her, while his fingers continued to thrust inside her.

The most intense orgasm Ruby had ever experienced took her, and her inner muscles clenched around his fingers, hungry for more. Hungry for him.

He withdrew from her then, fingertips and lips gliding up her body. Her skin tingled, nerve endings sparking from his touch, even though she lay sprawled and sated, incapable of moving.

She watched him silently as he knelt astride her. She didn't protest as he ripped her old t-shirt down the front and spread it aside.

He drew the straps of her bra down her shoulders. "Will you remove this torturous garment for me, Ruby?"

"Why?" she whispered.

"Because I want to see all of you."

"Why?"

He seemed lost for a moment. His head drooped as though

searching deep inside himself for answers. And then he looked up, gazing straight into her eyes. "I need to see you, Ruby. Please."

And she was lost. Devastated and afraid. And yet, a spark of hope remained. She arched her back and reached behind to unhook the clasps. She tossed the bra to the floor, baring herself fully to him, steeling herself to weather his disgust.

His eyes widened at the size of her breasts, and his blue gaze turned molten as he reached for her. He cupped the mounds in his big hands, kneading her flesh, tweaking her nipples and rolling them between his fingers. The fingers that stroked her flesh were gentle, and so reverent that tears pricked her eyes. He bent forward to press his lips to her flesh, drawing her nipple into his mouth, worshiping her breast with his lips and teeth and tongue.

She'd never thought her breasts were overly sensitive, or that having a man touch them would be pleasurable. Until now. With him.

"Kyan." She averted her gaze from his face and turned her head aside, uncomfortable with the intensity of his expression.

"Mmmm?"

"You don't have to stay, you know. I mean, thanks for the… um… what you did and everything. It was amazing. But you don't have to… you know."

"Make love to you?"

"Yes."

"Out of obligation?"

"Yes." Her voice wobbled with the huge effort it took to keep her pain and humiliation buried. She felt his hard shaft jutting against her stomach as he finished paying homage to her breasts and nibbled his way upward to gently lip the wildly beating pulse beneath her jaw.

"Oh, God." She hadn't meant to say the words aloud.

He stilled. "Look at me, Ruby."

She couldn't bring herself to turn her head and meet his

gaze. To see the pity in his eyes.

"Ruby."

A hand grasped her chin. Caring fingertips wiped away the tears that had stolen down her cheeks—tears of longing, bursting with wishes for what might have been if things were different. If *she* were different.

"Why are you doing this, Kyan? Are you that hard up for sex that you'd stoop to jumping me? Why?" The rush of words exited her mouth as a plea, and her anguish hung in the air between them like some malevolent entity poised to strike.

He frowned. And then his expression cleared, lips curving in a mischievous grin. He sat back on his heels and glanced down at his ready-for-action cock. "Something is certainly 'hard up'."

She bit back a giggle at the lame joke. He could say that again.

"And as for the rest, all I know is that I want you, Ruby. All of you."

"All of me?" She glanced down at her too-rounded stomach and pale, wobbly body lying spread-eagled beneath his firm, muscular, golden-skinned, godlike one.

"This?" Her voice rose, edged with disbelief. "Me?"

"You, Ruby. I find myself obsessed with you. I cannot banish thoughts of you from my mind. You—" He closed his eyes, jaw working as though he was fighting to find the right words. "You consume me. I do not know if what I feel is a result of the Crystal Guardian's bonding spell, but you consume me."

"Me, too," she whispered.

"And perhaps if I make love to you now, this obsession will fade and I will return to my normal state."

"You mean, crooking your little finger and being mobbed by girls?"

He grinned again, his eyes glittering like polished gems in the moonlit room. "Perhaps. I am only human, and a man, after all."

"Humph. Some life-partner you'll make. I can picture you making eyes at all the pretty girls behind my back. You'll be impossible." She grinned back because she couldn't help herself. His grin was infectious. It humanized the perfection of his face, made him fallible. More importantly, that grin made it seem possible that when all this supernatural woo-woo crap was over, they might remain friends.... Of a kind. At least until Kyan realized her feelings for him were not in the least bit 'friendly' and she wanted more. And that knowledge drove him away.

"So, my Ruby." He tapped her nose with the pad of his forefinger. "Where does that leave you?"

Her heart did a little pit-a-pat at his "my Ruby". And the pit-a-pat escalated to a gallop as he stroked a fingertip down the side of her breast, past the curve of her hip.

His hand came to rest on her thigh. Her body warmed beneath his touch. "Wh-what do you mean?" she managed to ask.

"I will be honest with you—more honest than I have been with any other woman. I cannot offer you anything beyond the Testing, for I know not what the future holds for us. Whatever we feel for each other now may be false. But I would have these few weeks with you, Ruby, if you would allow it. So I ask you this: Will you give yourself to me now? Is what I offer enough? For if it is not, then I will leave your bed. And you have my word that I will make no further intimate demands upon you."

"It's enough," she said. And it was the truth. Because for now, what Kyan offered was more than enough. More than she had ever dreamed.

He leaned in to kiss her, parting her lips with his tongue. And his hands... what they did to her, how they made her feel, was miraculous. When he entered her, slowly pushing his hard, thick cock inside her, it was all she could do not to scream his name. He filled her, and in this one way at least, they were perfectly matched, for she accommodated his considerable size. For a long, intense moment he didn't move. And then slowly—excruciatingly slowly—he withdrew, teasing her entrance with the tip of his cock until, craving him inside her again, she grabbed his butt and thrust her hips upward, demanding.

He gripped her hips and held her still, laughing down at her, and it was a laugh brimming with delight rather than derision. "So, Ruby. You do want me, after all. Perhaps now you will not be so quick to give me to one of your friends."

"Perhaps— Aaaah!" He thrust deeper inside her. "Perhaps not right away."

She waited until he filled her again, and hooked her heels around his thighs to keep him there, fully seated inside her.

They rocked together for what seemed like endless moments, Kyan suckling and fondling her breasts, Ruby stroking his back, his butt, and every part of him that she could reach. His cock twitched and pulsated inside her. And as each tiny movement triggered spasms of her inner muscles, she whimpered, until at last he moved, setting a slow, insistent rhythm. Each time he sank into her, his balls rubbed against her sensitized flesh and she writhed with mindless pleasure-filled gasps.

An age later, at her insistent urging, Kyan increased his pace, pounding deep inside her. He groaned, cried out her name. He came, and to her astonishment, his orgasm triggered her own. He lay prone atop her, his cock still lodged deep inside her, and at last she felt complete. For the first time in her life it didn't matter what she looked like, because she knew it hadn't mattered to him.

The man of her dreams rolled off her and curled up behind her, one arm draped over her hip. He nuzzled her ear. "Thank you, Ruby," he whispered.

She lay there listening to his slow, even breathing, wondering whether he was truly asleep, or lying there like she was, physically wiped but unable to sleep because of the chaotic thoughts buzzing through her brain.

She glanced at the clock, blinking at the time. Four-fifteen in the morning. For the past *hour* Kyan had coaxed responses and demands from her that should have had Ruby cringing with embarrassment and worry that brother might hear them from the next bedroom. But she didn't care what Mike might or might not have heard. All she cared about was Kyan.

Her last coherent thought before sleep dragged her down was that maybe, just maybe, Kyan really did care about her, and not just because of a spell. Maybe. Dreams, after all, were free.

KYAN WAITED UNTIL Ruby's breathing deepened and he was certain she slept. Only then did he roll onto his back, careful not to disturb her.

Disturbed. An all-too accurate description of his mental state right now. He stared at the ceiling, watching the shadows thrown by the gap in the curtains crawl and twist, wondering how this tryst could have gone so horribly awry.

He'd been motivated to seduce Ruby not only in tacit apology for his earlier coldness, but to bind her to him so she would be less likely to abandon him before the Testing took place. She had been correct to believe him angered by her suggestion to pass the bond to another woman—as though he were a side of meat. In another time and place he might have extracted a delicious revenge upon her for that suggestion—a revenge that involved teasing and tantalizing and leading her on until she begged for mercy, begged him to take her. But he could ill afford to play such games when the stakes were so high.

He'd hoped that bedding Ruby would lessen his growing obsession for her, clear his head, allow him to remain firmly in control. But he'd been a fool to imagine such an outcome when merely kissing her had made his world tilt on its axis.

His Ruby was a potent mix of endearing uncertainty and wanton female who knew what she wanted and, when sufficiently provoked, was not the least shy about communicating those wants. That combination, paired with the other qualities he so admired about her, was irresistible.

She held the power, here, not him. Not anymore. Because now he'd had a taste of her, now she'd given herself to him with a wholehearted abandon that stunned him, all his scheming was for naught. He was lost. He didn't know whether he could bear to leave and go his own way once the Testing was completed. He didn't know if he dared stay. And for Kyan, who had already lost everything that mattered to him, the thought of relinquishing his free will—depending upon a woman for whatever crumbs she deigned to throw his way—was anathema.

He could hate Ruby for what she'd done to him, what she'd reduced him to. Except that would be a lie. Because whatever happened between them in the future, he could not imagine hating her. Not his Ruby.

He could love her, though. Oh, yes. That was a distinct possibility. And that possibility, more than anything else that had befallen him since he'd tumbled into this world, scared him the most.

CHAPTER EIGHT

KYAN SHOOK HER awake. "Ruby."

"Go 'way."

"Ruby!" He tried yanking down the duvet and sheet but she grabbed a handful of bedclothes and held on. A fierce tussle ensued until his superior strength won out, leaving her curled naked in the middle of the bed.

"You will be late for your training session."

She groaned. "I'm too tired, Kyan. I'll have to start it tomorrow."

Silence reigned and she pried open one eyelid to reassure herself that he'd gotten the hint. The ambient temperature in her bedroom was cool, but not so cool that it prevented her drifting back to sleep. Which she was making a concerted effort to do when the mattress tilted, dumping her unceremoniously onto the floor.

"Hey!" She glared up at him through sleep-bleared eyes. "That was totally uncalled for."

He didn't strike her at all repentant, standing there, hands on hips, looking far too magnificent for her peace of mind. "If you wish to be fit enough to complete the challenge Mike tells me you have set yourself, then you must begin training as soon as possible. Today. Get up and get dressed, Ruby."

"Geez! Who died and made you my drill-sergeant?"

"You have five minutes to get dressed, Ruby."

"Or what?"

"Or I will drag you outside, as you are, and put you on your bike."

Naked cycling? In public? "You can't be serious."

"I am. Very serious."

Bastard. She scowled at him, only now noticing he'd already dressed in shorts, t-shirt and sneakers. He looked bright-eyed and bushy-tailed—as though he'd had a full eight hours uninterrupted sleep before bouncing out of bed, ready to face the day. She glanced at the clock. It wasn't quite five thirty. What kind of a person was *that* together this early in the morning?

She thought about curling up on the carpet and sleeping some more, but the gleam in his eyes made her reconsider. Kyan was obviously a man of his word. And she didn't want to be responsible for any unfortunate members of the public seeing her naked and requiring therapy. Not to mention if dragging was involved, as he'd threatened, there would be the distinct possibility of carpet burns.

She rolled to her hands and knees and crawled to the chest of drawers to fish out some old clothes. She sat back on her heels, clutching the garments to her front, and pinned Kyan with an expectant glare.

"What is wrong, now?" he asked.

"Couldn't you at least look the other way while I get changed?"

His drill-sergeant demeanor softened. "Very well." He turned his back. "Though why you feel shy now, after I have thoroughly bedded you, I have no idea."

Ruby managed a full-body blush as she struggled into her clothes. "That's different."

"Why?"

"Because it was dark and you couldn't see me properly."

"I have excellent nighttime vision, Ruby."

Shit. "Really?"

"Indeed."

"Oh."

"And I do believe I saw you naked when I tipped you from your bed," he said, his voice warm with amusement.

"Oh, yeah. Right." She shuddered. Bet he'd copped an eyeful—enough to put any self-respecting male off his breakfast. She sat on the edge of the bed to put on her socks and running shoes.

Kyan pivoted to confront her. "And from what I have seen, you are doing yourself a disservice, Ruby."

"Yeah. Right."

"Right." He extended a hand.

She stared up at him, ignoring his gesture. All the uncertainty that she'd banished during their intimate encounter came rushing back, tumbling from her mouth in a rush. "Oh, come off it, Kyan. There's no need to beat around the bush with me. I'm very aware of what I look like, and it's not pretty."

He grabbed her hand and jerked her to her feet so they stood face to face. Or rather, her face to his chest, given his superior height. She didn't mind. It was a very nice chest, after all.

"You are a very special woman, Ruby. Your body is a woman's body, all soft curves and generous, giving flesh. I enjoyed bedding you last night. And afterward, I felt—" His brows creased, and his gaze grew distant, as though he was searching deep inside for the right words.

"I felt as though I had discovered something precious—something I have been missing my entire life." His face filled with wonder, like a kid at Christmas time.

"Oh." Ruby was one-hundred-percent certain she was glowing, and that her face sported a dopey grin. Kyan had enjoyed making love to her. She'd fulfilled him in some deep and meaningful weird way.

He hugged her, and pressed a kiss to her brow. "Perhaps this bond is designed to fulfill spiritual as well as physical desires. If so, then I am content to accept the Crystal Guardian's choice."

Her pleasure twisted into a noose that threatened to strangle her with cold hard facts and obligations.

The bond—this so-called mystical power that had chosen *her*, an overweight, desperately lonely woman for this paragon of male perfection—was scrambling Kyan's brains, and overwhelming his natural inclinations. In real life, in Ruby's world, to a man like Kyan she would be nothing but a pity-fuck. Or a bet with his mates as to who could screw the most undesirable woman.

She desperately wanted to believe otherwise but the truth was, *nothing* Kyan felt for her could be real. It was all fake. A means to an end. A warped and potentially devastating lesson he had to learn before he would be released from the spell that had imprisoned him. Pair the handsome Adonis with the fat chick, and teach him to look beyond first impressions—that true beauty was more than skin deep, or some such bollocks. And that would be fine, Ruby thought, if she could disconnect her heart from her head and accept Kyan as a fleeting gift, a treat to be savored like an award-winning wine or the finest, most decadent Belgian chocolate that melted on her tongue. But that wasn't the case. Kyan had wormed his way into her heart and when he left, Ruby knew she would be broken and lost.

Someone, somewhere, had either grossly miscalculated or was indulging in a bloody good laugh at her expense.

She suspected the former. Only because she couldn't bring herself to believe anyone could be so cruel as to pair her with Kyan, knowing full well that her heart would be shredded when the Testing was over. But who knew for sure? Maybe the Crystal Guardian was a spiteful old bugger who enjoyed messing with people's lives and making them miserable.

Kyan released her and tugged on her hand. "Let us go, Ruby. Time is marching by."

She allowed him to lead her outside, where their bikes waited propped against the side of the house.

"And the training commences. Are you ready, Ruby?" He grinned at her, the sheer joy in his face eliciting a wan smile in return.

Somehow she summoned the energy to fling a leg over her bike. "Yep. I'm ready for anything." *Not.* But at least the perils of this bike ride would command all her concentration and prevent her from brooding.

AFTER RISKING LIFE and limb in the horrendous North Shore traffic, nearly toppling off her bike every time some impatient sod blared his horn, and having to practically sprint to the bus stop so she didn't miss her ride to work, Ruby's most heartfelt desire was to collapse behind her desk, stretch out her legs, and take a load off.

The instant she walked in the door she was greeted by a bunch of sideways glances. She figured her workmates were gauging the possibility she might faint again, and provide further entertainment. She smiled, murmured greetings, and headed for her desk, hoping that would be the end of it.

No such luck.

"How are you feeling, sweetie?" Liz perched on the end of Ruby's desk. The expression in her eyes promised the second Spanish Inquisition. "You look a bit buggered. Mike said it was probably a twenty-four-hour bug, but maybe you should go see a doctor—just to be sure."

Ruby hid a yawn behind her hand. "I'm fine. Merely a bit tired because I—"

"Didn't get much sleep last night?" Caroline sashayed into the reception area, smoothing her almost too tight, definitely too short, skirt down her thighs. She must have been lurking, waiting for Ruby to arrive.

"Do tell us *why* you're so tired, Ruby," Caroline said, winking at Liz.

"I'm tired because I got up early and went for a bike ride before work."

Caroline gave a ladylike snort and surveyed Ruby through slitted, disbelieving eyes. "That's not what I meant," she said. "I heard—"

"Gee, Caroline. What a great start to the week. It's—" Ruby glanced at her watch "—barely eight-thirty Monday morning, and already the gossipmongers are on the warpath. I'll have you know, I'm taking this triathlon seriously. Which is why I got up at five-freaking-thirty to go for a bike ride. If you don't believe me, you can ring Mike."

"I already did that," she said.

Ruby goggled at her. Bloody hell. "You're kidding, right?"

Caroline shook her head. "I rang this morning to check how you were, and whether you were coming in to work. And who do you think answered the phone?"

Uh oh. Ruby bit her lip.

"Duh," Liz said. "Mike answered the phone. He's staying the week, after all. What's the big fricking deal, Caroline?"

Please let it have been Mike who answered the phone. Please—

"Ruby's stripper." Caroline's tone was so triumphant one might have been forgiven for thinking she'd won the first division Lotto prize.

Ah, crap. Busted. Ruby was sooo going to have words with Kyan about answering her phone.

Liz's eyes widened until she resembled a startled owl. "That gorgeous guy from your birthday party?"

"Which gorgeous guy from whose birthday party?" David, the manager of the real estate firm, chose that moment to walk into Reception with a bunch of client files for Ruby to update.

"The stripper from Ruby's birthday party," Liz said.

"You had a stripper?" David fanned himself. "Way to go, sweetie! Wish I could have made it along."

David was—to borrow Ruby's mother's politically incorrect description—more fruity than a Christmas cake. He was obviously gay, and didn't give a toss who knew it. David would have beaten Caroline and the other women off with a stick for the honor of being first to squeeze Kyan's bum.

"Was he hot?" David asked.

"Sizzling." Liz sighed like she was going to melt into a puddle. "Wouldn't you agree, Caroline?"

"Yes, I would. And—" Caroline paused for dramatic effect "—if he was answering Ruby's phone this morning, where do you think he spent the night?"

Ruby hid a grin. Caroline was making an effort to sound upbeat and pleased for Ruby's good fortune, but it came across totally fake.

She abruptly realized she was the sole focus of three pairs of eyes. What was the question again? Oh. Yeah. She gulped. "Gee, I dunno. On the couch, maybe?"

It wasn't exactly a lie. She'd since discovered that Kyan had started off spending the night on the couch.

David's eyebrows formed impressive peaks of disbelief, and Ruby knew she hadn't convinced them. "Um, like, where any friend I haven't seen in years would stay if he needed a bed, and there wasn't a spare because my brother's using the spare room." Crap. Too much information. Now *she* was the one who sounded fake.

Caroline visibly perked up. "He's a friend?"

"From primary school. Lost touch with him when his family moved overseas. Didn't recognize him at first because I haven't seen him for years and he's changed his name. He calls himself Kyan now."

"Kyan *what*?" Liz had to ask. Bless her.

"Kyan… Davids," Ruby blurted, unable to think of anything better to use as a surname.

Luckily no one batted an eyelid at her lack of imagination under pressure. David even seemed rather chuffed by the stunning coincidence.

Liz goggled at her. "Bet you had kittens when you finally recognized him."

"Er, yes. He's um… grown up a bit since I last saw him."

"I'll say!" Liz said. And both she and Caroline giggled in perfect unison.

"You should have seen Kyan strip, David." Liz gushed like a teenager. "His physique is amaaazing. Biceps, pecs and abs to die for. Don't you agree, Caroline?"

"I was rather more interested in lower down." Caroline all but purred the words.

"Adequate?" David asked, a sly grin curving his lips.

"Oh, yes." Caroline ran the tip of her tongue over her even, white teeth. "Even though he didn't do the Full Monty, it was patently obvious he's very adequate indeed."

"And his eyes are this gorgeous shade of blue, and sooo compelling. I swear I nearly came on the spot whenever he so much as glanced my way." Liz sighed dreamily. "He's the most perfect-looking man I've ever met."

"Such a pity you've got a boyfriend, Liz," Caroline reminded her.

Liz came back down to earth with a thump. She heaved a sigh. "Yes. I mean, no! Geoff's a great guy." Flushing, she changed the subject. "You're between men, though, aren't you, Caroline?"

"Yes." Caroline examined her manicure. "I dumped Joseph last week."

"Ski Instructor Joseph?" David shook his head. "Shame. I rather liked him. That accent… oooh!"

"Joseph wasn't a patch on Kyan, though," Liz said. "Kyan's just… just—"

"Beyond words?" David arched his eyebrows, grinning at Liz's all-too-obvious infatuation.

"Oh, yeah." Liz sighed again. "He could sleep on my couch any time—if I didn't already have a boyfriend, of course."

David fanned himself with the latest Property Press. "You

should bring your stripper in for a visit some time, Ruby. I'd looove to meet him."

"Mmm." Ruby shuffled papers on her desk, wishing her colleagues would get down to work. It was becoming rather tiresome watching women—and men, too—reduced to giggling, brain-cell-depleted bimbos where Kyan was concerned. Thank God Jules was totally in love with Alex and seemed immune to Kyan's charms.

"Does he have a girlfriend?" Liz wanted to know.

"Who?"

"Kyan, of course!"

"No." Ruby snapped, before she'd thought the implications of that answer through.

"There you are, Caroline." Liz nudged her and winked conspiratorially. "He's single. Go for it."

Caroline's eyelids drifted half shut, and her smooth, immaculately made-up features morphed into a predatory expression. Ruby shuddered, reminded of a hunting hound who'd scented prey and was eagerly anticipating a feeding frenzy.

After last night, the last thing Ruby felt like coping with was watching Caroline trying to get into Kyan's pants. Time to improvise and salvage the situation. "I don't think he's interested in finding a girlfriend right now," she said. "Seeing as how he's still mourning the, er, tragic death of his fiancée."

"Oh, how awful!" Liz said. "What on earth happened to her?"

Ruby was saved from having to scour her brain for yet another lie when her phone rang. And even more lucky for her, the caller was Mrs. Liang, a demanding Chinese matron who insisted on being shown through new properties as soon as they hit the agency's books. Mrs. Liang categorically refused to wait for the advertisements to run in the local papers and the Property Press, and made a point of ringing every Monday morning without fail. All the agents hated dealing with her.

"Yes, Mrs. Liang," Ruby said. "We do have some new listings that fit your criteria. I'll email the links through for you to have a look at, shall I? Oh, you'd rather me tell you all about each one, and then you want to look through them all in person? Okay, no problem. I'll see which of our agents is free, and they'll arrange viewing appointments." On cue, Liz, Caroline and David heard their cell phones ringing and scurried off.

Ruby didn't mind dealing with Mrs. Liang, even though the woman could single-handedly waste an entire morning when she set her mind to it. All the staff knew she was rich as sin, and could buy half a dozen properties if she felt so inclined, but not one of the agents had come close to selling her anything. Mr. Liang spent weeks at a time in Taiwan, and everything had to be emailed to him for approval. Inevitably, by the time Mr. Liang got around to approving his wife's choice of mansion, the property had been snapped up by some other wealthy buyer.

At least, that was the official reason a deal had never been closed with Mrs. Liang. Ruby suspected the woman was lonely as hell, and used the pretext of buying a house as an excuse to get a bit of attention whenever her husband was absent on one of his business trips.

She settled back to haggle with Mrs. Liang. They both enjoyed this part of their "relationship". It was like being at a market, only instead of haggling over cheap clothes and knick-knacks, they were haggling over million-dollar properties. On a good day, Ruby managed to keep the number of houses Mrs. Liang insisted on viewing to under half a dozen. Her record was two. Today, however, her mind wasn't fully on the job and Mrs. Liang insisted on viewing four of the properties Ruby listed.

"But Mrs. Liang, the Lake Pupuke property doesn't have a pool. And you know Mr. Liang won't consider buying if it doesn't have a pool."

"Mr. Liang is not the boss," she squawked. "If I like the house with no swimming pool then too bad for Mr Liang! We will buy the house with no swimming pool!"

Oh dear. Now Ruby had offended her. "Of course, Mrs. Liang. As my mother always says, women rule the roost."

"Roost? What roost?" Mrs. Liang began muttering under her breath in Mandarin.

"I mean, women make all the important decisions," Ruby said. "Men might think they do, but it's really the women."

"Your mother is a sensible woman, Ruby. And you are a good daughter to listen to her. Now, you tell your boss that this week, I will almost certainly buy a house. You tell him."

"I'll do that," Ruby said. "And David will be very pleased to hear that, Mrs. Liang." *Though he won't believe it until he gets a signed Purchase Agreement, and the hefty deposit check clears the bank.*

"Now you will find me nice lady agent to show me these houses, Ruby."

Ruby grinned. Revenge could be so awfully sweet. "I'm sure Caroline would be—"

"Caroleen?" Mrs. Liang's outraged screech was so loud Ruby yanked the phone away from her ear. "I will not have that scrawny lady showing me any more houses! She is not a good person. Her soul is shriveled up just like her body."

Ouch. That was a bit harsh. Caroline was skinny, not emaciated. And she could be a bit self-involved at times, but Ruby wouldn't go so far as to say her soul was *shriveled*.

"No Caroleen," Mrs. Liang insisted. "I want Liz. She is very nice, very polite. You tell her, Ruby. She will show me these houses today, and I will buy one. She will get a nice big commission, heh?"

"I'll tell her right away, Mrs. Liang. I'm sure she'll be thrilled." Ruby hung up and went to give lucky Liz the good news.

After she'd commiserated with Liz for a bit, Ruby glanced

at her watch. She was taking an early lunch and there was only an hour and a half to go before she headed off to her first ever swimming lesson. Okay, so perhaps it had been crazy to sign up for a triathlon when she didn't know how to swim. But hey, how hard could swimming be?

RUBY SAUNTERED INTO the women's changing area and halted mid-stride when the ghastly truth about public swimming pools smacked her upside the head.

Oh God. Communal changing rooms. Unless she wanted to squeeze into a toilet cubicle, she'd have to strip off and change into her swimsuit in front of people.

She forced her feet into motion again, and treated herself to a fierce internal pep talk. *Come on, Ruby. You're a confident adult woman. You're completely fine with how your body looks. As long as you're happy, who cares what others think?*

Ah, who was she trying to kid? She wasn't happy. She faked it—only pretended not to give a shit about what others thought of her. She wouldn't be embarking on this get fit treadmill of pain and potential humiliation otherwise.

She slunk to the darkest corner of the room and deposited her bag on the bench seat. Head down, trying not catch the eye of anyone else in the changing room, she shucked her clothes and pulled on her new swimsuit. She sucked in a deep breath and wrapped her towel around her torso before turning around to face the world.

Turned out she wasn't the shyest, most body-conscious woman in the room. That label belonged to the pretty blonde teenager trying to strip off her wet togs... while completely draped in a voluminous towel... which kept slipping down at the most inopportune moments.

A wry grin twitched Ruby's lips. How ironic. This girl was still young enough to be completely devoid of cellulite, and instead of rubbing everyone's noses in her nubile-ness, she was too shy to show it off.

Ruby trailed a trio of elderly women out of the changing rooms and into the pool complex, momentarily distracted by the funny, flowery, old-fashioned swimming caps the women wore. They reminded her of an amusing birthday card she'd once bought for Jules. The card had featured a photo of four women poised to dive into a pool, all wearing swimsuits with little skirts designed to preserve their modesty, and flowery bathing caps—just like the ones these ladies wore. Inside, the card read: *It's official… we've become our mothers.*

The smile slid from her face as she was confronted by ghastly realization number two: There were men swimming in the pool, too. Lots of them. And as she headed for the area designated for swimming lessons, she discovered that her instructor was male. A very young male—hardly out of his teens.

Fabulous. Could it get any worse?

She watched him finish the lesson, and realized it *could* get worse. A lot worse. Because if he was going to teach her to swim, he'd have to touch her… like he was touching his current pupil, showing her how to position her arms as she floated on her back, tapping her stomach to encourage her to push her chest up so she didn't sink.

Registering for this triathlon to prove a now nonexistent point to her brother was all very well. And for all of a day, Ruby had felt intensely proud for doing a number of things that scared the hell out of her. Like shopping for her first new swimsuit in about a decade. And learning to ride a bike. She was even kind of looking forward to mastering the technique of jogging without giving herself two black eyes—something she would be coming to grips with tonight after work. But as the woman in the pool smiled at the young instructor, thanked him, and clambered out of the pool, Ruby wanted to run back to the changing room and throw up in the toilet.

Shit-a-flaming-brick. She'd signed up for a whole course of lessons, too. What on earth had she been thinking?

Her instructor beckoned her into the pool. Ruby clutched her towel and stared at him. She could almost hear her knees knocking.

He smiled. "Nothing to be afraid of. It's only water."

Easy enough for him to say. What did *he* know? Mere fear didn't even begin to cover Ruby's emotions at the moment. Try complete and utter horror.

"It's okay. Don't be scared, er—" Her far-too-youthful-to-be-taken-seriously instructor glanced at his whiteboard. "*Ruby*. Jump in and I'll have you floating before you know it."

She sucked in a deep, bracing breath. *It's now or never, Ruby. If you don't do this, you'll never learn to swim and you won't be able to do the triathlon. Then you'll hate yourself for being a coward. And your family, and all those people who've whispered unkind things about you when they thought you couldn't hear, will be proved right. And—*

And Kyan will never really love you. Because how could a buff, athletic, gorgeous guy like Kyan truly love someone who was fat?

That last insidious little whisper acted as a catalyst. Before she could chicken out, Ruby shed her towel and dived—or to be more accurate, belly-flopped—into the pool.

The horrified expression she glimpsed on her young instructor's face before she sank beneath the water was a huge clue that he might not have been exactly prepared for her to dive right in.

CHAPTER NINE

RUBY WEDGED THE phone more comfortably beneath her shoulder and chin, and sank deeper into the bubbles. "I'm telling you, Jules, diving into that pool was the stupidest thing I've ever done. Well, not quite as stupid as going jogging without buying a proper sports bra first, but pretty up there in the stupid stakes."

She groaned as the hot water penetrated her aching muscles. She had expected to be sore after her swimming lesson but half an hour jogging with her boobs bouncing all over the place due to lack of adequate support sure hadn't helped. Okay, so it'd only been five minutes of *actual* jogging because she'd been so winded that she'd power-walked the rest of the way. Briskly, mind you. But it was hardly an auspicious beginning to her dreams of jogging the entire leg of the triathlon course without taking a break.

Jules sniggered down the phone line. "God. Wish I'd been there."

"Oh, no you don't," Ruby assured her friend. "It was shades of Shallow Hal. Not pretty."

"Sorry, you've lost me."

"You know, that movie where they stuck Gwenneth Paltrow in a fat suit? There was this scene where she jumped into the pool, and half the water spewed out with such force that some poor little kid who'd been swimming in the pool ended up squatting in a tree."

Jules burst out laughing. "Oh come on, Rubes. You're exaggerating."

"Maybe. But it was pretty bad all the same." She winced at the embarrassing memory, and stifled another pained groan. "I made such a huge splash that I soaked a bunch of people walking by. You should have seen the look on Craig's face. The poor boy was horrified."

"You're imagining things, Rubes. I'm sure he's seen heaps worse bodies than yours squeezed into a swimsuit."

"He had that same expression on his face the entire lesson."

"What, and you don't think it had anything to do with the fact that you gave him a helluva scare when you jumped in and sank like a stone? Not to mention realizing you expect him to get you to a stage where you can swim in a triathlon in less than four weeks?"

"Okay, you win." Ruby sighed. "Poor Craig. He really drew the short straw. I wouldn't want to have to teach me to swim, either."

"What's really up, Rubes? It's not like you to sound so depressed. What's wrong?"

Darn. Jules knew her too well. "This is only my first day of training and I'm so exhausted I can barely move. How'n the hell am I supposed to get through an entire week, let alone four? I'm beginning to think I might not be up to this. And that I'm an idiot for signing up for this triathlon."

"You'll be fine, Rubes. Just take it easy and stop pushing yourself so hard. I looked on the triathlon website and most of the training schedules suggest training in only one discipline per day. None of the schedules mentions swimming, cycling *and* running every day. Little wonder you're feeling knackered."

"Yeah, but those schedules are for people who've got the full twelve weeks to train."

Jules huffed into the phone, and somehow managed to make the huff sound mega pissed-off. "No one's expecting you to break any records. It's an achievement for some women to merely make it to the start-line, let alone finish the course. And going by the stories from women who've done this triathlon before, it doesn't seem to matter whether you have to dog-paddle, wheel your bike, and walk the entire distance. It's all about participation."

"I know all that. But I can't help thinking I'm kidding myself. What on earth possessed me to think that I can do this? Maybe I should quit before I make a worse fool of myself."

"You can do this, Rubes—I know you can."

As Jules spoke a deeper voice echoed her words. "You can do this, Ruby. I believe in you. You have only to believe in yourself."

Ruby glanced up. "Kyan?" Yikes. She scooped a mass of bubbles toward her chest. "What the hell are you doing in here? Get out!"

"I brought you something to eat." He brandished a tray.

"Uh, thanks." *Not.* "Would you please leave it on the vanity unit and shoo? I need some privacy."

He ventured into the bathroom to deposit the tray, and when he pivoted, heading for the door, Ruby allowed herself to relax. But rather than leave her with a tiny shred of dignity intact, he leaned against the doorframe and surveyed her with a predatory gleam in his eyes. She couldn't tear her gaze away from him. He looked oh-so-sexy in bare feet, jeans that hung low on his hips and a black t-shirt.

"Kyan?" Jules' squawk yanked Ruby from a bunch of x-rated thoughts. "What's Kyan doing in the bathroom with you?"

"Evidently he's bringing me dinner," Ruby said.

"Awww, sweet. You know, Rubes, I reckon he secretly has the hots for you, and—"

"Gotta go. Bye." Ruby disconnected and dropped the receiver onto the bathmat. She scooted down beneath the dwindling layer of bubbles until water lapped her chin.

Kyan levered himself upright and sauntered toward the bath.

"Go away!" Her voice was a high-pitched squeak.

He hunkered down beside the bath to stare intently at her coverlet of bubbles. "I have never seen the likes of this substance before."

"It's bubble bath."

"Why do you bathe in these bubbles?"

"Because they smell good and, uh, make my skin feel nice and soft," she babbled, unnerved by his nearness. Having him watch her take a bath seemed even more intimate than sex.

"Hmmm." He reached out, skimming his fingers first through the bubbles, and then across her collarbone. Goosebumps trailed his touch.

"I think these bubbles do make your skin very soft. But to be certain, I will have to investigate further." He plunged a hand into the water and grabbed her ankle.

Ruby bit back a startled squeal. But she couldn't bring herself to resist as he coaxed her leg from the water and ran his hand up the length of her calf.

As he caressed her, Ruby's body went lax and her butt lost contact with the bottom of the bath. With a muffled shriek, she slid beneath the water. When she surfaced, ears full of water and eyes squeezed tightly shut, she vaguely heard Kyan apologizing. He tried to grab her slippery body and haul her upright, but it was an exercise in futility.

In retrospect, it was kind of inevitable that Kyan would topple into the bath and end up lying on top of her, just as Mike decided to investigate what all the fuss was about. "Having fun I see," Mike said.

Ruby swiped bubbles from her eyes with one hand, and tried to push Kyan away with the other.

Mike's grin was so damn wide it must have hurt his face. "I asked you to bring my poor, tired sister some dinner, Kyan. I didn't mean for you to help her wash her, ah, front."

Ruby sat up—modesty be damned—spluttering bubbles and gagging at the soapy taste in her mouth. She glared at her brother. "You, hand me my towel and get out. And you—" She pinned Kyan, who was hunched in the other end of the bath and apparently completely astonished by this turn of events, with a ball-shriveling glare. "Close your eyes and don't dare bloody open them until I say so."

"Why?" he asked.

"Because I'm getting out. The bath is all yours."

"Why doesn't Mike have to close *his* eyes?" Kyan asked.

"Because he's my brother, and he's seen it all before."

Kyan opened his mouth, but before he could counter with something embarrassing, like, "I've seen it all before, too" she cut him off. "I mean it, Kyan. Close your eyes. No peeking. Or else."

She must have sounded suitably annoyed, for he did as he was told without further argument.

Mike managed to smother his knowing grin as he handed her a towel. And then, without saying another word, he prudently vacated the room. Smart man, her brother.

Ruby wrapped the towel around her torso and padded from the room, leaving a trail of bubbly footsteps in her wake. The unaccustomed physical exertion was taking its toll. She was bone-weary, and almost too tired to think straight.

She headed for her bedroom. From the corner of her eye she spotted Mike fossicking in the hall cupboard for another towel, and felt a momentary qualm she hadn't thought of getting one for Kyan. She shut the door behind her. Somehow she managed to work up enough energy to towel-dry her hair and change into a t-shirt and knickers. Her arm muscles shrieked protests when she tried to reach behind her back, so she didn't bother with a bra. No one would be seeing her like this, anyway.

Famous last words.

Her head had barely hit the pillow when someone knocked

on her bedroom door.

"'S just me." Mike stuck his head through the doorway. "Want some dinner?"

"No thanks." It came out as a mumble. "Too tired to eat."

"You should eat something after all that exercise. You need to keep your strength up for tomorrow. And the next day. And the next—"

"Not hungry," she said. "Going to sleep now." She closed her eyes until Mike took the hint and left, quietly shutting the door behind him.

Ruby was doing a fair imitation of blissful slumber when her door opened again. Geez. "Trying to sleep here, Mike!" she said, without bothering to open her eyes.

"It is not Mike."

"What do you want, Kyan?"

"You are angry with me," he said, and there was a wealth of hurt and confusion in that bald statement. "Why?"

Ruby pried open her eyelids and stared at the ceiling. "I'm too tired for this right now, Kyan. I want—need—to get some sleep. Can we talk about it tomorrow?"

"If you wish."

Silence. He'd gone. Thank God.

"But I would prefer to know why you are angry with me now."

Crap.

"Otherwise it will be difficult for me to sleep tonight."

Bugger.

Ruby groaned. Hadn't he heard of sleeping on a little disagreement and letting it ferment overnight—or even days or weeks—until it was a huge rip-roaring big deal? That's how it worked with Ruby and her mum. Pamela Roberts would say something that Ruby took offence at, but instead of speaking up, Ruby would take it on the chin, seethe quietly, and file it away with all the other slights. Until, finally, her mum would say something that really pissed Ruby off, and Ruby would hit her with all the hurts she'd saved up. The joy of this method was that if Ruby didn't blow her stack too early, she had so much ammunition her mum ended up apologizing and being a reasonable human being for a month or so.

But that was her mum. And Ruby had thirty years of learning how to cope with her. Sort of. This was Kyan, the kind of man she had no experience in dealing with whatsoever. Somehow she didn't think she'd be escaping without some deep emotional scars this time around.

She rolled onto her stomach and buried her face in a pillow. It wasn't exactly comfortable, but it saved her from having to confront him.

The mattress dipped as he climbed atop it to straddle her hips. She tensed. Not again. She couldn't bear for him to try and make love to her again. Not now. Not when she was tired and aching, and so emotionally fragile that any display of tenderness would unleash a barrage of suppressed hurt.

He dug his fingers into her neck and shoulder muscles, kneading away the tension, and despite herself she loosed a sigh. It felt wonderful.

"Relax, Ruby. You are holding too much tension in your muscles. You will awake stiff and sore if you sleep in this state."

As Kyan's strong hands worked their subtle magic on her body, Ruby pondered why she'd overreacted when he surprised her in the bath. He'd only been bringing her dinner. It'd been a nice gesture. He hadn't deserved to be reamed because she was embarrassed at being seen naked. And it wasn't like he hadn't already seen her unclothed.

Her thoughts skittered over memories of making love with Kyan. And the eroticism of those memories flushed her skin and made her damp with desire. She shifted restlessly beneath his hands and they stilled mid-stroke.

She turned her face aside so she could speak without mumbling into the pillow. "I'm not angry at you, Kyan. I was… embarrassed about you seeing me in the bath. I'm sorry I yelled at you. I overreacted."

His palms rested on her shoulders, warming her skin through the thin cotton of her t-shirt. "You are not like any other woman I have known, Ruby."

"Yeah. I'm sure." She couldn't think straight with him so near. She shrugged off his hands and rolled onto her back, spilling him from his perch. He reacted instantly, in an elegant blur of motion that ended with him reclining on the mattress beside her, his head resting on a couple of her pillows. She tucked the sheet firmly between her armpits and wished that she possessed such feline grace.

"What were the women of your world like?" God. Dumb question. Doubtless his answer would tromp all over her sub-zero self-esteem.

"The women are as varied as desert blooms in an oasis."

Poetic, but not particularly informative. "Okay, so what about the kind of women you prefer, then?" *Geez, Ruby. How about you go get a hammer to nail shut your coffin, too?*

"For the most part, the women I chose were delicate-looking creatures, ever willing to please. Just as women should be." A smile tugged his lips. "Completely unlike you, my Ruby."

"Gee, thanks. You sure know how to flatter a girl. You'd better ask Mike for some pointers on how to chat up women or you're not going to get much action in *this* world."

He laughed. "You could never compare to my previous lovers, Ruby."

Ohhhh. That hurt. Much, much more than it should have.

She squeezed her eyelids shut to block out his painfully handsome, smiling face. She wished she could shut out his voice as easily. She wanted to curl into a tight ball and sob. Pride kept her lying rigidly beside him, jaw clenched against the angry, loathsome words she wanted to throw at him… if only she could think of something cutting to say.

"My ideal woman would use her feminine wiles to convey her interest in me," Kyan said, his tone conversational, obviously unaware of the pain he'd inflicted. "She took pains to act in a proper manner in public. And when I bedded her she was passive, allowing me to take my pleasure as I saw fit." He paused in his recitation. "Look at me, Ruby. I want you to know the truth of what I am telling you. You are not like the women I have previously chosen in any way, shape or form."

Ruby blinked her tear-stung eyelids and willed herself not to cry.

He waited, still and silent, and she wondered what she'd done to provoke this awful comparison. He obviously wanted to make it clear how he felt. He was honest, she'd give him that. Which was far more than she was being with him.

He grasped her chin, forcing her to gaze deep into his eyes. "The women I chose were never outspoken, never willing to argue their point with me for fear of causing offence. They were never feisty and courageous and determined. They were beautiful of face and figure, yes. But they were pale, insipid creatures compared with you.

"This body and this face have been both blessing and curse. And I admit, I have learned to use them to my advantage. I have been with many women, Ruby. But bedding them now seems little more than an unmemorable meshing of bodies to relieve my urges—" his voice dropped to a whisper and he leaned closer to press his lips to the corner of her mouth "—compared to making love with you. What spell have you cast upon me, my little sorceress?"

Ruby lay stunned and motionless while she processed his words. Her heart soared. He'd heaped compliments upon her, not the humiliations she'd expected. Beautiful compliments that warmed her soul, thawing the hurt that had lodged there. Banishing it….

At least for now.

Inevitably, typically, she extracted something he'd said and

twisted it into a self-deprecating comment. It was instinctive—
a reaction she couldn't suppress. "Little sorceress? Little? Not
hardly."

He kissed her again and she started to giggle.

He drew back, perplexed. "What is so funny?

"Me? Little? You really should get your eyes checked."

He rose to his knees, surveying her through narrowed eyes
while she burbled with laughter. Then he yanked down the
sheet, scooped her into his arms and tossed her into the air.
She squealed as he caught her and tossed her up again.

"Kyan! What are you doing? You'll give yourself a hernia!"

"You are little compared to me, woman," he said, disdain-
ing to catch her this time, and letting her bounce on the
mattress in a sprawling heap. Before she could catch her
breath, he covered her body with his. "A delicious little dumpling." He nuzzled her neck and mouthed the pulse at her
throat.

She wriggled. "Sure, you beat me in height but I bet we're
awful close weight-wise. Wanna hop on those sadly neglected
scales over there in the corner and see what you weigh?"

"You are spouting nonsense," he said. "And there is only
one way to stop a woman like you from spouting nonsense."

"What's that?" she said, grinning up at him.

His bright blue eyes darkened and he lowered his head to
capture her mouth with his. Delicately he teased her lips, but
there was nothing delicate about the hard shaft of his cock
pressing against her groin through his trousers. Heat flooded
her body and lust zinged through her nerve-endings. Her lips
parted in a moan of want and need and longing.

He licked her upper lip and then thrust his tongue into her
mouth, coaxing her to respond in kind.

He cleared his throat.

Huh? No. It wasn't Kyan who'd cleared his throat.

Kyan raised his torso, resting on his elbows so that he
could twist and glance over his shoulder. He tensed. And then

he went completely still.

Ruby craned her neck to see over him. Through desire-hazed eyes, she glimpsed her brother lounging in the doorway. Oh. Obviously Kyan hadn't shut the door behind him.

Ruby should have felt horrified that Mike had caught her rolling 'round on her bed with a man she'd met mere days ago. She should have been burning up with embarrassment, cringing at what her brother must surely be thinking. But she was too dazed by the emotions Kyan had coaxed from her to care about making a spectacle of herself in front of the brother she adored.

"Mike," Kyan said.

"Kyan." Mike's expression was as devoid of emotion as his tone. And for Ruby, that carefully neutral tone was like a slap upside the head.

What was she doing letting Kyan seduce her again? Was she truly that desperate to be loved, truly that pathetically needy?

She squirmed beneath Kyan's strong, muscular body. Now that Mike had seen Kyan and her like this it catapulted their relationship—such as it was—from pure speculation to fact. How could she look her brother in the eye tomorrow? Or Kyan, for that matter.

She tried to push Kyan away but it was fruitless as trying to shift a huge hunk of granite with her bare hands. He remained unmoved, merely bending his head to whisper in her ear, "Be still, Ruby. You are a grown woman and this is your house. Mike is a guest. If anyone should be ashamed, it should be him for walking in on you taking your pleasure with me."

Taking her pleasure?

Interesting way of putting it.

Kyan twisted again to meet her brother's gaze. The two men stared at each other, wordlessly communicating in some masculine fashion Ruby was unable to fathom. Then Mike turned and walked from the room, carefully shutting the door behind him.

"What was that all about?" she demanded.

Kyan turned his full focus on her once more, and nuzzled the incredibly sensitive little spot directly below her ear. "Your brother and I have come to an *understanding*, Ruby. And that—" he slipped a hand beneath her t-shirt to caress the underside of her breast "—is all you need to know."

She sucked in a deep breath, preparing to take umbrage at that chauvinistic statement, but all thought of argument fled when he rolled her nipple between his fingertips. Heat spiraled lazily through her pelvis. Then, as he pushed up her t-shirt and replaced his fingers with his mouth, the heat speared through her whole body. Every nerve-ending she possessed lit up, morphing into tiny fizzing firecrackers of almost overwhelming sensitivity.

It felt so good—*he* felt so good lying atop her, his warm weight pressing her into the mattress. Her worries, her self-consciousness, the censure she imagined Mike would heap upon her, receded. Her whole world was Kyan.

He stripped off her clothes and plunged his hard, eager cock inside her. And it seemed that she was *his* whole world, too, as he stroked deep inside her, growing thicker and harder until each thrust made her moan and writhe beneath him. He brought her to the point of orgasm again and again, always backing off and slowing his thrusts at the brink of her climax, never quite pushing her over the edge.

She wanted to scream his name. She bit her lips to keep the scream inside as she pumped her hips and hooked her ankles about his calves in a futile attempt to keep him deep inside her. She quivered with the need for release. She wanted him to fuck her hard and fast, instead of maintaining this leisurely, teasing, almost torturous pace. She grasped his shoulders and managed to whisper, "Kyan. Please."

The desperation in her voice gave him pause, allowing her to catch and hold his gaze. His eyes were half-blinded with lust—an expression she had never thought to see in any man's eyes when he made love to her.

He flexed his arms to lever his upper body away and hold himself poised over her. Her gaze slid from his face, down the length of his body, stopping where they were intimately joined. Her breath caught. His cock pulsed inside her and she gasped at the sensation.

"Am I hurting you, my Ruby?"

Her gaze flew to his face. The concern, the caring in his expression, brought tears to her eyes. "No. It's not that. It's just that I—" She couldn't finish, couldn't bare her soul to him even though she'd already bared her body.

"Tell me. Tell me what you want, Ruby. Tell me how to please you."

Please her? Couldn't he tell she was more "pleased" than she'd ever been in her life?

Tell him what she wanted? If he meant she should tell him what she *truly* wanted, how could she possibly do that?

She couldn't. Not when her deepest desire was to have him stay with her. Forever. So she settled for telling him what she desperately wanted right now, this minute. "I want you to stop teasing me and fuck me. Hard and fast. I want you to come inside me. Now."

He smiled. "That is easily arranged."

Taking her at her word, he set a rhythmic thrusting that stole her breath. He pounded his cock into her, and with each thrust, his groin rubbed against her swollen clit, drawing breathy gasps from her parted lips.

Pleasure rolled over her, through her, and it was as though some magical force had entered her and contrived to stimulate every part of her body, both internally and externally. Her inner muscles tightened around him, and clenched as her orgasm took her. He tensed. When he shouted her name, his voice was hoarse. And with one last deep thrust that slapped his balls against her and made her whimper, he came.

He lay draped over her for a time and she took comfort in their closeness—that he didn't feel the need to move away from her immediately the sex was over. Then he withdrew from her and flung himself on to his back beside her, breathing heavily.

She bit her lower lip hard, to the point of pain, but she couldn't help the tears. Silently she cried, hoping he wouldn't notice, that he'd roll over and fall asleep, leaving her to her misery.

His gentle touch intruding on her pain was a shock. He gathered her into his arms and held her tenderly as she sobbed. He didn't say a word. He cradled her to his chest until her sobs eased and she hovered close to sleep.

She believed he understood the root cause of her tears, and that was why he didn't try to comfort her with words.

Wise man.

She'd cried because for years she'd felt isolated and alone— even during sex, which was about as lonely as a human being could get. But with Kyan it had been different. Magical. And now she'd tasted his warmth, basked in the afterglow of making love with him, knew that he cared for her, it would be so much harder to lose him.

He kissed her eyelids and murmured, "Sleep now, my Ruby."

Sighing, she gave up trying to work it all out, gave up fretting over what the future would bring, and let sleep claim her.

CHAPTER TEN

K YAN WOKE RUBY before the alarm went off. God. If he harbored fond thoughts of her leaping out of bed, eager to start the day, he had another think coming. Right now, she couldn't summon the energy to knock the skin off day-old porridge let alone rolling of bed and climbing into clothes.

She peeled open one eyelid to peer up at him. *Of course* he was already dressed and ready to go. Worse, he was bouncing on his toes while he waited for her to wake up properly. She'd been so out to it she hadn't even heard him leave the bed. For all she knew, he'd been for a jog before coming back to wake her. He was obviously an alien—an alien in peak physical condition who possessed the stamina of… of… *something* that she was too sleep-befuddled to think of right now.

Ruby wasn't a morning person at the best of times—and definitely not until she'd had a caffeine fix—and Kyan radiated so much unnatural energy that she only felt more exhausted. But despite sleep deprivation, and muscles that shrieked for mercy whenever she moved, she crawled wearily from the bed. She told herself it was sheer dogged determination to stick to her training schedule but in truth, she didn't feel like a repeat of yesterday morning when he'd dumped her out of bed onto the carpet.

She didn't bother asking him to turn his back, or leave the room, while she dragged on her clothes. She was too damn knackered to give a damn about preserving her modesty. Besides, she reminded herself, Kyan truly had seen it all before. Multiple times.

Her mind chose that moment to replay a rather graphic vision of Kyan giving in to her demands of the previous night. She ducked her head to hide the flush that had bloomed on her cheeks, eyeing Kyan through the fall of her hair as she donned socks and sneakers. Way to not be quiet and submissive, and grateful as hell for whatever pleasure she could get during sex.

Mmm. Pleasure. There sure had been a great deal of *that*. And the more she thought about her personality transplant, the more she thought it was a good thing. There was nothing wrong with stating what you wanted. Kyan hadn't been put off by her assertiveness. He'd seemed to like it—

"You seem very pleased with yourself this morning, Ruby."

As she straightened—very very slowly, while biting her lips against a pained whimper—she caught a glimmer of a smile on Kyan's lips before he presented her with a guileless expression. She wasn't fooled in the least. It had been a smile of purely masculine self-satisfaction—a smug smirk, even.

"All right, Casanova. Let's go before I change my mind and crawl back into bed."

"Casanova? Who is this Casanova?"

"A man hailed as the world's most notorious seducer of women. So the story goes, no woman could resist him."

Kyan blinked. And smiled a slow, wide suggestive smile that made her tingle all over. "You are comparing me to this man?"

"Uh, well—" Ruby scratched her head. Jules always said you should never pay effusive compliments to men because their egos were inflated enough already. Ah, sod it. Kyan was an amazing lover. And Ruby had always been a pathetic liar. "Yes."

He stroked his chin. "I have been told that I am extremely knowledgeable in matters of intimacy."

"Oh? By who?"

"Many women."

Oh, really. "How many, exactly?"

He opened his mouth as though to enlighten her, and promptly snapped it shut.

Good decision.

She swept past him, out into the dark hallway, and waited by the front door for him to catch up. When he neared her, she grasped his arm and stood on tiptoe to whisper in his ear. She caught his sharp intake of breath. And she liked that she could affect him in such a way. She liked it a lot.

"Don't get too cocky, Kyan," she said. "Casanova also suffered from a number of nasty venereal diseases. In fact—" She paused, enjoying his shudder as her breath tickled his ear. "He was extremely fortunate his willie didn't shrivel up and fall off."

"His willie?" Kyan's voice was little more than a husky croak.

"His cock."

"Ah."

Ruby opened the door and ushered Kyan outside so she could trip the deadlock and leave Mike safely snoozing. Lucky bugger. She heaved a sigh and stomped off to the garage to liberate the bikes.

"There are often consequences when people sleep around with multiple partners," she advised Kyan as he fastened his helmet. "Weren't there sexually transmitted diseases in your world?"

He didn't answer. Perhaps he hadn't heard her. She hopped on her bike and set off on the course Mike had mapped out. Yesterday, Kyan had kept pace with her and called out encouragement. This morning he trailed her, and remained silent and subdued.

For a while she was okay with that. And then she got to thinking about consequences.

Ruby was on the contraceptive pill because it helped regulate her cycle. Her GP had recently suggested she change brands to one that was fully funded. She would have to check, but she might be in that crucial changeover period when women first started taking a new pill and weren't safe. Hence keeping the box of condoms Lani had given her, and stuffing it in her bedside drawer. Wishful thinking and all that, but better to be safe than—

She visualized that unopened box. And went clammy with shock.

Jesus, Mary and Joseph. She hadn't insisted Kyan use a condom. Even if she *was* in the safe zone for switching to a new pill, she should have insisted Kyan use protection. What the hell had she been thinking? Or, *not* thinking in this case. Obviously it wasn't only men who let their private parts rule their brains. One "come hither" glance from Kyan, and all her common sense had morphed into a brainless little bird and flown out the bloody window.

And now he had admitted to sleeping with numerous women, too? Shit. She was always so careful! Not that she'd had a great many partners to be careful with but— Shit.

She was so upset by her stupidity she didn't pay proper attention to the road ahead. She hit a pothole, swerved, and nearly clipped the gutter.

Her heart leaped into her throat as the bike wobbled and she struggled to regain control. Phew. That was close—too close. She called back a confirmation to Kyan that she was fine. A lie, of course. She wouldn't be "fine" until she got herself tested for sexually transmitted nasties. Chlamydia, gonorrhea, HIV… it didn't bear thinking about.

She shook her head, blinked, and realized she'd completed the circuit. She pedaled up her driveway, and it was far more than fatigue and abused muscles that caused her hands to shake as she stashed her bike and removed her helmet.

Kyan stood silently beside her. Waiting. Ruby swallowed,

trying to lubricate her dry throat. This wasn't going to be easy, but it had to be done.

"Kyan."

"Ruby," he said at exactly the same time.

"You first."

His brow was pleated. She didn't need to be a rocket scientist to know something was eating him. Yeah. She knew the feeling.

"How many men have you been with?" he asked.

"Huh?" Her jaw gaped.

Color stained his cheeks. He sucked in a deep breath then blew it slowly out through his nose. "How many bed-partners have you had?"

Sheesh. The nerve of him. Fists on hips, she gave him a look that should have frozen his balls. No way was she making this easy for him. She'd make him suffer. "Like, ever? Or only in the past year?"

He tunneled his fingers through his hair. "Ever."

"Three."

"Have you ever birthed a child?"

"No—obviously. Why?" She knew she sounded royally pissed off. She knew she was being unfair, considering she had been about to quiz him on the exact same subject. She didn't care.

He seemed uncertain how best to respond for a few seconds. And then he opened his mouth and dropped the clanger. "I wonder whether you are fertile."

"Whether I'm fertile? Whether. I'm. Fertile?" Color her gob-smacked. "It's a bit bloody late to be worried if you've gotten me pregnant now, Kyan." She flung up a hand to prevent him from speaking. "No, you listen up. Before you, I always used condoms, and even though we... uh, *didn't*, I'm on the pill so I'm pretty much protected from pregnancy." She hoped. But she wasn't going to fret about that possibility when the more pressing specter of some icky venereal disease was lurking. "I'm more worried about what disease you might have given me—you being the one boasting about multiple partners and being such a flaming stud and all."

"Me?" His nostrils flared and those gorgeous full lips thinned. He drew himself up, thrusting out his chest to stand straight and proud.

Ruby's eyes crossed. What were they arguing about again? Oh, yeah. "Yes, you."

"I assure you, I am not carrying any disease."

"How on earth would you know?" She curled her lip into a sneer to punctuate her words. "From what little you've told me about your world, you don't exactly have the latest in diagnostic equipment available. So how the effing heck would you know what you might have passed on when you screwed me, huh? You can't know. And you can quit looking all offended because *I'm* not the one who's slept with a shitfuckton of partners. That would be you."

He narrowed his eyes but whatever he'd been about to say was cut off when Mike stuck his head out the lounge window. "Would you two keep it down? It's barely seven in the bloody morning! Bring it inside—unless you want all your neighbors listening in on this particular conversation. Is that what you want, Ruby?"

Her ire deflated. The neighbors? Yikes! She grabbed Kyan's arm and towed him to the front door. She fished her spare key from her pocket, unlocked the door, and pushed him inside, intending finish off their "discussion" in private. The mouthwatering allure of freshly plunged coffee distracted her. She headed for the kitchen with Kyan hard on her heels.

Mike handed them each a mug. Ruby took a gulp. The hot beverage didn't do much to thaw the cold lump that'd lodged in the pit of her stomach. She didn't want to think about what she'd done—the stupid risk she'd taken.

Please God, let there be no such thing as venereal disease in his world.

She snorted at her folly. What bollocks. This wasn't a fairy tale, it was real life. And she was no longer the teenager who would cram another cream-filled lamington in her mouth in the vain hope the pain and hurt would disappear. She would eat her athletic shorts before she'd believe Kyan's people didn't suffer from at least some form of sexual nasty.

Mike drummed his fingers on the kitchen bench. "So. You wanted to know whether Kyan has any STDs."

"Um. Yeah. I guess you heard, huh?" How embarrassing. This was almost as bad as the time her mum gave her the birds and bees talk. Ruby drained her mug and poured another coffee. That last one hadn't even touched the sides on the way down.

"I do not have a disease of the privates, Ruby." Kyan slammed his mug on the bench. "Nor will I ever suffer one. My people have suffered no naturally caused ailments for centuries. At least, that was the case before I was… imprisoned."

Ruby barely prevented herself from snorting coffee through her nose. "Oh, go pull the other one, Kyan, it's got fricking huge church bells on it."

He frowned as he tried to decipher her meaning.

"She doesn't believe your people never get sick," Mike said, being helpful. A little too helpful, if the amused gleam in his eyes was anything to go by. She sooo did not want to be having this conversation in front of her brother and, damn him, Mike was well aware of that fact.

"'Tis true, Ruby," Kyan said. "Aside from magically induced ailments, and injuries caused by carelessness or inflicted during the course of a battle, my people suffer no illnesses. We are a long-lived people, with most living a span of nine *tehs* or more."

"*Tehs*?" Mike frowned. "Same root as *tehun*, which is a troop of ten men. So that would be a decade, right?" His eyes widened. "Your people routinely live past ninety?"

Kyan nodded. "That is the average, yes. Many live longer."

Mike's eyebrows disappeared into his hairline. "That's a pretty damn good average lifespan, don't you reckon, Rubes?"

"Yep, it sure is." *Especially for such a primitive people.* She left that thought unvoiced, reluctant to spark another argument. She knew Kyan was proud of his warrior status. And although he reacted like a kid at Christmas when confronted with some of the "wonders" he'd encountered, that didn't mean she wanted to rub his nose in her world's superiority. "Still, I find it hard believe they don't get sick. That's too far-fetched. Every human being under the sun gets ill at some time in their life. It's a normal state of being. Wouldn't you agree, Mike?"

"Mmmhunph," Mike muttered around a mouthful of hot buttered toast slathered with manuka honey.

"You believe you're immune to disease?" Ruby wanted to be clear because she was determined to get to the bottom of Kyan's outrageous claim.

Kyan rolled his eyes. Geez! He must have picked that up from Mike because it couldn't possibly be from *her*. "I do not merely *believe* we are immune to disease," he said. "I know it absolutely."

"Riiight." She would not roll her eyes. She wouldn't! But oh, it wasn't easy. "I hate to be the bearer of bad news, but that's impossible. Not to mention unnatural. I can't imagine any group of humans—however isolated—evolving like that without some outside influence playing a role. Like, say, a technologically advanced race of aliens inoculating them against every disease known to man."

Kyan had to be exaggerating. Or lying. How far could she really trust him? They'd had sex, sure. Okay, mind-blowing, amazing sex. Twice. But much as it pained her to admit, she hardly knew him at all.

Mike threw her a slit-eyed glare that conveyed disapproval of her sarcasm but Ruby ploughed on. "From what you've said, Kyan, I gather it wasn't always that way, right? So what changed suddenly? Somebody waved a magic wand and hey presto, no more illness?"

"You are very clever, Ruby." Kyan reached over to pat her on the wrist.

"Huh?"

"Although no wand was used."

She shot a glance at Mike. Hoh boy, this was gonna be good.

Kyan accepted the plate of toast Mike handed him, and settled on one of the stools by the breakfast bar. "Of course our good fortune is not a natural occurrence. Our priests banished illness forever with a powerful spell."

Ruby snorted, but before she could follow up with some scathing comment, he said, "And this one does *not* need pulling as it has no bells on it."

She blinked. "Huh?"

"I am telling the truth." Kyan hooked his ankles around the stool and pulled himself closer to the breakfast bar so he could butter his toast. "Never have I suffered an illness stemming from natural causes. Not even as a child."

"You do appear disgustingly healthy," Mike said. "In my professional opinion. As a medic."

Ruby shot her brother an evil glare for enabling Kyan's absurd claims of magical good-health spells.

Kyan took a huge bite of toast and licked the buttery crumbs from his lips.

Ohhh. Yum. Ruby crossed her legs and tried not to drool.

When he'd finished chewing, he said, "In your world, do you suffer from the ailment that inflicts upon you a congestion of the nose, an aching head, and sneezes?"

Mike rubbed his nose, as though he couldn't help reacting physically to the list of symptoms. "Sounds like you're describing what we call the 'common cold'. It's caused by a virus. No one's ever been able to cure that."

Kyan said nothing and merely smiled.

Mike's eyes went huge and his eyebrows shot upward. "You've never suffered a cold in your entire life?"

Kyan shook his head.

"Not even a sniffle?"

Kyan frowned at the term, so Mike demonstrated with what sounded more like a nasal snort than a sniffle. It seemed to get the point across for Kyan shook his head. "No. Not even a *sniffle*."

"God Almighty. What I wouldn't give for a spell to cure that." Mike shook his head and heaved a sigh. "Pity."

Looked like Ruby wouldn't be making that embarrassing appointment with her GP to discuss STD testing after all. She would get away with a discreet purchase of the morning-after pill at her local pharmacy instead. Yay.

Kyan licked melted butter from his fingers and she had to pinch herself to concentrate on his words, not his mouth. "As my people soon discovered," he said, "such powerful magic is not always benevolent. There are consequences, and a price to be paid."

"Wh-what—? What do you m-mean?" Watching him swirl his tongue around another buttery finger was playing havoc with her powers of concentration.

Kyan took a sip of his coffee and placed his mug on the breakfast bar with exquisite care. When he cast his gaze in Ruby's direction his eyes were distant. But whatever he was remembering reflected in his face, subtly shifting his perfect features into something ruthless and yes, even cruel. The über-confident, easygoing man who'd so easily and efficiently slotted himself into her world had vanished, leaving a warrior forged by the harsh realities of life in his home world. Right now, he looked capable of anything.

Ruby shivered, uneasy at the change, abruptly conscious of the vast gulf between them despite their physical intimacies.

Kyan laughed, and it was a mirthless, chilling sound. "Our priests did not wish commoners to learn of their folly. Thus, our histories do not record exactly what occurred. Only vague hints of the truth remain, buried deep, invisible except to those who are determined to seek the truth. Malach, our tehun-Leader, was such a one. And it took him many years to piece together the true chain of events. I caught him with a scroll he'd stolen from a temple, and coerced him to confess what he had learnt. Instead of offering my support, I recall jeering at him, suggesting he renounce his warrior status and become a priest if he was so enamored with old records and such."

He rubbed his hands over his face as if to rid himself of the unpleasant memory. "I told no one of Malach's discovery because I did not wish to believe him. In my heart of hearts, though, I knew it to be truth. But I thought... I thought if I did not allow myself to dwell on it, refused to speak of it, life could proceed as usual. I did not wish to believe my people were dying out due to covetousness and greed. Better we died in defense of our lives and our homes. Better we died with honor for a worthy purpose."

His voice throbbed with emotion, an emotion that stripped him of the raw sexuality that was so much an integral part of him, allowing Ruby a glimpse of the vulnerability beneath.

"What use is material wealth to a man?" he asked, and Ruby had the impression he was speaking to no one in particular, that this was a thought he'd often contemplated but never voiced until now. "Precious metals cannot replace the woman who carries a man's child. Jewels cannot replace the joy he feels when he gazes upon his firstborn."

Ruby ached for him. Her own guilt weighed heavily, making her hunch her shoulders. She had once thought Kyan shallow, of little substance—a to-die-for male body housing little else. She had been all too willing to judge him at face value and not look deeper, to the man beneath. And she'd harbored a vague sense of shame that she was so attracted to him, that she had allowed herself to be seduced by him. She'd justified everything she felt for Kyan by telling herself she couldn't be held accountable because she was influenced by "magic".

God she was pathetic, clinging to the belief that *all* handsome guys were arrogant pricks who got by on looks alone, and they'd only hurt her because they cared more about themselves, and their image, than anything else. Kyan was living proof that she was wrong. He was gorgeous, intelligent, caring. He was a man with deeply held morals, capable of deep emotions. He was the antithesis of shallow.

What more could a girl ask for?

While Ruby wrestled with seeing Kyan in a whole new light, Mike was focused on more important matters. Like life and death, and the decline of an entire race of people. "What do you mean your people were dying out?"

"In their o'erweening pride, our priests sought to meddle with the natural laws of life and death." Kyan's expression was so grim and bleak that Ruby shivered and rubbed her arms. "They conjured visions of other worlds—such as yours—and they coveted the riches of those worlds. Thus they hatched their plans for invasion. When our Lord Keepers demurred, doubting the wisdom of such plans, the priests vowed to cast a spell that would make our warriors invincible. And so the seeds for our own destruction were sown." He paused, his jaw clenching so tightly the tendons of his neck distended. Ruby could see a pulse beating on his temple.

"We should have known the gods would not let our arrogance and greed go unpunished."

"But the spell worked, didn't it?" Ruby said. "Your people don't ever get sick and they live long lives. That doesn't sound like a punishment to me."

"The spell did not work as the priests envisioned. For one, it affected *all* our people, not merely the warrior caste. And my people may have henceforth enjoyed rude health and longevity, but we were not invincible by any means. A sword thrust could still kill a warrior, just as a broken neck could kill a commoner who tripped and fell. But the true punishment for attempting to cheat death was that our women bore only male offspring." Kyan laughed again, and this time it reeked of despair and sadness. "At first we rejoiced in this unexpected side-effect of the spell our priests had wrought. Every man's desire is for strong, healthy sons to carry on his name, yes? Is that not true in this world, also, Mike?"

"Yep," Mike said. "Even in so-called civilized countries, sons are desired to inherit and carry on the family name."

Ruby didn't get it. She knew she was missing something crucial. "So, what happened?"

"What do you think happened?" Mike said. "Think about it, Ruby. Each Styrian female eventually went through menopause and couldn't bear any more children. And when the last generation of women died, there were no more children born at all. Period. So—"

Ruby gasped as the full import hit her. "Only men were left, and all your people began dying out? That must have been devastating. Surely there was something your priests could do?"

Kyan levered himself from the stool to stand before her, gazing into her eyes. "Of course they found a solution, Ruby. My people did not die out, otherwise I would not be standing here today."

His tone was dangerously light but she wasn't fooled for an instant. He caressed her cheek with his knuckles, and despite the tension surrounding them, even that feather-light touch provoked a rush of desire that made her shiver. She pressed her thighs together, embarrassed by the wholly inappropriate reaction in the face of Kyan's anguish.

"How could we survive without women to bear our children and replenish our population?" he asked. "Why would we even *want* to survive without women to slake our needs? Our priests knew we needed women and of course, they knew exactly where to find them."

Kyan's hand stilled, and he cupped her cheek. Some unnamed emotion flickered in his eyes. Her body recognized and understood the emotion, even if her brain could not yet give it a name. Her skin grew cold beneath the warmth of his palm.

"What did your priests do?" she asked.

"They opened a portal to other worlds, as they had originally planned. Your world was one of them."

"Why?"

"So that instead of stealing your metals and other riches, we could steal your women."

Comprehension smacked her like a physical blow. She wanted to fling his hand away, break the connection that they shared. "To use as breeding stock?" The shrillness of her voice echoed the horror churning in her stomach.

Kyan tilted her chin and placed a gentle kiss on her lips. Ruby's brain began sending those inappropriate, lust-fueled messages to her body again, and she reared back, almost falling off her stool.

Kyan turned away from her to address Mike. "You should not be surprised to learn what lengths men will go to in order to survive," he said. And then he left the room.

Ruby let him go. She heard the squeal of the front door hinges, then a slam that made her wince. But she didn't follow him.

CHAPTER ELEVEN

MIKE REFILLED HER coffee mug while Ruby stared out the dining room window and wrestled with her emotions. Kyan had been a trafficker of humans—specifically fertile young girls and women, which for some reason made it so much worse. Ruby could imagine all-too-vividly how they would have been used like broodmares until they were too old or worn out to bear more children. He'd been a slaver—a monster. And yet....

Any adult who possessed a television and tuned in to the evening news had seen graphic video footage of humankind struggling to survive. None of it was pretty. All of it was disturbing. Despots reigned. Other countries intervened for the greater good—so long as "the greater good" benefited them. Wars were fought over disparate beliefs or natural resources. And those caught up in the conflict were forced to confront how far they would go, what they were prepared to do, in order to survive.

Fear, desperation and suffering forced even the most moral, compassionate person to resort to baser instincts. How were Kyan's people, fighting for survival in the only way they knew how, any different?

Unfortunately, the only way to definitively answer that question would be to ask the women the Styrians had stolen and used as breeders, which was obviously not an option. But here and now, given the information she had been given, Ruby could understand what had driven Kyan's people. She didn't like it, not one little bit. But she understood the motivation behind the acts.

She grabbed her rapidly cooling coffee and intercepted Mike peering intently at her. And before he schooled his expression to blankness, a bunch of little clues clicked neatly into place. "You bloody well knew all about Kyan's past, didn't you, Mike? He told you everything. And I'm guessing this is why he and the rest of the Crystal Warriors were imprisoned by the Guardian—as punishment for their crimes. Why didn't you tell me?"

"Would it have made a difference, Rubes?" Mike extracted a lump of frozen bread from its bag and pried the individual slices apart.

"A difference? Of course it would have made a goddamned difference." She snatched the bread slices from him and shoved them into the toaster. All the coffee sloshing round in her empty, exercise-hyped stomach was making her feel queasy.

At least, she hoped it was the coffee, and not because she was pregnant—

"Why?" Mike asked.

Ruby pulled herself together. No way would she be showing signs of morning sickness already. But she made a mental note to stop by the pharmacy before work for that morning after pill. She'd heard they could make you feel really crappy. Hopefully she wouldn't feel too sick to train tomorrow—

Mike clicked his fingers in her face. "Why would it have made a difference, Ruby?"

"What? Oh, yeah. Duh, because no way would I have slept with Kyan if—"

"You've slept with Kyan?"

"Yes." She flushed and tried to hide it by peering into the toaster slots as if to check what was taking the bread so long to toast. "What do you *think* we were doing when you walked in on us? Reciting poetry?"

"Sheesh. I had no idea my own sister was such a tart."

She lifted her chin, preparing to mount a defense, and then realized Mike was trying not to smile and thoroughly enjoying making her squirm. Bastard. "Before you get into tease-your-poor-sister-unmercifully mode, if I'd known he was a... a—"

"Soldier, doing what he was ordered to do? Trying his utmost to save an entire race of people?"

"I hate you when you're so fucking eloquent this early in the morning."

"Language," Mike said, imitating their mother so skillfully that Ruby shuddered.

She grumbled beneath her breath, knowing her brother was right. Kyan had been a soldier, following orders. And that made it even more difficult to judge him.

The toast shot up from the toaster and Mike grabbed it before it landed on the bench.

"Hey, that's mine," Ruby said. "Hand it over."

"You would have slept with him anyway." Mike slapped her hands away. "You need to have something more substantial than toast to keep your strength up. Go microwave an egg or something."

"I'll have you know that me sleeping with Kyan was not a foregone conclusion."

Mike drizzled manuka honey over his toast. "Puhlease. He's so hot for you he can't keep his hands off you. And then there's the whole needing you to save him from a fate worse than death aspect. You didn't stand a chance, Rubes. Of course you were going to sleep with him."

Ruby popped two more pieces of bread in the toaster and, while Mike was otherwise distracted with extracting the last dregs of coffee from the plunger, snitched both pieces of his honey toast. She licked a drip of honey from her fingers... and gave up trying to gather the scattered pieces of her dignity. "Yeah. You're right."

Mike scowled at his empty plate. "And from the sounds I've heard coming from your room the last two nights, he's not too shabby a lover, either."

She blinked at him, mouth agape, face burning. "Eeeeuw! I am so *not* discussing my sex life with you, Mike. You're my brother. It's just… wrong."

"Bet you'll tell Jules all about it—in such graphic detail it'd make a man's hair curl."

"That's different. Well, it would be if I'd told her about Kyan and me. But I haven't. I've told *everyone* he's an old friend from primary school."

Mike regarded her with slitty-eyed, single-minded focus. "How come?"

No point trying to prevaricate when her brother was in full blown inquisition mode. "I don't feel comfortable telling Jules. Or anyone else, for that matter."

"Why? I figured you'd want to show him off. You know, rub the Stick Insect's nose in it for all it's worth."

"Much as I'd adore rubbing Caroline's nose in the fact that even someone like *me* can hook a hot man, I'd prefer to keep my relationship with Kyan private. It's nobody's business but ours." No way did she want to admit her fears to Mike. Gut-twisting, heart-wrenching fears that, once they'd passed the Testing, Kyan would have no further need for her and he'd take off, leaving her looking like a gullible idiot. Leaving her feeling a whole heap of things she didn't want to examine too closely.

"He's not like that, Rubes," Mike said, obviously reading her thoughts in that uncanny way he'd had since they were kids.

"You really think he's hot for me?" she whispered, daring to hope.

"Yep. Hard to miss, really."

Her flush of embarrassment morphed into a warm glow of contentment—for all of two seconds before the doubts crept in. "Mmm."

"What're you 'mmming' about?"

Ruby gnawed her thumbnail, struggling to put the worry pricking her mind into words. "This bonding thing you told me about in the café. What if there's more to it than we've been told? What if there's more to it than haphazardly match-ing a Crystal Warrior with his chosen life-mate?" She wound a lock of hair around her finger and tugged. Hard. Until her eyes watered. "I mean, what if Kyan accidentally chooses another girl? Or his chosen mate isn't having a bar of it—like that Chalcedony chick's mother. Bet you anything *that* wasn't supposed to happen. I mean, what if there's no... *connection*? Life-mates. Bonding. What about free will? I can't help think-ing there's an important bit of information missing from this puzzle."

"You think too much." Mike's gaze slid away, and he bus-tled about cleaning up the breakfast dishes.

He was hiding something. "Mike, what—?

"Are you happy when you're with Kyan, Ruby?"

"Happy?"

"It's a simple question. How do you feel when you're with Kyan?"

"I–I feel great. He makes me feel, I dunno, like a different person."

"Complete? Like there was something missing and now you're whole?"

She stared at her brother, wondering how he'd managed to sum up her innermost feelings so accurately. Spooky. "Yeah. I feel whole."

"Like I do with Annie." He hung the dishcloth over the tap and dried his hands. "You'd better get ready for work. It's pushing seven thirty."

"Shee-iiit!" Ruby rushed from the kitchen to shower and get ready. And as she dressed she thought, *Neat change of subject, bro, but you're not fooling me.* She knew how to find out what Mike was hiding, though—if she dared.

WORK STARTED OFF BADLY and went downhill from there. She'd been running so late she hadn't had time to go to the pharmacy, so that was preying on her mind. Liz just about drove Ruby crazy with her incessant bitching about how Mrs. Liang would never buy a freaking house in a month of Sundays no matter how many houses she was shown, and how much effort Liz put in. David kept dropping not-so-subtle hints that he'd like Ruby to introduce him to Kyan so he could check firsthand whether Kyan was AC or DC. Hah. Like a man who made love to women like Kyan did could ever bat for the other side. And Caroline insisted on bringing up Ruby's monthly get-together with Jules, and pretending to be all teary-eyed at being excluded.

Yeah, right. Like Caroline had ever shown the slightest interest in going out to see a chick-flick with them before. It was so not her scene, she'd informed Ruby the first couple of times Ruby had invited her to come along.

Uh oh. Here she comes again.

"What movie are you and Jules going to see on Saturday, Ruby?" Caroline asked, as she contrived to wander past Ruby's desk.

"Don't know. Haven't decided yet." Ruby kept her eyes glued to her keyboard and tapped away industriously.

Caroline didn't take the hint. She exhaled. Loudly. "It must be so nice to have a friend like Jules. Someone to go to the movies with you when you don't have a boyfriend to take you."

"I'm sure you've got plenty of guys lined up, Caroline. You always go out Saturday night." *And every Monday morning, you regale us lesser beings with how much your date spent on you, and how perfect he is, blah blah blah.*

Caroline sniffed, and somehow managed to make it sound both ladylike and woebegone. "Not this Saturday. I'm still pining after—" she paused theatrically "—Joseph. Breaking up with him really hurt, you know?"

"Joseph?" David slid to a halt outside the door to his office. "Do my ears deceive me? I thought you dumped him."

Ruby gave up pretending to work and fixed her gaze on Caroline. This should be good—

"I did," Caroline said. "But that doesn't mean it doesn't hurt right here." She fluttered a hand over what she probably imagined was her heart.

"It's the left side," Ruby said.

"Huh?"

"Your heart. It's on the left side of your chest."

Caroline chose to ignore that. "I mean, even though Joseph had become rather predictable in bed," she said, "we had, like, a *connection*."

Yeah. Like from Joseph's wallet directly to Caroline's perfectly manicured fingernails. And how the hell could a man be predictable in bed after only a couple of weeks? Actually, scratch that. Ruby so did *not* want to know.

"I feel so lost and alone now Joseph is gone." Caroline sighed again, and this time she gave it her all, right down to an Oscar-worthy droop of her shoulders. "Weekends are the worst, don't you find, Ruby? It's awful being all on your own the entire weekend, with nothing to do except imagine everyone else out having fun with their friends." Cue crocodile tears glittering in her eyes.

Oooh, she was good.

Both Liz and David cast glances at Ruby. Glances that screamed, "You're a big bad meanie for not immediately inviting Caroline along on your girls' night out with Jules."

Great.

Ruby could feel the invitation hovering on the tip of her tongue. She ground her teeth together and swallowed it. "Yeah," she said. "Weekends can really suck when you're on your own." God knows *she'd* suffered through enough of them.

Caroline trailed her fingernails across Ruby's desk. And when Ruby remained silent, Caroline sniffed a little more… and then reached across to grab a tissue from the box on the desk, and use it to dab artfully at her eyes.

Liz and David were goggle-eyed by now, anxiously waiting to see how Ruby handled the pressure.

"You know what I miss the most about Joseph?" Caroline asked, her voice catching just a little.

Ruby surprised herself by managing not to fall into that trap. Instead, borrowing Caroline's idea, she extracted a tissue from the box and blew her nose. Loudly.

Unfortunately, Liz fell for it hook, line and sinker. "What?"

"Do tell," David said. "I bet you miss his gorgeous big Swiss—"

"Accent," Caroline interrupted, ignoring David's snigger. "The way Joseph used to say my name made me feel sooo special. I really, really miss that." A single perfect tear rolled down her cheek.

Ruby rubbed her temples, groaning inwardly. Jules would be pissed off to the max but she couldn't take the drama any longer. Jules would just have to deal. "Fine, Caroline. If you've nothing better to do Saturday night, of course you can come with us. Don't blame me if you're bored out of your tree, though. All we do is watch a movie and guzzle popcorn. It's hardly exciting stuff."

Caroline smiled. "I'm sooo lucky to have a friend like you, Ruby. Let me know when and where, okay?"

"Okay." Ah, crap. She was such a soft touch.

Mulling her options didn't provide any inspiration. And it didn't help she had a lot of other stuff on her mind. Thankfully she got her head together before her lunchtime swimming lesson, which proved a vast improvement over the previous one because she managed to stay on top of the water for the duration. But that was pretty much the highlight of the workday, which turned out to be one of those days when she was busy as heck, but never seemed to accomplish anything.

All the way home in the bus, Ruby replayed that fateful conversation with Caroline in her mind. It was either that or obsess over the awkward conversation with Mike this morning. And the one before that, with Kyan.

No, best to wipe the disturbing subject of Kyan from her mind, and figure out how to survive breaking the news about Caroline to Jules. Or whether she should even mention it at all. If Caroline showed up on Saturday, it would kinda be obvious what Ruby had done. And maybe, if she was really lucky, Jules wouldn't make too much of a fuss in front of Caroline.

Hah. Delusional, much? Jules couldn't *stand* Caroline. Of course she'd make a fuss. Either way, Ruby was doomed.

Mike's rental was nowhere in evidence when she got home. He and Kyan were still off somewhere, doing whatever it was they did while Ruby was at work. And by the time she headed off on her jog for five minutes, walk for five minutes, jog for five, walk for five, cardio session, Ruby was almost grateful for the distraction provided by the straps of her very unsuitable bra, which were chafing something wicked.

Still no sign of Mike's SUV. She fished the door key from her pocket and unlocked the front door. But instead of making a beeline for the shower, she paused, resting her forehead on the doorjamb. She'd been trying not to think about this moment all day, and now it was about to lunge and bite her on the bum.

What on earth was she going to say to Kyan? Presuming he wasn't still with Mike, of course. In which case she'd have a while longer to fret. But… Kyan could be home right now, waiting inside for her to show her face, and she didn't have the foggiest clue how to even begin to apologize for being such a bitch to him.

Suck it up and deal, Ruby. She straightened her shoulders and headed inside to face the music.

Her house was eerily quiet. She wandered through to the kitchen. Empty. Ditto with the bedrooms. Typically, Mike hadn't left a note to say when he and Kyan would be back, either. Hah. They were probably both sitting in some fancy pub, drinking beer and fending off feral women. Nice for some.

Her gaze caught on the tissue paper-wrapped bundle left abandoned on the phone table in the lounge. And when she picked it up, she was vaguely surprised to discover the pieces of kyanite crystal hadn't vanished.

She plopped onto the couch and carefully unwrapped the bundle. She didn't know what she expected to see—perhaps that something about the broken crystal had fundamentally altered. Like the color or the shape—*something* to indicate it was no longer a prison that had trapped a man for hundreds of years.

But it was just as she remembered: An unremarkable, silvery blue, blade-shaped hunk of stone that had broken in half. Nothing special. Certainly not something that screamed supernatural otherworldliness.

She turned the two pieces over in her hands, investigating how they fit together. Her heartbeat escalated until it thudded in her ears. Her breath caught in her throat. She fitted the two halves together and held them, waiting for—

Something.

Nothing changed. Her world didn't turn on its head and realign. The two pieces didn't magically fuse into one whole piece of kyanite again.

She let the crystal pieces fall into her lap and leaned back, closing her eyes. And a vision rolled through her tired, vulnerable mind.

KYAN RECLINES ON a pile of brightly colored cushions. His bored gaze rakes a bevy of naked girls who all wait, heads bowed in demure silence. He clicks his fingers imperiously and the girls step aside to reveal a plump feminine figure, swathed head to toe in layers of gauzy material.

Kyan jerks his chin at a girl with huge doe-like eyes, and she steps forward to grab a trailing tail of material. She tugs it, gathers the excess material in her arms and tugs again, repeating the action, causing the draped figure to spin like a drunkard as the material unwinds.

One last tug and a woman is revealed. Now she is naked, too. Dizzy and dazed, she loses her balance and plops to the sand, landing on her ample rear in an inelegant sprawl of pale limbs and bare flesh.

Kyan stands, and raises his hand for silence. He is about to make his final choice. The younger girls titter at the woman, at her, for Ruby is the woman now struggling to her feet... and all she can do is stare at Kyan and hope with all her heart that he will choose her again.

Her hopes are dashed when Kyan chooses one of the graceful young girls. And when he does finally spare her a glance, his lips are pursed with disgust.

He turns his back. And as he strides from the tent, the female he has chosen slung over his shoulder, tears well and course silently down Ruby's face. She—

Uhhh!

Ruby's eyelids popped open and she cast a quick gaze the length of her body. Thank God. She was still fully clothed, slumped on her couch with the crystal pieces laying her lap.

She swept them aside, onto the couch cushion, and told herself that it'd only been a daydream—her imagination playing tricks on her.

It had felt so real though—the gauzy material wrapped so tightly about her body. The panic she'd felt as she was spun around and had to struggle to stay upright. The sand grazing her naked buttocks as she fell. The blissful coolness of the shelter provided by the awning—such a stark contrast to the harsh sun beating down outside, and the burning flush of humiliation that even now warmed her face.

She grabbed the TV remote and channel-surfed. But so far as distractions went it was a failure, especially when all she noticed were slim, glossily perfect female newsreaders, or equally slim, pretty young things acting out teenage angst in locally made soaps.

Her wandering gaze lit on the phone. Before she could talk herself out of it, she dialed international directory services and asked for Chalcedony Laureano's phone number.

As she waited for the call to connect, her stomach tried to crawl up her throat. This was probably a bad idea—really bad. Did she truly want to know *everything* Chalcedony had discovered about Wulf, Kyan, and the rest of the Crystal Warriors? How would that knowledge change the way she felt about Kyan? Could she reject him if it was in her best interests to do so, or was she even now, in too deep?

"Hello."

The unexpectedness of the masculine voice booming from the phone receiver startled her into nearly dropping the phone. "H-h-hello," she squeaked.

"Who am I speaking to?"

Shee-it. This *had* to Chalcedony's husband. Lord Wulf, Ruler of the Moving Sands, or whatever the land he had supposedly ruled over was called. "Ah, it's Ruby Roberts here. Is… is… Chalcedony Laureano there, please?"

"Chalcedony is asleep."

"Asleep?"

"'Tis very, very early in the morning."

Oh, crap. She'd completely forgotten to factor in the US-NZ time differential. "God. I'm sorry to wake you. I'll ring back later."

"Perhaps I may help you, Ruby."

"Um, well, I don't want to keep you from your bed."

His chuckle was a low rumble. "You are too kind. However, as 'twas my turn to convince our daughter to sleep rather than play in her crib, I am wide awake. What is wrong, Ruby? Is my kinsman's behavior troubling you?"

"Wh-whose behavior?"

"Kyan's." His voice turned cold and harsh—obviously there was no love lost between Kyan and Wulf.

"Um, would I be right in thinking you know exactly who I am, and what I'm going through with Kyan?"

"You would be correct. I know all about you, Ruby, for Kyan was quite… *effusive* in his description of you. And from what I hear, you are far too good for the likes of him. Are you bonded? Or is there yet a chance you might escape my kinsman's wiles?"

Whoa. He really *really* didn't think much of Kyan. "I'm not entirely sure, Mr., uh, Lord um—"

"You may call me Wulf, Ruby. I am not Lord of anything in this world of yours. I am ruled by my wife, and lately, my daughter, who has wrapped me around her tiny finger. Such is the fate of Wulfenite, former Lord Keeper of the Shifting Sands fief."

Was that a hint of laughter in his voice? Certainly, his deep affection for his wife and daughter was evident. Lucky, lucky Chalcedony.

"Do you wish to know about the bond, Ruby?"

"Yes. Please tell me everything you know. Everything."

He was silent for a long, excruciating moment. "Are you certain, Ruby? Ignorance is oftentimes a more blissful state than full awareness of the consequences of one's actions. Or inactions, as the case may be."

"Yeah. I'm sure. Please."

A sigh gusted down the phone line. "Very well. The bonding is twofold, Ruby."

"Twofold? I thought that once we were chosen as lifemates, that was it?"

"Nay. First, there must be an exchange of true names."

"Oh, right. We might have done that one already. Did you

and Chalcedony suffer any, ah, unusual side effects with that one?"

"Uttering each other's true names rendered us both unconscious for a time. I do not recall it being a particularly pleasant occurrence."

"Me, neither. When I woke up it sorta felt like someone whacked my head with a cricket bat."

"I do not know of these *cricket* bats, but I do remember feeling as though a horse had stomped on my head."

"Yeah, that's the one. And Kyan passed out, too. So I'm guessing we've exchanged true names."

"I believe so."

Oh. Strike one. "Okay, what's next?"

"Bonding intimately."

A blush heated her face and slowly crawled down her neck and chest. She fanned herself with a hand, grateful Wulf couldn't see her reaction. "Um, how intimately?"

"Sexual intercourse," he said.

"Ah." Talk about consequences. Just not quite the consequences she'd imagined.

"I gather you've already—" he paused as though searching for words that would not give offence "—allowed Kyan to seduce you?"

"Yeah. So I suppose we're bonded then. No way around it." She wasn't sure whether to be thrilled or horrified.

"That is not necessarily the case. How many times, Ruby?"

"Excuse me?"

He huffed a sigh. "I apologize for my bluntness, however this is important. How many times has Kyan seduced you?"

A corner of her mind found it interesting that Wulf presumed *Kyan* had done all the seducing. She debated being offended. But only for a second. She'd never have had the guts play the seductress. "He and I, uh, we—" God! "Twice."

"That is good news."

"It is?"

"You are not yet irrevocably bound."

"We're not? But I thought I had no choice. I thought that after four weeks I'd face some sort of a test, and there was no way I could get out of it."

"As Chalcey explained to your brother, unless you engage in sexual union with Kyan three times, you are not irrevocably bonded. You have only to refuse Kyan's advances from this moment forward, and at month's end there will be no Testing. Chosen life-mates or no, Kyan will be drawn back into his namesake crystal, and once more become a prisoner of the Crystal Guardian's spell."

"Three times? It takes three times? We're not bonded yet?" She slumped lower on the couch. And Mike knew this. Yet for some reason he hadn't revealed this... this... extremely perti-nent fucking fact. How could he not have told her? And, more to the point, why? This was her heart he was playing with. Her happiness. Shit—her life!

Her thoughts roiled and seethed. And when the surge of anger and betrayal faded enough to be bearable, Mike's moti-vation became all too clear. He was a St John's medic—a lifesaver. And to his mind, by not telling her, by letting her think she had no choice but to await the Testing, he was mak-ing certain Kyan had the best possible chance to survive.

But what about her? How would *she* survive when all this was over, and Kyan hooked up with some hot babe who was more his type? What happened to *her* when there was no magical attraction binding Kyan to her? When Kyan finally saw her for who she was, and all she saw in his eyes was pity, not even Mike would be able to pick up the pieces and put her all back together.

"Ruby." Wulf's deep voice, oozing compassion, cut through the hurt. "What are you going to do?"

"Do? About what?"

"About Kyan."

"I don't know." The sigh shuddered through her. "I truly

don't know."

"'Tis difficult, I know. Unless Kyan has fundamentally changed, he is a man who is overly reliant on his handsome face to lure women to his bed. Last I knew of him, he was too concerned with his own pleasures to pay much heed how his actions affected others. 'Twas not always so, but—" He paused. "Perhaps that is a tale for another time. Please know this, Ruby. I would not wish for him to suffer the rigors of the crystal again. I would not wish that hell on any man."

"That place he was trapped in," she whispered. "I felt it— experienced what Kyan felt. For a short time only, but it still haunts me. It's indescribably horrible."

"'Tis more terrible than you could ever know," he murmured.

"So I guess it's up to me, then. Ruby to the rescue. Now there's a bloody laugh. Me, rescuing someone like Kyan? Hilarious."

"Do not denigrate yourself, Ruby." Wulf used one of those stern, lecturing tones that parents used on their children. "Perhaps my kinsman is not beyond redemption. Perhaps he is capable of learning what it means to give yourself wholly to another, to be truly joined in mind, body and soul. Kyan spoke of you with more wonder in his voice than I have ever heard him describe a woman. I believe you are special to him."

"Yeah. Thanks to the Crystal Guardian and his delightful little magic spell. Kyan would never have given me a second glance otherwise."

"Perhaps so. One thing I have learned in this life is that the Crystal Guardian somehow sees deep into our hearts and our souls. Pieter did not choose you on a whim, Ruby. The old man recognizes the kind of love we are each searching for. Even if we are not consciously aware we are searching for it, he knows."

"I hope so," she whispered. God, she hoped with all her heart that she was the woman Kyan truly needed. Wanted.

"In truth your dilemma is a simple matter, Ruby. If you choose not to initiate the full bond for whatever reason, then Kyan is not the man for you. He must still have important lessons to learn before another mate is chosen for him. Or not."

That "or not" chilled her to the bone. Those two little words were loaded with the real possibility that returning to the crystal meant Kyan's death. From what Ruby recalled Mike saying, no one knew for certain. And no one had heard of a Crystal Warrior being given a second chance.

"If I don't he might die," she said.

"Perhaps. Though that has yet to be proven. And remember, Ruby, that Kyan is first and foremost a warrior. He has faced death many times. More importantly, this choice is yours, and yours alone, to make."

"And boy, doesn't that just suck the big kumara."

Wulf chuckled. "Yes. It sucks indeed."

"One last thing, Wulf. Does Kyan know about this three times the charm when it comes to sex with me thing?"

"You fear he knows and is using you to save himself."

"Yes." It cost her dear to admit that. "So, does he know?"

"That depends."

"On what?"

"On whether your brother passed on all the information Chalcedony imparted to him. She felt it important that he had all the facts as we know them. However, to afford you some measure of choice, some degree of protection, she did not reveal the full nature of the bonding to Kyan. And neither did I."

"Oh. That's good." And it opened up a whole new can of worms, too. "Thanks, Wulf. For everything."

"And does it aid you now to know what is in store for you both?" he asked.

She caught her lower lip between her teeth. "Maybe. I hope so."

"And I am full of hope for you, too. Be happy, Ruby."

"You too, Wulf."

"Ah, but can you not tell? I already am."

He rang off, leaving Ruby smiling... and wondering where her brother's loyalties lay.

Mike knew *everything*. But whether he had revealed what it took to make the bond irrevocable to Kyan remained to be seen. The only thing Ruby was sure of, was that Mike had an agenda of his own. And she would have to be an idiot to believe Kyan didn't have an agenda. Was he making love to her because he *wanted* to, or because he believed he had to?

Come to think about it, did Kyan even know sex was involved at all in the bonding process?

She snorted. Duh. Of course he knew. That had to be the reason for that serious little man-to-man exchange when her brother had surprised Kyan and Ruby making out in her bedroom. Kyan must have been tacitly seeking permission from Mike to continue with his seduction. Meaning, Kyan *was* using her to save himself.

Not that Ruby could blame him.

Bottom line? She still had a choice—for now. Two steamy hot sex sessions down, one more to go before her choice was stripped from her.

And that was another thing. If she *did* choose, and three times proved the charm, when the Testing finally came what if she failed? She wasn't much good at physical stuff. Aw, heck. To be honest she royally sucked at the physical stuff.

Ruby covered her face with a cushion to muffle her groan. Shit. If she was the only option Kyan had, he would be back in his crystal before he could blink. He was so screwed.

CHAPTER TWELVE

DESPITE HER MANY worries, Ruby crashed the instant her head touched the pillow and slept right through the night. She woke with Kyan wrapped blanket-like around her. He must have snuck in very late last night and decided her queen-sized bed was a better option than the couch. Doubtless he wanted to keep up the pressure, remind her of how good they were in aforementioned bed. After all, he couldn't risk her getting away.

She lay very still with her eyes tightly shut, pondering why he hadn't attempted to seduce her for the third time and make certain the bond could not be revoked.

Hang on. Could he have—?

Nah. No matter how exhausted she was, no way would Ruby have slept through *that*.

She cracked her eyelids to check the alarm. Five minutes to go. Might as well sneak out and get the bike ride over. Kyan didn't need to escort her. She could manage on her own.

She reached out to switch off the alarm before it shrilled. But before she could inch from beneath the covers, Kyan's arms tightened around her. She was so in tune with him that she noted his breathing change. It wasn't a reflexive action. He was awake.

Bugger.

She rolled within his embrace to face him. He opened his startling blue eyes and gazed at her. A frown creased his brow.

It was as though he sensed that she was hiding something from him, knew something had changed. He sucked in a deep breath and exhaled the tension from his muscles. His eyes grew shadowed, distant. And then he released her, and shuffled across the mattress, giving her space.

The gap between them was mere inches but it yawned like a chasm.

"You are angered because of my past," he said. "Because of the women we stole from your world."

"No, it's not that— God. That's a lie. Kind of. I mean, I *do* have a problem with that. But there's something more important. It's not that I don't care about all those poor women, you understand? But I haven't had time to figure out how I truly feel about all that stuff yet. So you're off the hook. For now, anyway. No, this is something else. Something really big. For me, anyway." Sheesh. She was babbling like an idiot.

"What is troubling you, Ruby?"

Crunch time. Okay. She would hit him right between the eyes with it and watch him squirm. "You don't feel anything real for me, Kyan. You could never consider loving someone like me under normal circumstances. You're only sleeping with me because you're afraid that if you don't, the Crystal Guardian will send you back to the crystal."

He winced. "I do not know what I feel, Ruby. Every time I try to analyze it, every time I convince myself what we have is real and true, I look at you and I wonder."

"How a man like you, who could have your pick of gorgeous women, could be involved with someone like me?"

He sighed, and it ached with sadness. "Not that, Ruby. Never that. As is your way, you again underestimate your appeal to men. No, I wonder why I have been chosen for you. Why me? Because, as my gods surely know, you deserve better."

Mouth agape, Ruby watched him roll out of bed to sit slumped on the edge of the mattress, elbows on knees, face buried in his hands. His little speech had knocked her for six. She'd expected smooth denials and suave declarations, not this stark admission that had throbbed with pain and self-loathing.

She shuffled her bottom up the mattress until she could lean against the headboard. And then she sucked in a deep breath, and addressed his vulnerable, naked back. God. Why did he have to make this so hard? Why couldn't she hate him for deceiving her?

"I know about the bonding process, Kyan. I know the significance of us having sex. One more time and we're irrevocably bonded. Then, if we pass the Testing, you're free and the Crystal Guardian can never imprison you again. I thought—" She wound a finger through a lock of her hair and tugged until her scalp hurt. The small pain helped ground her, helped her formulate her thoughts. "I thought exchanging true-names bonded us and brought on the Testing. I thought I didn't have a choice."

"Mike told you everything." He sounded resigned.

Her heart twisted into a painful knot that made her fist her hand and rub her breastbone. Kyan *did* know everything. He'd been feeding her lines to ensure he got into her knickers.

When she could bring herself to speak again her tone was flat and cold—a last ditch effort to disguise the pain of lost hopes and dreams. "It wasn't Mike who told me. I know why he didn't come clean, though. He's a medic—a healer. He can't stomach the thought of standing by while you're imprisoned again to suffer, and maybe even be put to death by the Crystal Guardian. Mike thinks I'm your best shot to get out of this mess. I'd be pissed off at him except—"

Except Ruby knew Mike only wanted her to be happy. He believed *Kyan* made her happy. And the bugger of it all was that Mike was right. Kyan did make her happy... when he wasn't making her miserable.

Kyan glanced over his shoulder at her, curiosity overcoming whatever else he happened to be feeling right now. "Who told you of the bonding?"

"Wulf. I rang him last night."

"Ah." A wry smile twisted his lips. "Wulf and I have often clashed. We are too different to like each other overly much, my kinsman and I."

"He cleared some things up for me, though."

Kyan turned his face to the wall. "And?"

Ruby scooted forward on her knees until she knelt behind him. She stroked her palms over his shoulders, trying to soothe away the terrible tension in his muscles. When that failed, she entwined her arms around his chest and held him, resting her chin on his shoulder. "*And*, I now know that if I can find the strength to resist you and we don't make love again, you'll be returned to your crystal."

He shuddered beneath her hands. She wasn't sure whether he was affected by her touch or the threat inherent in her words. It wasn't a true threat. It had no teeth because she knew that even if she could resist him, she didn't have it in her to leave him to his fate.

She couldn't let him off easily, though. He'd complimented her for speaking her mind, so damned if she wouldn't say her piece. "And if you *are* taken by the crystal, it could be a good thing, Kyan. You might have another chance. No one knows for certain whether the Guardian will kill you, or even whether he can. He might simply find you another woman—one far more suited to you than me."

"Perhaps I do not wish to take that risk."

The words stung but she couldn't blame him. He'd not asked for this—any of it. Sure, Ruby bemoaned not having a choice but Kyan had never had a choice, either. Until now. Not that it was much of a choice. Her, or insanity. Not to mention, the high possibility of death.

She ran her palms over his chest. There was nothing sexual about her touch. It was more about comfort—hers and his.

"What if you are the only woman for me, Ruby? What if

there is no other?" He grasped her hands, stilling them. And she felt his heart beating steadily beneath her hands.

"And perhaps," he said softly, "what I truly want is you, Ruby."

Ohhh. His words sank into her, warming her soul, banishing the hurt. She didn't have a chance. If she hadn't been a goner before, she sure was now.

Her choice was clear. She couldn't be responsible for Kyan's suffering and possible death. He was too vibrant, too alive to be caged and twisted by pain and suffering. He was the whole package. The almost perfect man—a dream come to life. And part of that package, an intrinsic part of Kyan's makeup, was his knack for knowing the perfect words to say to make her feel precious and wanted and worthy of love.

When he'd uttered that heartfelt sentiment, he had been completely caught up in the here and now. So, deep in her soul, she was certain that his words weren't lies. They were the truth—at least for that one precise, precious moment in time. Whether he meant them later, when the cold, hard reality hit, remained to be seen. But for Ruby, "later" was rapidly becoming something of little consequence.

Right now, Kyan made her feel like no other man had ever managed—or cared—to make her feel. Sexy. Desirable. Worthy of being loved. Her uncertainty about what tomorrow—or next week, or even next month—might bring could go to hell. *Now*, she would willingly take the first step toward saving Kyan. She would give him her body—such a small price to pay to save his life.

Relax and enjoy, Ruby. You've taken the morning after pill. Introduce him to condoms and safe sex, and everything will be peachy from now on. It wasn't as though making love with him again was something unpleasant to be endured. It was mindblowingly amazing. A beautiful experience to be treasured. One that would give her a bunch more wonderful, tendernessfilled memories that she could treasure for the rest of her life.

So she refused to worry about the future. Instead, she would grab hold of *now* and hold on tight.

His murmured words dragged her back to reality—to her bedroom, and the man she was embracing tightly, desperately, as though she would never let him go…. As though she would never give him up. "Perhaps I want all of you, Ruby," he said. "And especially your heart."

He twisted, pushing her back onto the bed and trapping her there with his body. He levered himself onto his elbows to better examine her face. "What say you, Ruby?"

He must have seen what she truly felt in her eyes—the flare of desperate hope, warring with the agonizing doubt she couldn't hide no matter how hard she tried to kid herself.

She pulled his head down to kiss him. She touched her lips to his, soft, butterfly kisses at first, and then hard demanding ones. She put everything she had into them, needing to erase the pain she saw in his eyes.

He responded passionately, taking control, kissing her until she was drowning in him, overwhelmed by him. Until she would have given him anything and everything she had to give—body and soul. She would have let him do whatever he wanted with her, and to her, the bond and the consequences be damned. She wanted him. And right here, right now, she didn't care about anything else.

But instead of taking it to the next level, he rolled off the bed and stood staring down into her confused, passion-hazed eyes.

"What's the matter, Kyan? Don't you want to have sex with me again so we can finalize the bond?"

"Oh, yes." The conviction in his voice caressed every inch of her, skating tiny lust-fueled shivers down her spine. "I want you, Ruby. I want to bed you. I want to make love to you. But when you next offer yourself to me, it will not be from obligation, or because you feel you need to save me." He turned away.

"But... but... Kyan!" The wail tore from her throat and echoed, mocking her.

He pulled on his clothes.

"Why are you doing this? Do you have a freaking death wish or something? What if Chalcedony's mother is right, and if we don't bond, you get sucked back into that goddamned hunk of rock? What if the Crystal Guardian *can* kill you?" Ruby knelt on her mattress, hands clasped like a religious supplicant begging for salvation. "Kyan, please. Come back to bed and let's get this bonding crap over with. I want to—"

He whirled to face her. "Is that all I am to you, Ruby? Something to be 'gotten over'?"

"No! I didn't mean it like that. I—"

"If you are only willing to bed me again in order to complete the bonding, then I am not interested." He pulled on his socks and sneakers, stamping his feet to check for comfort, just as he did with his boots. Must be a warrior thing.

"I will not be used," he said, driving the final nail into his metaphorical coffin.

Ruby lowered her hands into her lap and sat back on her heels. "*Excuse* me? I can't possibly have heard you right. I thought you just implied that I was using you."

"That is correct."

"You stupid, brainless, dim-witted, idiotic... *man*! I've just given you carte-blanche to have your wicked way with me so we can be bonded and prepare for this Testing which could save your bloody life. And you think I'm *using* you? How the freakin' heck do you figure that one? Now's not the time to get all moral, Kyan. We're talking life and death here—yours. So get your bum back over to this bed and fuck me, okay?"

To drive her point home, she lay back on the mattress and shimmied her hips in what she hoped was an inviting fashion. The t-shirt and granny-pants she wore possibly didn't present the most alluring of pictures but beggars couldn't be choosers. She was all he had.

He stalked toward the door. "No."

"No?"

"No."

Ruby's skin prickled white-hot with fury. *Bad move, Kyan.* This was gonna get ugly. "Oh, I get it. It's a control thing, right? I can't initiate sex with you, because you have to be in control of the situation. You have to tease me 'til I'm gagging for you and then you'll deign to have sex with me again. You wait 'til I'm a big lusty bundle of wants and needs before you jump me. And I'll be sooo grateful to you for giving me another orgasm. It's all about what *you* want, when *you* want it."

"That is not true. I—"

"We couldn't have a woman, or worse, a woman like *me* calling the shots, now, could we? That would change the natural order of the universe, wouldn't it?"

"Ruby, I—"

"And your other Crystal Warrior mates might laugh at you, huh? They'd say that Kyan's lost his mojo. Why else would he let a woman like *me* seduce a man like him?"

Of course it could be that he truly doesn't want to make love to you, that damnable little inner voice whispered. But why now, when she finally understood all the terms of the bonding and the consequences? Why now, when she'd finally committed to saving him? Hadn't that been what he wanted from her all along?

She didn't realize she was crying until the tears trickled past her chin. She blotted them away with the hem of her t-shirt. Crying over Kyan. Again. How humiliating.

Through the blur of tears she watched him stride toward her. His fists were clenched as though he wanted to strike out at something.

Her, probably. Well, that would be one way to ensure she went right off him in a big bloody hurry. She tensed, pressing herself against the mattress, waiting for... for... whatever punishment was about to rain down on her.

He climbed onto the mattress and crawled toward her on all fours. It might have been an incredibly erotic fantasy come true, except that she felt so miserable and wretched she wanted to curl up into a ball and howl.

He didn't touch her. He settled next to her and rolled on his back to stare at the ceiling. "What am I to do with you, my Ruby? I am trying to be gallant, and put your needs above my own. I do not want you to offer yourself to me for the wrong reasons."

She sniffed. "And how is wanting to save your life—or at least, giving you the best shot to actually *have* a life—the wrong reason? You knew about the conditions of the bond when you made love to me before—twice. And yet you had sex with me anyway. So how is this time any different?"

"Ahhh. That is where you are mistaken, Ruby. I did not make love to you because of the bond. I made love to you despite it." He leaned over to press a quick kiss to her brow before crawling off the bed.

Huh?

He strode to the door and paused, glancing back at her. "Hurry up, Ruby. We have a bike ride to complete before breaking our fast."

Men. God. Ruby would never understand them in a million years.

CHAPTER THIRTEEN

J ULES ALWAYS CLAIMED that after an argument, make-up
sex was the best sex ever. Passionate and hot and oh-so
intense that you wandered around with a goofy, dazed
smile plastered all over your face for days afterward. Unfortunately, by the time Saturday morning arrived Ruby still hadn't
gotten to test that claim.

Instead of sleeping on the couch, Kyan had continued to
share her bed. And snuggle. But no more than that. The man
sure knew how to torment a girl.

Speaking of torment, every night, her mind had replayed
erotic images of Kyan making love to her. Every night, she lay
in bed, teased by his tantalizing masculine scent. Inevitably,
her lust-ridden girly bits would start to tingle. Now they'd had
a taste of Kyan, they weren't letting her hear the end of it. Her
inner muscles would clench with anticipation. Her body
remembered him, and it reminded her in shockingly vivid
detail how wonderful it was to have him inside her, stroking
deep. And no matter how fiercely she admonished her brain to
quit with the x-rated show-and-tell, every cell in her body
yearned for him to make love to her again.

Waking up each morning was the worst torture, though.
The instant she peeled open her eyelids and her brain began to
function, she would be treated to an eyeful of Kyan parading
naked around her bedroom with an upstanding erection so
pulsatingly proud, it made her want to dive back under the

covers and whimper.

He might be able to ignore said proud erection, but she couldn't. *He* might be able to resist using that erection for the purpose it was intended, but she couldn't put it out of her mind it so easily.

Ruby hadn't dared attend her Thursday evening clay sculpture class. She'd been terrified her hands would go on autopilot... and she'd end up sculpting Kyan's impressive cock. Lani would doubtless approve wholeheartedly of that, but Ruby didn't believe fondling a wet clay penis would do much to help her sex-deprived, Kyan-obsessed state of mind.

There's a saying: "Hell hath no fury like a woman scorned." Yeah, well, it was total BS. Because Hell hath no fury like a man determined to do the right thing. Geez. She'd only endured *four* sex-free nights. How was she supposed to survive another three weeks of deprivation? She would go stark raving insane.

Ruby had organized her training schedule so she got to sleep in Saturday mornings—no waking up at a sparrow's fart and crawling out of bed to go cycling in the dark. Yay. And as she'd collapsed between the sheets last night, she'd entertained visions of lazing in bed until the respectable hour of nine, then heading out for a bike ride, and finishing the morning with a leisurely breakfast upon her return. No "drowning" lessons were scheduled over the weekends, so she'd planned to go for a jog around four in the afternoon, when it was cooler. As a bonus, if she had plans for the evening, she would have plenty of time to recover from the run before heading out. It wouldn't matter if she had a late night, either, because Sunday was her rest day from training. Double yay.

It was a nice plan. Except she had woken at five-freaking-thirty on the dot, and couldn't get back to sleep because of Kyan's bloody great huge erection snuggled into the cleft of her bum.

Not even a substantial pair of granny-panties helped

dampen the sensation of a certain part of his anatomy throbbing and twitching against her aching, exquisitely sensitive
girly parts. And God, it was so very tempting to ditch her
knickers and press up against that hard cock—take him inside
her while he was still asleep and his guard was down.

She couldn't do it, though—couldn't take away his choice.
Damn her overblown morals.

This morning there was another sensation to cope with,
too. The horrible kind she got when she knew she'd forgotten
something really important.

After thirty agonizing, frustrating minutes, she'd had
enough of trying to soothe her brain and body back to sleep,
and she gave in. Decision made, she rolled out of bed onto her
hands and knees.

From there, she slowly crawled on all fours toward the
wardrobe and steeled herself for what came next. Compressing
her lips tightly together so she wouldn't groan and wake Kyan,
she reached up and used the wardrobe's door handle to haul
herself upright.

Success. She rested there for a while, balancing on the balls
of her feet, working up the courage for the next part of what
had become a familiar morning routine. And then, millimeter
by millimeter, she lowered her heels, gritting her teeth and
breathing through the pain of stretching her calf muscles until
her heels were flat on the floor.

All the unaccustomed exercise had taken its toll, and her
muscles were in full-bodied, shrieking revolt. Tuesday, she'd
been a mite stiff. But by Wednesday morning, her intense
training sessions had begun to catch up with her. Big time.
She'd even taken to wearing heels at work because if she wore
flats, each time she got up from her chair she had to lurch
around on her tiptoes until her calf muscles stretched out
again. And as for her shoulders after all the swimming.…
Ouch. Even typing hurt. And reaching into the cupboard for a
coffee mug had brought tears to her eyes.

To be blunt, the stretching fucking hurt. But she persisted with it because it meant she could function. Kind of. Huh. Just as well the wardrobe door handle was sturdy, otherwise it might have broken off from all the abuse she'd been dealing to it lately, and then she'd be totally screwed.

As she dressed, swallowing groans of pain, she glanced at the lump in her bed.

Kyan yawned widely, and met her gaze with an amused gleam in his eyes.

Bastard. "Coming for a ride, oh mighty warrior?"

"A ride with you is always foremost in my mind," he said, smiling as her face heated.

Sheesh. Double entendre, much?

"Have you had a change of heart, my Ruby?"

He sounded so hopeful she couldn't help but feel flattered. Damn him. "What? You think that overnight, I've decided I don't give a rat's arse about saving your life? Sorry to disappoint you, Kyan, but my offer still stands. I'll willingly sleep with you to finalize the bonding and that's the end of the matter. Don't suppose you've changed *your* mind?"

"No."

"Then we have nothing more to discuss." Unless, of course, he wanted to discuss it. In which case she'd very likely burst into tears, get down on her knees, and plead with him to change his mind. Which would not be good.

Well, the sex part would be good—excellent, in fact, if Jules' theory on make-up sex was to be believed. But sex was never a good way to resolve problems. Unless you happened to be a Crystal Warrior, in which case it might just be the only way to resolve your problems. Or not. Because it might create a whole heap more, depending on what the Testing and subsequent life-mate stuff entailed.

God. What a mess. Ruby raised her hands to tie back her hair and the ache of yet another abused set of muscles stabbed her. *Owww.*

"I thought you would sleep a while longer this morning," Kyan said. "Is this not a day of rest with no work scheduled?"

His voice was still husky with sleep, and he surveyed her through lazy, half-closed eyelids. Ruby had to force herself to turn away, and take deep breaths. It was either that or launch herself onto the bed and use her superior, er, *weight* to pin him down while she took advantage of him. Too, there was the distinct possibility that if she belly-flopped on to her bed, she might damage both Kyan *and* the bed. She couldn't afford to buy another one right now.

"Couldn't sleep," she mumbled, fumbling with the laces of her shoes. "You coming or not?"

His eyebrows raised and his grin turned wicked.

Ruby mentally reviewed her question. Uh oh. Heat flushed her face. Again.

Kyan said. "Alas, no. I am not coming. At least, not this morning. Perhaps later. After we… *talk* some more." He rolled onto his stomach and damned if the sheet didn't slide all the way down his spine, exposing the cleft of his muscular bum. He lifted the aforementioned buns of steel from the mattress, adjusted himself, and flopped back down, sighing and wiggling his hips in an effort to attain maximum comfort.

Oh. My. God.

On jelly-like legs, Ruby fled from the room before her blush overtook her whole body… and she was tempted to sink to the floor, stick her hand down her exercise pants, and stroke herself until she came right there, on the carpet beside her bed.

THE ONLY GOOD THING about the bike ride was that it cured her lustful thoughts. In fact, they were completely squelched in the space of ten minutes. Right now, the only throbbing going on was a direct result of having her girly bits mashed against the supposedly ultra-comfortable, non-chafing, gel-covered saddle. Nothing quite like the cold, hard reality of a bicycle saddle to cure lustful thoughts.

To make absolutely certain, though, Ruby did the unthinkable, and completed her circuit twice.

She stowed her bike in the garage, and couldn't dredge up any sympathy whatsoever for her neighbors when the garage door screeched like a banshee as it closed. She let herself into her house, and snuck back into her bedroom to grab some clean clothes.

Kyan was still snoozing, his lips curved in a slight smile.

It would be nice if he was dreaming of her. But it was more likely to be the harem of young women Ruby had seen in that awful, humiliating dream. *Damn him.* She debated having a cold shower to completely cleanse her mind of any lustful thoughts, but in the end she couldn't bring herself to be that masochistic.

When she emerged from the bathroom after a long, hot shower, she heard voices coming from the kitchen.

"This is life or death, you bloody fool." Mike's voice. "Why haven't you completed the bonding process with Ruby? What the hell's your problem?"

Mike's tone conveyed worry for Kyan—a man he barely knew—while his words conveyed complete disregard for his sister's virtue. Nice to know he had his priorities straight. Ruby lurked out of sight, curious to hear Kyan's response.

"I refuse to take advantage of your sister's misguided desire to save me."

Mike snorted. "It's just sex, dickhead. Ruby likes you. And you seem to like her, too, if the noises I've heard coming from her bedroom are anything to go by. You've already done the deed twice, so what's the fricking problem?"

"The problem, Mike, is this." Kyan's tone was so short, sharp and tightly controlled, Ruby suspected he was trying very hard not to lose his temper. "In my previous life I could have any woman I wanted. And I had many."

"So? All the guys I know would clap you on the back and call you a lucky dog."

"Indeed. And I would take my pleasure and move on to the next attractive female without a backward glance, or a care for who I might hurt. But when I encountered your sister, everything changed. And when I learned the terms of the Guardian's spell from you, I was not displeased. It would be no chore to take your sister for my life-mate. But now she has bewitched me. And each time I make love to her, I want her more. Not just her body—all of her."

"And this is a bad thing, how?" Ruby could hear Mike's frustration.

"I cannot bond with Ruby."

"Why the fuck not? If she's talked to Wulf, as you say, then she understands exactly what's at stake. And from what you've told me, she freely offered to complete the bonding, and she'll do her best to help you pass the Testing. I don't see what the fucking problem is, Kyan. Do you have a death wish or something? Christ!"

Something crashed onto the breakfast bar, followed by a muffled expletive and running water. It wasn't a stretch to envisage Mike taking his frustration out on his coffee mug and sloshing hot coffee all over himself.

There was an extended silence, and Ruby found she was holding her breath. She let it out with a whoosh when Kyan finally spoke.

"Your sister deserves a chance to find a love that is true and real. I *think* I am in love with her, but I cannot be certain what I feel is real. Ruby deserves better than that. She deserves better than me—a be-spelled man who cannot be certain he truly loves her for who she is. She does not deserve to be compelled to bond with a man due to a curse—to have her choices taken from her."

"I get it. She's my sister, and all I want is for her to be happy. But Kyan, how do you know what you're feeling *isn't* real? It could be. Wulf and Chalcedony's love turned out to be real. And they're both happy. Why couldn't you and Ruby be happy, too?"

Ah, Mike. Her brother was such a sweetheart. And such a sap when it came to romance. But it was ludicrous to expect everyone to be as blissfully happy as he and Annie were. Not everyone managed to find that perfect person for them—their soul mate. Sometimes people had to settle. And sometimes, it was far less heartbreaking to remain single.

"There is one other factor to be considered." Kyan's voice cut through Ruby's maudlin thoughts.

"Yeah?"

"Ruby has made her desire to bed me again abundantly clear. But despite her knowledge of the bonding process, she has never once told me she loves me. Or that she desires us to remain together for the rest of our lives. And until your sister can tell me that, and I can look deep into her soul and know it for the truth, I will resist her allure with every fiber of my being. In this decision at least, I will have a measure of control. I find the thought of her being manipulated by anyone, or anything, repugnant. Her choices will be hers to make. And that is my final word on this matter."

He wanted her to admit her true feelings for him? To his face?

Ruby did consider it—blundering into the kitchen, confessing her growing love for Kyan, telling him he was her dream man, and that even though they'd only known each other a few days, she hoped they could make a life together. Yeah. Like, for about five seconds until commonsense prevailed.

A couple of years ago she had thought she'd found the perfect man—a fitness trainer she met when she finally caved and took up a three month gym membership her mother had given her. He'd been kind and sympathetic about her embarrassment over working out in public. They'd talked, and he admitted overcoming a weight problem of his own. She'd dated him for six months. And she'd believed her unconditional adoration for him was mutual. So when he proposed, she accepted.

He turned out to be a crusader—a fitness freak who thought he could change the world, one overweight person at a time. Beginning with her. And not even a month into their engagement, the harping started.

"Are you really going to eat all that?"

"You shouldn't snack between meals."

"I'm going for a run—you should come too, the cardio will do you good."

"These protein shakes are great—sort out your metabolism and stop the cravings. Shall I buy you some? It's on special at the moment."

On and on the barrage of not-so-subtle hints went, until finally, Ruby called off the engagement. She wanted a husband who loved her, not one who thought she was his "good cause". Or worse, a free advertising campaign for how great a fitness trainer he was.

Last she heard, he'd latched on to another chubby woman, and nagged her into losing heaps of weight and getting ultra-fit. They'd even started up their own weight-loss program. She hoped they were very happy together.

She snorted softly. Yeah, riiight.

It was all very well to secretly lust after Kyan, to wish they could be together forever, and hope he would grow to love her. But admitting that to him face-to-face was another matter entirely. And what she'd just overheard complicated every-thing still more.

He thought he *might* love her, but wasn't sure whether the feelings were his own or influenced by the spell. She got that. And yet, before they made love for the third time and sealed the bond, he wanted her to bare her soul? The man had some ego.

Kyan had mentioned control. Perhaps she hadn't been too far off when she'd gotten stuck in and given him a piece of her mind. Perhaps it *was* all about control—or rather, his lack of control over his circumstances since he'd appeared on her doorstep a week ago.

Hang on…. She performed a mental check. Yep. It'd been exactly one week since she'd first met this man who was now doing her head in.

One week? That realization was like a slap in the face with a cold wet dishcloth—more than sufficient to make her swallow any potentially humiliating declarations, and saunter into the kitchen as though she hadn't a care in the world.

"Morning," she said, making it chirpy and carefree… and heading straight for the coffee plunger in case her expression revealed otherwise. "Couldn't waste a beautiful morning by lazing round in the sack either, huh? What're your plans for your last day in Auckland, Mike? I'm going to the movies tonight with Jules. You two gonna watch the cricket match on the telly? Oh, and by the way, what time's your flight tomorrow? I'll come and see you off if you like."

She swigged her coffee and almost choked at its bitterness. "This tastes funny. Did you buy soymilk, Mike?" A glance at the container of milk showed her that wasn't the case. "Huh."

"It's trim milk," Mike said. "That's all you had in your fridge. But we only opened the pack of coffee yesterday."

"What are you looking at me like that for?"

"No reason." Mike suddenly became very interested in spreading Marmite on his toast.

Ruby sniffed her mug and then took another experimental sip. It smelled divine but tasted disgusting. Her stomach roiled. She ditched the coffee and opted for a breakfast of banana on toast instead.

"Not feeling up to scratch, huh?" Mike was still shooting her weird glances.

"Must be all the exercise—you know, detoxing and stuff."

"Yeah. That must be it. So what movie are you and Jules going to see?"

"*Kong*. It's a rescreening and it's supposed to be awesome, so I really want to see it on a big screen."

"Yeah. I wanted to see it when it first came out but Annie wasn't fussed. If it's anything as good as Lord of the Rings, the special effects will be mind-blowing."

"What is this *movie*?" Kyan asked.

Ruby screwed up her nose and racked her brain for the easiest way to explain the concept. "Um, a movie is like the stuff you've seen on the telly. Only with a movie, a bunch of people pay to sit in a special, darkened room and watch the film on a huge screen. It's really cool. Sometimes it's almost like you're there, in the movie, with the actors."

Kyan's eyes lit up. "That would be a wondrous thing to see."

"I've an idea," Mike said, looking far too pleased with himself.

Uh oh. Please don't say it. Please don't say—

"How about we come to the movies with you and Jules? Jules can bring Alex along—I didn't have much of a chance to catch up with him last Saturday because I got in so late. What d'ya reckon, Rubes?"

"Um...." She cast about for a valid excuse to keep the boys at home. "Don't you want to watch the Black Caps give the Aussies a run for their money?"

"Naw. It's a given the Aussies will thrash us. Their form is stellar right now, and we're just not firing. Besides, it's only the first match of the series so I'll watch the replay tomorrow night after I get home." Mike turned to Kyan. "What would you rather do? Sit at home and watch a bunch of guys whack a small ball around a grass field with a wooden bat, or go out with the girls to watch a giant gorilla terrorize a bunch of people and yank planes out of the sky?"

Ruby closed her eyes and prayed Kyan would opt for the wonders of cricket.

"I choose the giant gorilla."

Rats. *Of course* a big gorilla going ape-shit and destroying things would appeal to a warrior.

"It's settled," Mike said. "Ruby, how 'bout you ring Jules and tell her to invite Alex along?"

"But Alex might want to stay in and watch the cricket. And he might have already seen *Kong*."

Mike shrugged. "He can meet us for a pub dinner after the movie."

Again with that niggling sensation she'd forgotten to do something important. Something she should have done days ago.

And then it hit her. Ruby's stomach roiled, ruining the taste of her bananas on toast. Bugger. If Ruby had told Jules immediately after she'd screwed up and invited Caroline along to movie night she might have gotten away with it. But she'd left it until practically the last minute. Not even ultra-imaginative Jules would be able to come up with a valid excuse to exclude Caroline now.

Jules was never going to forgive Ruby for this. She was going to be really pissed off. And the absolute last thing Ruby felt like doing tonight was trying to keep the peace between Jules and Caroline. Plus, there was the added stress of maintaining the flimsy fiction of Kyan being an old school friend in front of Jules, her far too astute boyfriend, and Caroline.

Running through worst-case scenarios was doing her head in. Things were bound slip out. Things that were better off remaining hidden if she, Kyan and Mike didn't want to look like candidates for a mental hospital—a fact that obviously hadn't occurred to her brother.

"I think it's a really bad idea to expose Kyan to my friends," Ruby said. "You know, under the circumstances."

"Why? He blends in okay now he's not decked out in leather. Besides, if they do find out, Alex and Jules are the sort of people you want on your side. I don't see the big deal."

"Caroline is the big deal."

"Caroline?"

Ruby rolled her eyes at his obtuseness. "You know. *Caroline*. Skinny twig with big boobs who thinks she's God's gift to men. Goes through boyfriends like soap on a rope. Won't take no for an answer."

Mike scratched his head. "Sorry, I don't follow."

"I said she could come along on our girls' night out. She put me on a spot at work. And I sort of felt sorry for her, because she'd just kicked her last boyfriend into touch and she said she was lonely. So I caved."

Mike blinked. "And Jules was okay with that?"

"Erm, not exactly. I haven't told Jules the good news yet."

Her brother let loose a bark of laughter. "You are hip deep in the crapper, Sister Dear. Better get it over with and ring Jules right away." He made shooing motions with his hands.

He was right, dammit. Ruby slunk off to eat copious amounts of humble pie and confess her crimes to her best friend. Geez. Could this day get any worse?

CHAPTER FOURTEEN

C OULD THIS DAY get any worse? Hah. Talk about a
dumb question. Really, really dumb. The short answer, Ruby decided, was a resounding affirmative.
And just for fun, Fate, that heinous, capricious bitch, really put
the boot in.

Jules was mega-pissed, and took a heap of placating before
she forgave Ruby for being such a wimp to let Caroline manipulate her. Then, while on her afternoon jog, Ruby tripped
in a pothole on the footpath, resulting in some nasty scrapes
and grazes... and an unpleasant encounter with Mike, a pair of
tweezers, and the numerous tiny pieces of gravel embedded in
her skin. And finally, after enduring the excruciating sting of
the hot water cascading over her bleeding knees and scraped
hands while she showered, Ruby discovered she had no clean
underwear. She'd planned on putting a load of washing
through this morning, but the day had gotten away from her.

Worse, the only underwear option she could come up with
turned out to be the screamingly red lace g-string Lani had
bought for her birthday. It was either that or go commando.

Ruby opted for the g-string. And a glance in the mirror at
her bum, exposed in all its pale, dimpled glory, was enough to
make her want to weep. God. If she accidentally flashed anyone wearing *this*, all humankind would collectively shudder.

"Your undergarment is very fetching," Kyan said from the
doorway.

"Christchurch, Kyan! Don't you ever knock?" Ruby backed up and perched on the bed before he could glimpse her backside and choke on his compliment. Only then did it occur to her she was topless because she hadn't gotten around to checking whether she had a halfway decent clean bra. She crossed her arms over her chest, trying to make the gesture seem casual, like she wasn't trying to hide.

Kyan stroked his fingertips over the wooden doorframe.

Ruby shivered, imagining those fingertips stroking her.

"We do not have such grand entrances in my former world," he said. "Wood is scarce."

"Good try, Kyan. But it's still polite to ask permission before you enter my room, especially if I'm recently out of the shower and I'm likely to be getting changed."

"I do most humbly beg your pardon," he said, his voice oozing sincerity. Then he ruined it all by grinning and waggling his eyebrows. "Are you trying to tempt me with that brief undergarment, Ruby?"

"Sorry to disappoint you but I'm only wearing this thing because all my comfy undies are in the wash."

"A pity," he said. "Because I find myself mightily tempted."

Hmm. She dropped her arms to just beneath her breasts, and arched her back slightly to better display her considerable assets. It might have been a bit more convincing if she hadn't groaned when her sore back muscles twinged. Oh, well. A girl had to work with what she had. "Really?" she cooed. "Perhaps you'd like to sit here." She patted the mattress. "And we can discuss your temptation a bit more."

He laughed but made no effort to leave his doorframe. "You are far too transparent, Ruby."

"Fine. Whatever." She straightened her back and rolled her shoulders. *Ow!* Slowly. "Then I'd appreciate it if you would leave. I have a difficult decision to make, and I'd prefer to suffer through it without an audience."

"Oh? And what decision might that be?"

Ruby sagged forward, propping her chin on her hands. "Only *the* most difficult decision every woman in the entire damn world has to make on a daily basis—what the hell to wear. Scram. I need to concentrate on the task at hand."

"I do not understand what your problem is in this respect, Ruby." He waved a hand toward her wardrobe. "This entire structure is stuffed full of clothing. How can you not have anything to wear?"

God. He was so literal at times. "I mean I don't have anything I *want* to wear."

His perplexed expression screamed that he still didn't get it. Fine. She would explain the concept and once he understood her problem, like any normal male, he'd bugger off and leave her to it.

"I want to be comfortable," she said. "Especially if I'm going to be sitting down for a couple of hours watching a movie. Hence my dismay at discovering unless I go commando, I'm going to have to put up with scratchy red lace and this stretchy stuff flossing my bum." She snapped the silicon strap around her hip for emphasis. "I also want to look dressy, like I've made an effort to look nice. But not too dressy, otherwise it'll look like I'm desperate."

He quirked an eyebrow, obviously still not comprehending her dilemma.

"*Desperate* in this case means trying too hard to attract a man. And Caroline is coming tonight, so I don't want to dress in the same-ole-same-ole safe clothes all my friends have seen me wearing a hundred times before. Caroline always looks immaculate. And she makes me feel— Well, anyway. I've no time to get into all of that. Bottom line? I want to look good— like I care about my appearance, but not like I care too much. But if I wear something other than my safe going-out pants and a top that hides all the stuff I want to hide, I'm afraid that's exactly what I'll end up looking like."

"Exactly how is it that you will end up looking?" he asked.

"Like I don't care about my appearance!"

Kyan threw back his head and laughed. "I had no idea choosing clothing was so fraught with pitfalls. However, I have a solution. While you locate an undergarment for your breasts, I will choose your clothes."

"Oh, really?" It was Ruby's turn to laugh. Visions of being swathed head to toe in a sarong-like thing, à la desert haute couture, skittered through her mind. "I don't think that's such a good idea, Kyan."

"Trust me, Ruby. I know what flatters the female form." He sauntered over to her wardrobe, yanked open the doors, and began rifling through the outfits she'd managed to collect over the years.

Trust him? No way were they were at the stage of their "relationship" where she'd let him choose her clothes. Sooo not a good idea to give guys that kind of power. But she was out of options, so she decided to humor him. With one proviso. "If I don't like what you choose, or it's not suitable, I'm not wearing it, okay? I'll swallow my pride and go for my black high-rise pants, my favorite purple drapey top, and my black boots. Deal?"

"'Tis a deal," came his muffled reply as he delved deeper into the cavernous wardrobe. He'd have the devil's own job finding something that actually fit her. She never threw anything out—not even items that were too tight. There was always the chance she might lose some weight and be able to squeeze into them again. So Ruby reckoned the chances of Kyan coming up with something she actually liked, that actually *fit* her, were almost nil.

While he was occupied, she sidled over to her dresser, keeping her rear end pointed away from his direct line of sight should he happen to glance up from the Herculean task he'd set himself. She pawed through her drawers. Damn. All hope of finding a clean bra that wasn't too hideous was fading fast. She was used to wearing mismatched underwear, but the plain white or skin-toned bras she favored seemed like ridiculous options when paired with a red lace g-string. If only she hadn't worn her good black bra out cycling this morning because the straps didn't chafe. Exercise sucked in so many ways.

She was about to give up and go for a skin-toned bra when she unearthed a glossy black box hidden beneath a pile of socks and pantyhose.

The logo on the box belonged to a shop that specialized in sex toys, racy dress-ups, and even racier lingerie. What the heck? She certainly would have remembered buying something from *there*.

She peeked inside the box, pushed aside the tissue paper, and as soon as she spotted the froth of red lace, she clicked. A gift from her ex-fiancé. Red crotch-less undies and matching see-through lacey bra. Well not matching, exactly. It didn't have cut-outs for her nipples or anything sleazy like that, thank God.

Sheesh. She still couldn't reconcile the man who'd bought her naughty underwear—in the right size and everything— with the man who'd constantly nagged her about her weight. And even now, the sight of this lingerie twisted her stomach and made her skin feel clammy.

She shrugged off the bad memories. This was an emergency. She couldn't afford to have too many principles. She ripped off the tags and ladled her breasts into the bra before she could change her mind. It wasn't the exact shade of red as her g-string, but hey, who'd be getting up close and personal enough to notice?

The very man she wouldn't mind getting up close and personal with chose that moment to slam the wardrobe doors shut and turn to her with a smugly satisfied smile… which slowly slid off his face as he looked her up and down. That smile was replaced by the smooth blankness of expression Ruby had come to realize signaled Kyan was hiding some strong emotion.

"Here." He handed her a floaty black skirt with stencils of large hibiscus flowers outlined in a gorgeous coppery color, and a v-necked black sleeveless top with a clever gathering detail down the front, which Ruby seemed to recall hid a multitude of sins.

She wiggled into the skirt and top, and then caught sight of herself in the mirror. "Oh!"

He handed her a pair of mid-heeled sandals in a color that matched the copper tracings on the skirt. Exactly.

She slipped them on, and then examined her reflection again. Critically.

"Well?"

She beamed at him. "Excellent choice, Kyan. I'd forgotten I had these tucked away. I think I look pretty—"

"Wonderful," he interrupted, in such a clipped tone that Ruby ceased admiring herself in the mirror and turned to ask what the hell was eating him.

"I am going to shower," he said.

"Uh, okay." What had gotten up his nose? What on earth had she done now? "See you soon?"

"Yes. Soon." He pronounced the words like knells of doom, and then he stalked from her room.

Men. She would never understand them. In fact, she might even make that statement her new mantra to help regulate her breathing while she was jogging.

Breathe in while chanting, "Men. I'll. Ne-ver." Then breathe out while chanting, "Un-der-staaaaaaand. Them." Yeah. That could work.

She twirled before the mirror, craning her neck to catch sight of her rear view.

Final verdict? Classy. Almost hot, at a stretch. At least, so long as you didn't mind a well-padded rear. And thankfully, the skirt was long enough to adequately cover the big hunks of sticking plaster Mike had applied to her grazed knees after he'd finished doctoring her.

She smiled at her reflection, feeling confident for the first time in years—so confident that she adjusted her boobs to further enhance her cleavage and practiced a sultry, come hither smile in the mirror.

Kyan was not going to be able to resist her tonight. They were going to have sex. Wild, passionate, uninhibited sex. She was going to complete the bonding. And nothing was going to stand in her way.

KYAN TURNED THE shower mixer to full cold, stripped off his clothes, and stepped beneath the water. He turned into the ice-cold stream, letting it pound his body and pummel his aching, throbbing cock into submission.

Gods. Garnet Ruby Roberts would be the death of him. He'd never met a more stubborn, frustrating, desirable woman. If he'd stayed in her room a second longer he would have ripped her clothing from her body, bent her over the dresser, and plunged his cock into her until she climaxed screaming his name. She would have gone nowhere tonight because after he'd taken her hard and fast, he would have tumbled her to the bed and taken his time with every inch of her delectable body. She would have spent the entire evening in bed. With him.

After he had taken his fill of her, he would have cradled her until she drifted off to sleep, and thanked every god he could think of for allowing him this bliss. The only thing that had given him pause was an almost paralyzing fear that when this was all over, Ruby would revile him for forcing the bond on her and taking away her choice.

She believed that bedding him to cement the bond was the right thing to do because it was his only chance of escaping the sorcerer's spell. But Kyan didn't wish her to share her body with him because it was "the right thing to do". He believed in his heart that to successfully pass whatever test the Crystal Guardian devised, he and Ruby must share more than merely a strong physical attraction. Why else would the spell revolve around the concept of bonding for life? The old sorcerer was far too canny to be fooled by outward appearances and false declarations of undying love. He would look deep into their hearts to dig for the truth of their commitment toward each other.

Kyan knew his own heart. It was Ruby's that he doubted. And he wanted—needed—to be more to her than an obligation.

He'd heard the deep love and affection in Chalcedony's voice when she'd spoken of Wulf, and he'd inwardly sneered to hear echoes of the same in Wulf's voice. Wulfenite, Lord Keeper of the Shifting Sands fief, a ruthless warrior who tolerated no weakness, cooing over a woman and the child she'd borne him? How the mighty had fallen. But now, mere days later, Kyan would sacrifice a limb to hear that same affection in Ruby's voice when she spoke of him, and to watch her grow big with his child.

He understood enough about this woman—*his* woman—to know that uttering three little heartfelt words would convince her to finalize the bond. But that was no longer enough for him. For once, instead of living in the moment, Kyan was looking toward the future. A future with Ruby…. Provided the Crystal Guardian had chosen truly, and they did not loathe each other on sight the instant the curse lost it power. Provided everything Wulf and Chalcedony had revealed about the curse was true.

Kyan thrust his face beneath the cold water, ignoring his stinging skin. When he blinked water from his eyes, with clarity of vision came understanding. Ah. Perhaps that was to be the Crystal Guardian's ultimate punishment—to show him the pain and ultimate joy of loving a woman, only to have her reject him. Kyan wouldn't put it past the twisted old bastard to devise such a revenge.

So be it. If fate decreed that Ruby turned her back on him once the Testing was done, it would be no more than he deserved.

He adjusted the mixer to warm. Little point in freezing his stones, he decided, given the cold water hadn't made his cockstand any easier to bear.

In truth, he knew the root cause of why those three little words would have to be torn from his throat before he would willingly utter them. Because secretly, in his innermost heart of hearts, Kyan did not believe himself worthy of being loved. His handsome face, his superbly honed physique, his physical prowess—they meant nothing. He hid behind them, used them to his advantage, and despised himself for doing so… just as he despised those who were taken in by such superficial qualities.

What was inside a person mattered. And inside, he felt ugly, sullied. He always had.

His first memory as a child was his mother's shame that her son had been mistaken for a girl. She had dragged him to their tent, held him down, and hacked at his hair with the sharp blade his father used to shave his whiskers. That hadn't been the worst of it. She'd then shaved Kyan's head, and hadn't been gentle or careful about it. She'd cut him, and the blood had run into his eyes. He'd swiped his hands across his face, seen the blood on his skin, and, believing himself mortally wounded, had begun to howl with terror and fear.

"Be silent!" she told him, her fury so great that she'd sprayed spittle into his face. "I will scar your face and rub ashes into the wounds. Then no one will mistake you for a girl. You will thank me for this one day."

Only his father's fortunate return had saved Kyan from that particular fate.

"Any scars the boy bears will be earned in skirmishes and battle!" his father had roared—after disarming his mate, of course. He knew how lethal she could be with a blade.

Kyan shuddered, recalling how his mother had eschewed any form of weakness. She'd used her beauty and her sly intelligence to get her way, and then sneered at those she had manipulated. She taunted her mate for giving in to her demands, provoked him until he lost his temper, and then, only then would she find him worthy of her intimate attentions. She stayed with him because she knew he was enthralled by her fierce beauty, and because, in her way, she loved him.

Not so, her son. What little love she had to give was lavished on her mate. She despised her son for being pale and sickly. For being clumsy and un-athletic. For his face that was too fine-featured for a male—even if he did strongly resemble *her* in looks. She belittled him and slapped him down until he cringed whenever she glanced his way. And his fear of her only made her despise him more.

Kyan had soon learned to use his face and body and silver-tongued charm to cajole women into giving him what he wanted. But getting what he wanted didn't guarantee happiness. He often wished he'd been born ordinary—a man who didn't set female hearts aflutter. Life would have been far easier if his peers had not continually prejudged him on his looks alone. And he did not believe Ruby would be so reluctant to embark on a deeper, more meaningful relationship if he was nothing special to look at. Then, she would not feel so threatened by him. She would see him for what he truly was— a man who believed himself in love with her but was too afraid of rejection to tell her three simple words to her face.

"I love you." That would be all he needed to say to prove to Ruby that she was not a means to an end, a woman he'd settled for because he had no choice in the matter.

Three little words that would change everything… and yet, he could not bring himself to utter them.

He wanted her to bare her soul to *him* because he believed—hoped—that if he could hear those words on her lips, gaze into her eyes and know she told the truth, he would find the courage to tell her that he loved her in return. Then, and only then, he would allow the bond to be finalized, and be ready to face the Crystal Guardian's Test. And once the Guardian had thrown his worst at them and they had prevailed, Kyan would show Ruby how much she meant to him. He would get down on his knees to beg her to be his forever. And pray that she did not reject him.

Begging a woman to stay with him, to love him?

Giving a woman that degree of power over his future happiness?

This is what Garnet Ruby Roberts had reduced him to. And to borrow one of Mike's favorite sayings: He was screwed.

CHAPTER FIFTEEN

RUBY PERCHED ON a spindly-legged, indescribably uncomfortable excuse for a chair, and sipped her chardonnay. God. Right now she craved that lovely drunken state of semi-oblivion. Unfortunately, drunkenness wasn't an option because she was the designated driver. She'd figured it would hardly be fair to insist Mike limit what he drank on his last night in Auckland. Plus, she was watching what she spent because she'd offered to pay for Mike and Kyan's meal and drinks. It was the least she could do after the money her brother had spent buying Kyan clothes. And a freaking bike.

Speaking of Kyan and money, she might have to find him a part-time job so he could help out with expenses. Yeah. That would be interesting.

The evening was warm and humid, and they'd opted to sit outside in the pub's courtyard. Ruby wished the heavens would suddenly open and teem with rain. Thunder and lightning would be a bonus. Or perhaps hail. Then they could all go home. Then she wouldn't have to watch Caroline's immaculately lipsticked mouth giving her cocktail garnish oral. Or her beautifully buffed French-tipped talons brushing up and down Kyan's arm. And his thigh. In fact, any part of his anatomy she could reach.

Ruby also wished Caroline would shut the fuck up and quit subjecting them all to her oh-so-terribly-witty tales of her exploits with men. It was a mystery to Ruby that, instead of Caroline coming across like a total skank, her dating stories only appeared to make her audience-of-one more sympathetic to her current man-less plight. Poor Caroline, so misunderstood by men who continually got the "wrong impression" about her for some reason. Poor Caroline, who was only looking for the right man to settle down with. Or a no-strings-attached fuck with a bad boy type. Take your pick.

Ruby hid a yawn at yet another of Caroline's "funny" little stories. And, as she covertly observed her workmate, she mulled Caroline's compliment. She'd made a huge fuss over Ruby's outfit, then ended by marveling that it could be, "Sooo flattering. Considering."

Ruby had always thought of Caroline as a friend—not a particularly close one, but a friend all the same. But what sort of a friend took such delight in putting others down? Like the time they'd gone shopping and Ruby had worn jeans, and Caroline had loudly proclaimed, "I'd love to be able to wear jeans like you do, Ruby. If only they didn't make my bum look so big." This from a woman with a nonexistent bum. Of course, Ruby ended up feeling totally self-conscious, imagining passersby snickering and wondering how on earth a woman like her had found a brand of jeans to fit her.

Why had she ever believed Caroline was her *friend*? Was she completely brain dead? Or merely so desperate for friends she'd overlooked the sad fact that Caroline made herself feel good by putting Ruby down. Not only that, but if even half Caroline's stories about her past experiences with men were the least bit true, she was dangerously promiscuous. And surely that wasn't something to boast about.

Alex and Mike were no help. They stuffed their faces with beer-battered fish and chunky chips, and ignored Caroline wherever possible. If a response was demanded, they muttered some platitude to keep the conversation rolling and went back to their beers.

At least Jules had finally forgiven Ruby for inviting Caroline along. Unfortunately, forgiveness didn't extend to Jules slapping Caroline down a few rungs for Ruby's entertainment. Instead, Jules, replete with squid rings and a large helping of potato wedges, was on her best behavior, and confined her reactions to rolling her eyes while Caroline continued with the most blatant come-ons Ruby had ever had the misfortune to witness.

It was all Ruby's own fault, of course. She should have laid public claim to Kyan instead of insisting they were old school friends. Now she'd backed herself into a corner, leaving Ms Stick Insect With No Soul free to make a play for Ruby's guy.

Caroline made cow eyes at Kyan while she toyed with the stem of her cocktail glass in a suggestive manner. Ick.

Worse, Kyan seemed enraptured by her—especially the aforementioned oral foreplay with the skewered fruit hanging off the side of her cocktail. The atmosphere about them snapped with sexual attraction

What was the name of the drink Caroline had ordered again? Oh yeah. A Slutty Temple. How appropriate. It was enough to make Ruby want to puke.

She took another sip of her chardonnay and grimaced. Definitely time to stop drinking. Besides, what little wine she'd drunk tonight hadn't tasted that great. Perhaps the bottle was corked.

"I'm okay to drive if you want another one, Rubes." Mike broke off his "discussion" with Alex about whether the Aussies would give the Kiwis yet another drubbing in the cricket. Alex was a staunch Black Caps supporter. He had faith they'd win the test match regardless of how badly they'd performed lately. Hah. Privately, Ruby suspected the Kiwis would yet again snatch defeat from the jaws of victory.

"Nah." Ruby shook her head. "I'm right, thanks. Tomorrow may be a rest day but I don't want to be nursing a hangover."

"How's your training going, Rubes?" Alex asked. "From what Jules tells me you've set yourself a pretty rigorous training schedule. I'm surprised you're still upright."

"Funny you should say that, 'cause first thing in the morning I'm in flaming agony." She rolled her eyes at her folly and gave a mock laugh. "Have to literally crawl out of bed and pull myself up on the door handle, and sorta hang out until I can convince my muscles and ligaments to stretch so I can put my heels flat."

"Ouch!" Alex winced in sympathy. "Bet that's a sight for sore eyes."

"It certainly is," Kyan said, cutting Caroline off mid-compliment. He reached across the table to squeeze Ruby's hand. "But even though she is in considerable pain, she continues her punishing training regimen. She is very determined, my Ruby."

"And isn't it sooo nice of you to get up early and drag Ruby out of bed each morning." Caroline all but purred the words. "You're such a sweetie, Kyan. I'm sure Ruby would never be able to stick to an early morning routine on her own without you to encourage her."

Ruby buried her nose in her empty wine glass. "Would be a damn sight easier to get up early if Kyan's raging hard-ons didn't keep me awake." Ooops. She hadn't meant to say that aloud. Maybe no one had heard. *Maybe. Please?*

When she couldn't wring another drop from her glass, she glanced up.

Alex and Jules tore their gazes from Kyan's face to gave her knowing looks. Jules even gave her a thumbs up. And Mike was unsuccessfully attempting to smother a grin.

They'd heard. *Crap.*

Ruby dared a glance at Caroline. And got the distinct impression that if Caroline had been a cat, she'd be coughing up a fur ball right about now.

Caroline's gaze dropped to Kyan's hand, still resting on

Ruby's—a gesture that spoke of intimacy. Her nostrils flared, scenting a victim ripe for belittlement.

Ruby hunched in her chair. Wait for it—

"You naughty girl, Ruby!" Caroline's laughter was sharp as broken glass. "You should have told me you and Kyan were *that* sort of friends."

"Huh? What sort of friends do you mean?" Too late, Ruby caught Jules shaking her head, warning her not to fall into the trap.

"Comfy-fuckers."

"Excuse me?"

"Oh, you know what I mean. Friends who indulge in com-fy-fucks because one of them feels sorry for the other one. It's so sweet of Kyan to indulge you. And I'm sure you're very grateful to him since it's been so dreadfully long since you've had a boyfriend. Isn't it?"

Ruby felt the heat that painted her cheeks crawling down her neck. She tried to pull her hand from Kyan's grasp but he refused to relinquish it.

"Christ Almighty, Caroline." Jules stared at Caroline like she was something disgusting Jules had scraped off her shoe. "You really are a nasty bitch. I don't know why Ruby puts up with you."

"That's a bit harsh, Jules," Caroline drawled. "I'm merely stating the truth. Kyan can have his pick of girls. So why else would someone like him be interested in someone like... Ruby?"

"Let's go home." Mike stood so abruptly he rocked the ta-ble .

"Alex and I have had enough, too. Haven't we, babe?" Jules grabbed her purse from under her chair and stood.

"Sure have," Alex agreed. "Caroline, thank you for living down to my extremely low expectations of you. I'd like to say it's been a pleasure but I'd be lying."

Ruby stood, awkwardly, since Kyan had remained seated

but still refused to release her hand. "Uh. Yeah. I think it's time to call it a night." Like, before she grew a pair and bitch-slapped Caroline into orbit.

Caroline latched on to Kyan's arm. "You don't need to rush off though, do you? I can drive you home."

Ruby stared down at him. "Stay with Caroline if you want, Kyan. It's up to you."

Caroline leaned over to whisper something in his ear. It didn't seem have the effect she'd hoped, for she sat back, pouting.

"You are wrong, my Ruby," Kyan said. "'Tis up to you. It has always been up to you."

Under any other circumstances, Ruby would have been thrilled to itty bitty pieces that Kyan's attention was wholly directed toward her. And if she hadn't been certain the bonding process was as yet incomplete, she'd might have believed this evening's debacle was the Testing come early.

Jules and Alex shifted uneasily beside their chairs, aware that something big was going down but not sure what the deal was. Mike cleared his throat as if willing Ruby to say the right thing, do the right thing. But what the hell was the right thing? What was right for Kyan, wasn't necessarily the right thing for Ruby.

Or was it? She didn't know.

"I— I—" A huge lump formed in her throat. Her chest felt so tight and achy it was a struggle to catch her breath. So she stood there, gasping like a landed salmon and paralyzed with indecision.

Her gaze flicked to Caroline.

Caroline met her gaze with a triumphant smirk.

Ruby's stomach plummeted to her toes. Here she was, publicly embarrassing herself over a man. Again. She couldn't compete with someone like Caroline. She couldn't hold onto a man like Kyan. She was a fool to even try.

She yanked her hand from Kyan's grip and fled. Her heart

pounded in her ears as she ran through the courtyard. And even though she knew she should stop running, go back and confess the truth to Kyan, her fears prodded her onward.

She was a coward. If he stayed with Caroline tonight, Ruby would only have herself to blame. If Kyan slept with Caroline, she wouldn't blame him, but she'd never forgive him. Or herself, for not fighting to keep him.

But if she couldn't bring herself to tell Kyan how she truly felt about him, how would he ever figure out how he truly felt about *her*?

The despair that engulfed her was like a well-aimed body blow from a pro fighter—so painful that she couldn't cry because the tears choked off before they could form. Just like all those important things she wanted—needed—to say to Kyan choked off before she could voice them.

She stumbled across the road to her car, and then realized she'd left her purse—and her car keys—back at the pub.

Shit. Shit. Shit! She swiveled mid-step, caught the heel of her sandal in a pothole, and fell to all fours in the middle of the road, scraping her already grazed hands and knees. The pain was excruciating. But it was physical pain, and that she could deal with. Unlike the emotional anguish of knowing she'd screwed up and ruined everything.

She heard someone call her name and she glanced up, squinting in the headlights of an oncoming car that had just rounded the corner.

"Ruby!"

Mike's voice. He sounded panicked. Silly. Nothing to worry about. Of course the driver of the car barreling toward her had spotted her. No way was he going to hit her—

Oh, fuck....

Chapter Sixteen

Ruby's throat felt desert-dry and scratchy. It didn't seem to be working properly because she couldn't speak. She worked up enough saliva to swallow. Ugh. Bad move. Tasted like something nasty had crawled into her mouth and died.

She tried to pry open her eyelids but they were glued shut. *Gawd.* Must have been one helluva night. And she must have cut off the circulation in her left arm because it didn't want to do what she was telling it to do. She tried her right arm, managed to get it up to her face and rub her eyelids.

She blinked. And stifled a gasp as the figure looming over her swam into focus.

Mike. Her pulse-rate calmed to something resembling normal.

"Hey, sis." Mike looked rough—really rough. His eyes sported dark rings and bags he could cart a kitchen sink around in.

"You look like something the cat dragged in," she croaked. And discovered that speaking was another bad move because it made her cough—dry hacking coughs that knifed her chest and built pressure in her skull until she thought her head might explode. She closed her eyes, willing the coughing to cease.

Mike muttered something about getting someone.

"Sorry, what?" She opened her eyes again to squint at him.

"Here." He did something out of her line of sight and the back of her bed began to rise.

Clue number one. However cool it might seem at the time, a bed that raises its back at the flick of a switch is not normal.

Then Mike handed her a cup with a straw bobbing in it, which she had to grasp with her right hand because her preferred left hand was encumbered by a bunch of tubes and stuff.

Clue number two. Tubes and stuff dangling from one's arm is definitely not normal. Or pleasant. And the instant she noticed all the tubes, her arm started to ache and throb like it'd been fed through a wringer.

She sipped her water, sighing as it soothed her raw throat. And then, when the door to her room opened and a nurse entered the room, clue number three smacked her upside the head.

She opened her mouth to ask what the hell had happened to land her in a hospital bed, but the nurse was too quick and popped the thermometer into her opened mouth. After a minute or so, the nurse removed the thermometer and noted the temperature on Ruby's chart.

She had a chart? *Crap*. This so was *not* looking good.

"I'll have Dr Pillay come and examine Miss Roberts as soon as he's finished with his rounds," the nurse told Mike, totally ignoring Ruby. Then she exited the room.

Sheesh. Some bedside manner.

Ruby rolled her eyes, which took a mammoth effort. God. Why was everything she asked her body to do taking so long to… to… *do*? She had just opened her mouth again to ask when her mum rushed into the room.

Pamela Roberts' hair was a mess and her lipstick was crooked. More than anything else, that finally convinced Ruby whatever happened to her had been no joking matter. "Mum," she croaked.

Her mum hugged Ruby. Her whole body shook with sobs. "Oh, Ruby. Mike said you'd be coming out of your—"

"Mum," Mike snapped.

"Ah, waking up soon," their mother amended. "I've fetched your father, darling. He was just grabbing some hot drinks. You gave us such a scare!"

Her mum called out to someone lurking outside the room. "Oh for goodness sakes, do come inside. We're family! No one will object to three family members being in the room at once. And if they do, Mike will sort it out with the person in charge. Won't you, darling? Doctor to doctor?"

Mike wisely said nothing. So far as their mother was concerned, he was a fully-fledged doctor, and that was that.

"Mike's a St John's medic, Pamela, not a doctor." Ruby's long-suffering father entered the room, juggling two polystyrene cups. "How many times do I have to explain that to you?"

Her dad was here, too? Oh God. It had to be really, *really* bad to have pried both her parents from their peaceful Nelson home to brave the "evils" of Auckland.

"Pamela, you're hurting her arm." Her dad had noted Ruby's grimace as her mother's extended hug tweaked the needle of the drip in her left arm.

Her mother reared back, her expression stricken as she scrambled off the bed. "I'm so sorry, darling." Her face creased into the scrunched up moue she made when she was trying not to cry.

"Mum, it's—ahhh!" The cuff of the automatic blood-pressure monitor had tightened viselike around Ruby's upper arm. It'd been placed just above the drip and the increased pressure wiggled the needle in her vein. It hurt—a lot— snatching her breath and leaving her sweaty-browed and panting.

"Hurts, huh?" Mike said, his tone oozing sympathy. "Sometimes it's not very comfortable when the cuff is on the same arm as a drip. I'll move it to your other arm—see if that helps."

Her heart skipped a beat and she flinched away from his

hand. She hated needles at the best of times.

"Chill, Rubes. You've already got a line set up in the vein of your right arm, but I'm only moving the cuff, not the drip, okay?"

"O-okay." Even so, she squeezed her eyes shut while he mucked about with the equipment and swapped the whatever-it-was-called to her right arm.

Her dad handed her mum a cup, and the two of them perched on the end of Ruby's bed, sneaking concerned glances at her in between sips of their tea.

"Why haven't those dreadful marks on her arms gone away?" her mum asked.

"Medics don't have time to be gentle when we're trying to save lives," Mike said. "We just shove the line in. Often there's a bit of heavy bruising which can take a while to disappear."

Ruby raised her now unencumbered left arm to take a look. Faded yellowing bruises smudged six-inch-long trails down the inside of her arm. Gross. No wonder it felt like it'd been mangled.

"They've faded a lot, Ruby. You looked like a druggie for the first week or so."

Her stomach gave a sick-making lurch, and the fine hairs on the nape of her neck stood to attention. The first week? "How long—" pause to clear her throat "—have I been—" cough, splutter, hack "—stuck in here?"

Mike's gaze slid away. He scratched his chin, and exchanged significant glances with their father.

"How long?" Another fit of coughing was the only thing that prevented her from throwing a really stellar tantrum.

Her mum patted her back and proffered the cup of water and straw again. "You've been in a medically induced coma for the past three weeks, darling," she said.

All Ruby's fight drained from her, leaving her weak and shaking and scared. Three weeks? "No way."

"Yes, way." Mike stared her through narrowed, intent eyes.

"What's the last thing you remember?"

"Uh, a giant ape? Wrecking stuff?"

"Excuse me?" Ruby's mum looked a little wild about the eyes after that statement.

"King Kong. Good. That's really good." Mike smiled a relieved kind of smile.

"It's a movie, Pamela," her dad said quickly, to prevent his wife from rushing off in search of a neurologist.

"Anything else?" Mike asked.

"I remember—" Ruby searched her befuddled mind. "I remember being pissed off with Caroline."

"Language!" her mum said.

"Sorry, Mum."

"And?" Mike prompted.

"Lights. I remember bright lights and—" Images careened through her brain. Car headlights. Struggling to her feet. The tortured screech of tires. The vehicle's bumper smashing into her. Her body flying over the bonnet, weightless for a split second before she hit the car's windshield. The sickening shattering of glass. A glimpse of the driver's shocked white face before she slid off the car's bonnet and onto the road. Numbness, followed by a burst of agonizing pain. And then— thankfully—oblivion.

"I remember the crash," she said. "It was quite… bad."

"Yep." Mike had never been one to mince words.

"Tell me."

Her dad reached over to squeeze her hand. Ruby clutched it like a lifeline while Mike listed her injuries.

"Ruptured spleen. They removed it. Fractured ribs. Two broken legs. Concussion—hardly surprising. Cuts and grazes all over you. And that's only the minor injuries. You're lucky to be alive, Rubes." He exchanged another one of those looks with their dad, but Ruby was too shell-shocked to call him on it.

She sucked in a shaky breath and peeked beneath the sheet.

Sure enough, both legs were in plaster—the left to mid thigh, and the right to just below her knee… which was covered in still-healing scabs. Ick. And of course, as soon as she acknowledged both legs were broken, they began to ache and throb with a vengeance. Worse, now she knew there wasn't a hope in hell of getting to the little girls' room under her own steam, she wanted to pee. Desperately.

Ruby slumped against the hard hospital pillows. She tried to cover her face with her hands, but the movement tweaked the drip in her right arm. It wasn't until her mother handed her a tissue that she realized she was crying.

"Are you in pain, darling? Shall I buzz the nurse?"

"N-no. I'm just tired." Ruby blew her nose and squirmed, trying to suppress the urge to pee. No way was she doing that with an audience.

Mike murmured something to their dad, who stood and said, "Pamela, let's go grab some lunch before the rush."

"I'm not hungry, dear."

"You can sit and watch me eat, then. We'll be back in half an hour, Ruby. Can we bring you a sandwich, Mike?"

"That'd be great. Thanks, Dad."

"Ruby?"

Her mother's too-wide smile cued Ruby that another embarrassing mother-daughter moment was imminent. "Yes?"

"Look on the bright side, dear."

Bright side? Shit-oh-dear. Who was she trying to kid? "Okay."

"You've lost heaps of weight. A liquid diet obviously agrees with you."

Her dad threw Ruby a sympathetic glance as he dragged his wife from the room.

Mike stared after them, his jaw sagging.

Ruby started to giggle, but had to stop and clutch her ribs. "Ow! God, she's unbelievable."

"She is that." Mike heaved a sigh and shook his head in

mock-despair. "It's been… interesting. I'll get you the bed-pan."

"That obvious, huh?"

"Only to me." He grinned. "You know, being practically a real doctor and all."

Ruby gauged the distance to the bathroom at the far end of her room. "Don't suppose I could try crutches?"

"With two broken legs? In your dreams." He maneuvered the bedpan beneath her bottom, and turned his back while she tinkled into the pan. In the end she felt far too happy to have an empty bladder to be embarrassed when he removed the offending object and put it out of sight. "Nurse'll sort that out later."

"Thanks."

"Ruby, there's something I didn't mention."

"I figured as much."

"Dad suspects, but won't come right out and ask because then he doesn't have to lie to Mum. She'll have kittens. And I wanted to spare you that until you're recovered. But—"

"Spit it out, Mike. The tension's killing me." Weak joke but the best she could do right now.

"Har bloody har." Mike summoned the barest hint of a smile. He puffed out a long breath. Ruby's foreboding intensified, pressing down on her like a physical weight.

"When the results of the first lot of tests came back," Mike said, "they showed you were pregnant. Only barely, but the tests were positive."

She took a moment to digest his words. "Pregnant? How? I mean, I know how, but— That's impossible. I haven't slept with anyone in two years. How could I be pregnant?"

Hang on. Her skin prickled with heat. But the heat didn't last. It drained away, leaving her cold and shivering. So very cold, right down to the depths of her soul. "You said I *was* pregnant. So I guess…. I'm not any more."

"You started spotting a couple of days ago and then you

miscarried. I'm so sorry, Rubes."

A lump of despair settled just beneath her heart. "'S okay, Mike. I mean it wasn't like it had time to grow into a... a...." She squeezed her eyes shut against the overwhelming pain. But that only made it worse. All she could see was a baby with blond curls and blue-blue eyes—which was crazy because she had neither. And then her senses really started playing tricks on her because she could even smell a milky baby smell reminiscent of a newborn infant.

"It wasn't a real baby yet," she whispered. "It was just a tadpole, right?" *Don't tell me the truth. I don't want to hear the truth right now. Just give me platitudes and lies. Please.*

"Not even a tadpole, really." Mike was doing his best to come across all staunch but this had hit him hard, too. After all, he'd lost a potential niece or a nephew.

Ruby managed a watery smile for his benefit. "I'll be okay. It's not like I knew what was happening." Lies. She wouldn't be okay. She wanted to curl up into a ball and howl for what she'd lost. But she couldn't put Mike through that. She wouldn't. She'd fall apart when he was gone, and there was no chance of her parents walking in on her.

"Ruby, do you remember who the father was?"

She tried her best to remember but it was all a blank. "Must've been an immaculate conception," she joked. "Obviously a totally forgettable experience."

Mike wasn't smiling at her sad attempt at humor. "I need to give you something."

"A present?" She tried to push herself up higher on the pillows. "For me? You shouldn't have. But hey, I'm glad you did."

He reached into his jacket pocket and grabbed something—two large shards of bluish-gray stone. He pressed them into her outstretched hand.

"What're these?"

"Don't you remember?"

She stared up at Mike, noting how tired he seemed. No, it

was more than fatigue. It was a deep sadness that made her want to hug him and tell him everything would be all right. Her vision blurred. And superimposed upon her brother's face she saw another face. A man's. He was so beautiful he stole her breath. She glimpsed piercing aquamarine eyes—haunting eyes that were tantalizingly familiar—before the face dissolved into her brother's familiar features.

Ruby frowned. She had recognized that face, dredged it up from her subconscious. But the memory hovered just out of reach.

She turned her attention to the stones in her hand. She ran her fingers over the jagged edges where they'd broken.

Not *two* stones. One. She fitted them together. And the memories smacked into her.

"K-Kyan." The loss overwhelmed her. She gasped, choked, couldn't catch her breath.

Mike buzzed for the nurse, and then grabbed the oxygen mask dangling from the panel at the head of her bed. He fitted it over her face and began to talk her down. "Breathe, Ruby. Listen to me and just breathe, okay? Good. Now breathe in… and out… in… out… That's it. Good girl."

She'd managed to get her breathing under control when the door burst open and a compact man of Indian descent strode to her bedside. He checked her vitals and, apparently satisfied, raised his eyebrows at Mike.

"She was hyperventilating, Dr Pillay. She insisted on knowing what happened to her and I think was a bit much for her to cope with all at once."

"Not surprising given the circumstances," the doctor said. "Miss Roberts, you need to rest. You've suffered a major trauma and you need to take things slowly. I'm giving you a sedative."

"No!" Her protest was muffled by the mask so she ripped it off. "No. I need to find Kyan."

She sounded shrill. She wouldn't get anywhere with the

doctor if he thought she was hysterical. She sucked in a deep, steadying breath and spoke slowly and clearly. "Mike, where's Kyan?"

When he didn't answer, she struggled to sit up but was restrained by Dr Pillay. She felt the sharp prick of a needle in her arm. "No! I can't go to sleep yet, dammit! I need to find him. Where's Kyan, Mike? Is it too late? Where. Is. He?"

"He visited you every day and stayed with you for as long as he could, Ruby. But his time was up. He had to… go."

The faces of the two men—Mike's anguished, the doctor's coldly assessing—wavered, lengthening and distorting like some desert mirage. Coldness seeped into her bones. "It's not fair," she whispered. And then it was difficult to get any words out because her teeth had begun to chatter. "We d-didn't even h-have a ch-chance to b-bond… to be t-tested. It's n-not fair!"

The frost crept over her. It froze her soul and she drifted away.

Chapter Seventeen

RUBY BREATHED IN the chilly early morning air and winced. Auckland was gleefully inflicting its residents with an unexpected cold snap that had everyone unearthing their heaters and warm clothes. It was so cold her sinuses ached, and despite her thermal socks, her feet felt like ice blocks. But she was one of the few not moaning about the weather. The cold didn't alter anything for her—she hadn't felt warm in forever.

She trudged along the footpath, relieved beyond measure that her injuries had finally healed enough to allow her to get out of the house on her own. Not to mention convince her mum to return home to Nelson. She loved her mum… in small doses.

During the months of rehabilitation, her mother's fussing—well-meaning though it had been—had almost driven Ruby to drink. Thank God for Jules, who'd visited Ruby every Saturday morning and pushed Pamela Roberts out the door to "go shopping, catch a movie, take time out for yourself".

Jules didn't believe in fussing. She let Ruby blob out, and feel however she wanted to feel. No judgments and having to hold it all in around Jules. Ruby didn't have to watch her language or pretend that she was okay. They talked whenever Ruby felt up to talking, and when she didn't, when it all got too much and she felt like she would lose her hard-won control and burst into tears that might never stop, they watched chick-flicks and guzzled ice cream.

It took a month of those precious Saturdays before Ruby plucked up the courage to reveal Kyan's background to Jules. She'd half-expected Jules to suggest she needed therapy, but Jules took it all in her stride.

Perhaps her best friend had already wangled the truth from Mike. Ruby didn't ask. She was simply grateful to have someone to confide in. And facing up to how she'd truly felt about the Crystal Warrior who'd stolen her heart, and fathered the baby she'd lost, was better than any therapy. So was knowing that Jules believed her, and believed *in* her. Jules understood why Ruby had acted as she had. And Jules understood why sometimes, when the memories of what she'd lost, and the heartbreak of what could have been, crashed down on her, Ruby needed someone to hold her while she cried.

Slowly, the heavy, crushing guilt she lived with had become almost bearable. Slowly Ruby's soul had begun to heal along with her body. And, as the months passed, she no longer cringed when her mum chided her yet again for letting "that handsome young man who came to visit you in hospital" get away.

Her mum believed Kyan was a friend who'd been staying with Ruby until his work permit ran out and he had to fly back home. According to Mike, the instant Pamela Roberts had laid eyes on Kyan sitting by Ruby's hospital bed, holding her hand and talking to her, she'd been smitten. She thought he was gorgeous—eminently suitable to marry her daughter and present her with a horde of equally gorgeous grandchildren.

Funny how her mother, for all her harping on about Ruby's weight, couldn't see how ludicrous that scenario would have been.

Thankfully, Ruby's mum now had far more important things to think about than the potential husband her daughter had let slip through her fingers. Mike and his fiancée, Annie, had set a date for their wedding. The prospect of her son's marriage, and the opportunity to angst about Annie's age, and how they'd better have children before Annie turned thirty and her eggs started to dry up, sent Pamela Roberts into paroxysms of delight and consumed her every waking moment.

Ruby kicked a stone and watched it skitter across the grass verge of the footpath, and then bounce onto the road. She was thrilled for Mike and Annie. They were so happy together—a true match made in heaven. And now, with the gift of time, wondering whether *she* could have ever been as happy with Kyan—if only they'd been given a chance—didn't hurt so much anymore. At least, that's what Ruby told herself.

As she rounded the last corner before home, a flash of gold caught her attention.

An elderly man, dressed in jeans and boots, with an incongruously bright gold scarf tucked into the neck of his white shirt, strolled toward her. And, as he passed by, the memory of where and when she'd seen him before sliced through her brain.

Her birthday party. She'd glimpsed him from the window.

"Hey!" Ruby turned on her heel and limped after him. "Hey! Please stop. I'd like to ask you something."

Even when she'd finally caught him, he paid her no mind whatsoever, seeming oblivious to her puffing along beside him, trying to match his stride. It was as though she didn't exist for him.

"I'm sorry to bother you, but I really need to ask you something important."

When he still didn't respond, she was goaded into grabbing his arm and forcing him to a halt. Only then did he finally condescend to notice her.

A knowing smile quirked his lips. "Yes, Garnet Ruby, I imagine you do need to ask me something important. But first, I have something important to show you."

He disappeared.

No, that wasn't right. *She* disappeared. Well, she was definitely *somewhere*, just no longer on the footpath near her home. Ruby had been transported to someplace else entirely—a place she'd never visited before. She recognized it just the same. Because she'd seen it in a dream.

"I HAVE TO do this, Ruby," Kyan said. "'Tis our custom. I cannot remain mated to a woman incapable of bearing children."

Shadows played upon the billowing silken walls of the tent. From her nest of brightly colored brocade pillows, Ruby gazed up at the implacable face of the man she loved. "Kyan. Don't do this. Please! We can try again. I carried this child longer than the others. Maybe the next one will be to term. I—"

"No."

She heard the wind whistling over the dunes. She recognized that sound. The Storm Season had begun. Outside, many days ride via the swiftest mount, a mighty storm was brewing. It was newly birthed and tremulous, not yet a danger to the denizens of the Shifting Sands fief. But that would change. Soon.

"Kyan, please!" She swallowed her tears, knowing he'd view them as lack of control, a weakness.

He raked his gaze over her. His tightly clenched jaw, and a tiny tic beneath his left eye, were the only signs he found her insistence on pleading her case, rather than silently accepting her fate, distasteful.

"Of what use is a woman who cannot bear children?" he said. "My people are a dying race. Children are our future. Even if the only children born to us are male, I must father sons. 'Tis my duty. That is why I bid for you on the Choosing Block, Ruby—for your abundant breasts and your wide, child-bearing hips. Gods know, I did not Choose you for your beauty."

His cruel words shattered her heart.

She had believed him different from the other men of this

world. She had believed that a man who was always judged, always expected to behave a certain way because of his appearance, would not judge a woman on looks alone. She had told herself he saw beyond her ample flesh and had Chosen her for love. She loved *him*, after all. And she had believed he might grow to love her, too.

"I refuse to stand on the Choosing Block and submit to another Choosing, Kyan." The humiliation of standing half-naked, displayed for all to see, prodded and subjected to jeers and laughter, would be more than she could bear. Her fragile self-esteem still bore the mental scars of that experience, even as her left shoulder bore the brand.

"Very well. That is your choice. You are aware of course that because our contract will not be renewed for a further term, I am no longer responsible for you." He waited for her nod. "However I am not completely without a heart. I will send females to assist you in your packing and resettlement."

Bitterness enveloped her—more smothering than the unrelenting heat of the desert. How big of him to make that concession considering all she'd been through in the past year.

In two days hence, the tented city would be dismantled. All inhabitants would shelter in caves for the next three moon-cycles until the Storm Season passed. All except Ruby. She would not spend her remaining years slaving alongside those worn-out older women who undertook menial tasks that favored women disdained.

"That won't be necessary." She lifted her chin, daring him to ask whether she would rather remain here and let the storm take her, daring him to give her the chance to explain that she would rather that than suffer the agony of watching him fulfill his obligation to increase the population—filling other younger, prettier, more fertile women with his seed.

But Kyan no longer cared enough to ask. He quirked an eyebrow at her, and his lip curled. He obviously doubted her ability to pack her belongings and ready herself for travel.

He was right, of course. He always was. Only two days ago she'd miscarried for the third time, and she was weak as a newborn fennec kit.

"As you wish, Ruby," he said. And then he turned and strode from the tent.

"No, Kyan. Not as *I* wished." Her heart ached with a hurt so profound she was numb, beyond even tears. The wind trilled an eerie death-knell. She closed her eyes and lay back against the cushions, willing the wind to find her and put an end to her suffering.

RUBY PRIED OPEN her eyes. Her heart thudded like she'd just run a four-minute mile. She cast her gaze down herself, surprised to discover she was huddled on the footpath, arms tightly clasped about her torso as though trying to protect herself from… something.

The old man loomed over her, his piercing gaze taking in every little nuance of expression as she clambered to her feet. It took everything she had left to suppress her fear and confront him. "The Crystal Guardian, I presume," she said. "Nice to meet you at last, Pieter." *Not.*

He cocked his head, staring at her as though he would see into her soul.

The best form of defense was offence. Well, maybe not when you were dealing with omnipotent sorcerers, but it was all she could come up with right now. "Where the hell have you stashed Kyan, you old bugger? I want him back."

"And what if he does not want you, Garnet Ruby?"

"Tough." She curled her lip in what she hoped was a credible I-don't-give-a-flying-fuck sneer. "We didn't have a fair shot at bonding because of my accident. It's a pretty impossible task to initiate sexual intercourse to complete a bond when you're in a coma, don't you think? You might want to bend your fancy rules a bit, Pieter."

"I don't make the rules," he said, sounding resigned and

saddened and bone-weary. But she wasn't going to think about that right now. She didn't care whether *he* was suffering. She only cared about saving Kyan.

She rattled on, needing to voice her demands before she lost her nerve. Or broke down and cried over that terribly real vision. "Send Kyan back and give us our allotted time. If we don't do the wild thing for the third time, or pass your rotten testing, fair enough. *Then* you can take him. But not before I've done my best to save him."

Pieter seemed unmoved. "And what you've seen doesn't convince you, Garnet Ruby? How could a woman like you, an infertile woman, hope to hold a man like Kyan?"

Bastard. She hadn't told *anyone* about that unhappy complication from her accident. "Ah. So that's what that lovely little scene you chose to show me was all about. Epic fail, Pieter. Because my worth is not measured by my ability to have children."

She had to believe that. Just as she had to believe that it wouldn't matter to Kyan, either.

"Listen to me old man. My infertility isn't the end of the world—not in *this* world, anyway. If you'd done your research, you'd know there are plenty of kids out there who need good homes and loving families. I can adopt a child."

"And what if Kyan does not want someone else's child? What if he does not want you, Garnet Ruby?"

"Just 'Ruby' is sufficient," she said, lifting her chin and wielding the only weapon she had left: Her dignity. "And that's for me and Kyan to work out. Which I promise you we will when you give him back to me."

She wanted to wipe the smile from his smug face. How dare he smirk at her, like this was some joke. She grabbed him by his shirtfront and shook him. And if she hadn't still been recuperating, she'd have unleashed all the fury boiling inside her and kicked his arse.

Horrible old prick. How could he bear to live with himself

after all the suffering he'd put her through—put them through!

Kyan.

Chalcedony and Wulf.

Chalcedony's mother, and Malach, the Crystal Warrior she'd rejected.

"Who died and made you God?" she hissed, releasing him. "And just so you know, I choose to believe Chalcedony and Wulf's version of life in the Shifting Sands fief. And I choose to believe in Kyan, too. I don't believe that fantasy crap you showed me about his world. The man I knew wouldn't be so cruel. The man I knew loved me. And he didn't care what I looked like, or whether I could have children. Give. Us. Another. Chance!"

He straightened his shirt and adjusted the silken scarf around his neck. And then he smiled. "Your wish is my command," he said.

Uh oh—

Chapter Eighteen

CAR HEADLIGHTS BLINDED HER. She struggled to her feet. The tortured screech of tires and the acrid smell of burning rubber filled the air. The vehicle's bumper smashed into her. She flew over the bonnet, weightless for a split second before she smacked the car's windshield. She caught a glimpse of the driver's shocked face before she slid off the bonnet. Numbness. A burst of agonizing pain. And finally—thankfully—oblivion.

Oblivion was dark. No, more than mere darkness—an absence of everything. She was sightless, deaf and mute. Cut off from any and all sensation. She screamed and fought until she believed she would go mad but the nothingness was absolute. And then….

A feather-light thought brushed her bruised and battered psyche.

Kyan.

She searched for him in the nothingness of the void. She couldn't touch him, for touch did not exist in this time and place. But a part of her soul reached out and snatched the essence of him to her. She had no weapons, nothing physical that she could use in her fight to free him. Nothing except her innermost thoughts and dreams, hopes and desires. And her love.

Time drifted and Ruby fought her silent battle to free the man she loved from his crystalline prison. She would not let go. She refused to give up. And finally, she sensed a spark of awareness that latched on to her and joined her lonely battle.

An eternity later, Kyan awoke. And in the dark recesses of her mind he whispered her name. "Ruby."

"I love you, Kyan."

"I know. I have always known. And I love you, too, Ruby. More than life itself." And when he kissed her, she could feel his lips and his warmth pressed up against her, taste his unique masculine scent curling through her, see the love in his eyes.

They consummated their love, bodies and souls united in an unbreakable bond that transcended even a goddess-invoked, centuries-long curse. And when Ruby awoke to her own reality, she was lying in a hospital bed with Kyan bending over her.

"How long have I been unconscious?" she whispered.

"A week has passed in real time," he said. "Welcome back, my Ruby. And thank you for saving me." He stroked a straggly hank of hair back from her brow, and then gently brushed her lips with his. "Thank you for loving me."

"My pleasure."

His answering smile was that of a man gazing at a woman, lusting after her in the worst way, and wondering when he'd get a chance to jump her bones. And if not for her broken legs and cracked ribs, yadda yadda, she would have invited him to do just that.

Happiness buzzed through her veins. *She* was the woman he lusted after. *She* was the one he loved. They had been given a second chance. And Ruby intended to be out of her hospital bed in record time, so as not to waste a single second of their miracle.

She shifted on her pillow, trying to get comfortable. Kyan raised the head of the bed, and reached over to plump the pillows for her. When he straightened, he held something in his hand.

"What is it?" she asked.

He didn't answer, merely held it out to her.

Ruby recognized it immediately. It was his kyanite crystal. And it was whole.

WHEN THE FOUR-WEEK deadline passed and Kyan didn't vanish, the last of Ruby's nagging fears dissolved. As her rehabilitation and recovery progressed, it became obvious the Crystal Guardian had planned a different kind of Testing for her and Kyan—a lifetime sentence. Pieter had a wicked sense of humor, she would give the old bugger that.

When Kyan arrived, Ruby was in the pool with the hospital physio. She hid a grin, wondering how he'd cope with *this* test.

"Hey babe." She smacked her lips together and blew him a kiss as she slowly breaststroked the width of the pool.

"Hey yourself." He smiled in that breath-stealing way of his.

Laura, Ruby's physio, had to fan her suddenly flushed face. "He's so gorgeous!" she said, not-so-*sotto voce*.

"Yeah, I know." Ruby clung to the poolside rail and slanted the smitten young woman an ear-to-ear grin. "Can I take five, Laura? I've something important to tell him."

"Oh! Right. Sure, Ruby. I need to uh, grab a drink to cool down, anyway. It's stifling in here this morning. Someone must have turned up the thermostat." She swam to the side of the pool and climbed up the ladder—a blonde, blue-eyed goddess of a woman, with a stunning figure.

Kyan never even spared her a glance. His killer-blue eyes were all for Ruby.

"Kyan, I need to tell you something."

His brow creased with worry. He squatted on his haunches to stare intently at her. "Not more complications to delay your recovery, I hope?"

"Complications. Hmmm. I s'pose that's one way of putting it."

He offered a hand to haul her from the water. "Do not keep

me on tenterhooks, Ruby. Tell me what is troubling you. Please."

She grasped his hand. "I'm pregnant. We're going to be parents."

Kyan stilled mid-heave. And because he still had hold of her hand, when Ruby fell back into the water, he took a swan dive.

She surfaced, spluttering and coughing, to see him treading water. She brushed the sopping wet hair from her eyes and searched his face for a reaction to her news.

His face broke into a huge grin. He whooped and fist-punched the air. And then he paddled over to scoop her into his arms.

"A baby? *Our* baby? My Ruby, you have fulfilled my every dream!"

Funny that, because he'd fulfilled every single one of hers, too.

EPILOGUE

RUBY ARRIVED AT Orakei Domain just as the news headlines were announced on her car radio. She parked, and grabbed the box containing her gear. Once she'd dropped it at the designated area, there was nothing to do except mill around with the other competitors. Butterflies the size of albatrosses flapped in her stomach. She'd peed before leaving home but she desperately wanted to go again. Her nerves were getting to her big-time.

The Waitemata was living up to its literal Maori-to-English translation of "Sparkling Water". The sun was out, and there wasn't a cloud to mar the sky. Even so, Ruby shivered as she waited by the start-line.

Start time came, and with it, an interminable agony of cross-legged anticipation. The starts were staggered, so Ruby still had to wait her turn. Then her group of competitors were off, and she didn't have time to worry about nerves anymore. She waded until she was thigh-deep in the water, then threw herself forward and began swimming madly. Or, to be quite honest, considering her still limited abilities, it was more of a mad flounder than actual swimming.

The swim began at the Hammerheads restaurant end of Okahu Bay, and ran parallel to the beach. Ruby wasn't a competent enough swimmer to head for deeper water to get clear of the other swimmers, so she had to contend with face-fulls of seawater flung up from the frantically swimming women churning along beside her. Still, if she needed to rest, or it got too much for her, she knew she only needed to stand up because she wasn't anywhere near out of her depth.

She'd promised herself she wouldn't stand up, though. And she didn't. It seemed to take forever, but she swam the entire three-hundred-meter course without taking a break. And then she was out of the water, rolling her aching shoulders as she loped up the beach to the grass reserve. She basked in the shouted encouragement from both onlookers and the marshals, who were pointing competitors in the right direction.

She had collected her bike and was running with it toward the transition area exit, when she realized she couldn't recall stopping to put on her running shoes. Her stomach lurched. For a frantic instant she thought she'd have to turn around and go back, but then she glanced down. Nope. She'd done everything right. She'd even remembered her helmet.

The ten kilometer cycle course along Tamaki Drive was relatively flat, but a couple of ks in, her leg and thigh muscles protested the abuse she was heaping upon them. Ruby kept her head down and pedaled for all she was worth. Mind over body. And, as she'd proven while recuperating from her accident a second time, she was very strong-willed indeed.

This leg of the course seemed to pass more quickly. And before she knew it, she had reached the end of the cycling course and was racking her bike in the same place she'd collected it at the beginning of her ride. Again, she hadn't stopped to rest once along the way.

One more leg to go. Mentally, coming on the end of the swimming and cycling legs, this would be the hardest one for Ruby—a three kilometer run that began up the seaward side of Tamaki Drive toward Auckland City.

She removed her helmet, jammed a cap on her head, and again decided not to waste time by pulling on shorts and a t-shirt. She didn't care that she wore only a swimsuit. How she looked, or what other people might think of her, wasn't what this was all about.

She set off at a slow jog, too keyed up and concentrating too fiercely on keeping her breathing even to appreciate the stunning views.

By the time the end of the course was in sight, Ruby's shuffling movements could barely be termed running at all. She focused on the fence-lined chute leading to the finish archway. Onlookers clapped and cheered. She heard her name, and spotted her little cluster of personal supporters jumping up and down and screaming at the tops of their lungs. Mike and Annie, Jules and Alex, Lani, her workmates, and even her parents, who'd flown up from Nelson to be here today.

She crossed the finish line. And as she received her medal, she felt so damn proud of what she'd accomplished she thought she might explode. Even though every competitor who completed the course received a medal, Ruby felt like a winner.

She spotted Kyan pushing his way toward her, their year-old daughter clasped tightly in his arms, and Ruby didn't just *feel* like she'd won, she knew in the depths of her soul that she had.

Sarah grinned at Ruby. "Mama," she crowed, and kissed Ruby with sticky, lollipop-red lips.

A flash of bright gold caught Ruby's attention. She nudged Kyan.

Across a seething mass of competitors and onlookers, they gazed at the old man who'd manipulated their lives. Kyan inclined his head. Ruby waved. Despite all the pain and anguish Pieter had caused, how could they not forgive the man who'd given them Sarah?

Pieter acknowledged them with a raised hand and a satisfied smile before he vanished.

A cool breeze whipped straight off the sea. It whispered to Ruby of other men—men who might still be trapped in cold hard crystalline prisons, awaiting their chance of redemption.

She shivered. She'd had a taste of Kyan's prison. And every now and then she woke in the night, her face wet with tears, her throat scratchy and sore as though she'd been screaming. She hoped with all her heart the other Crystal Warriors would find life-mates who loved them enough to fight for them and set them free. Whatever their crimes, none of them deserved such a terrible punishment.

Ruby turned to *her* Crystal Warrior, her life-mate and the love of her life. He didn't care that she hadn't yet shed the extra pregnancy pounds she'd put on, and even when she did, she'd never be slim. He didn't care that her body was scarred from the car accident. And he didn't give a damn that she was sweaty and in dire need of a shower. When he hugged her close and a camera flashed in their faces, instead of feeling self-conscious, Ruby gave the reporter exactly what he wanted—a genuine mega-watt smile.

~*~

About the Author

MAREE ANDERSON WRITES paranormal romance, speculative fiction romance, fantasy, and young adult books. She lives in beautiful New Zealand, home of hobbits, elves, and kiwis—both the fruit and the two-legged flightless variety. Her first novel for young adults, the multi-award-winning Freaks of Greenfield High, was optioned for TV by Cream Drama, Inc., Canada. She recently released the fourth book in her Crystal Warriors series, and is currently working on a third book in the Freaks series.

For more information about Maree's books, please visit her website at: http://www.mareeanderson.com

Glossary of Kiwi Terms & Slang

Arse—ass, bottom

Arsehole—asshole

All Blacks—New Zealand's national rugby team

Aussie—Australian person

Bench (i.e. kitchen bench)—counter

Black Caps—New Zealand's national cricket team

Bloody (e.g. "Bloody hell!")—a mild expletive

Bollocks (e.g. "some such bollocks")—rubbish; stupid thing i.e. emphasizing something considered ridiculous

Boot (of a vehicle) —trunk

Bugger—a mild swearword

Bugger off—tell someone to go away

Buttie (e.g. bacon buttie)—buttered bread eaten as a sandwich with a filling, such as chips or bacon

Bum—bottom

Chips—crisps; thin-cut deep-fried potato wedges usually served with battered fish

Coffee Plunger—French Press

Crikey—a very mild expletive

Crook—sick, unwell

Do (e.g. "a private do") —function, party, celebration

Doss down—sleep in a rough or makeshift bed

Dressing gown—robe

Duvet—comforter, quilt

Fat chance—unlikely (that something will happen)

Jandals—flip-flops, thongs, Japanese sandals

Kiwi—flightless bird native to New Zealand, national icon; slang for New Zealander

Knackered—extremely tired; broken, not working properly and beyond repair

Kumara—sweet potato (a root vegetable that is usually eaten boiled, roasted or baked)

Mum—mom

Numnit—idiot, dummy

Paracetamol—mild analgesic used for the relief of pain and fever, available at pharmacies and supermarkets (Panadol is a common brand)

Pissed—drunk

Pissed as a chook—very drunk

Pissed off—angry, annoyed, irritated

Plunket—an organization that provides support services for the health and wellbeing of children under five

Plonked (e.g. "plonked herself down on the chair")—plunked

R.N.Z.A.F.—Royal New Zealand Air Force

Serviette—napkin

Sod it—mild expletive.

Sodding (e.g. "no need to sodding well rub salt in the wound")—mild expletive, like "bloody"

Stoush—a fight or brawl

Sucks the big kumara (e.g. "Wow. That really sucks the big kumara.")—expression used when you run out of luck and things aren't going your way

Sussed (e.g. "hasn't got it sussed yet")—figured out

Takeaways—takeout

Tap—faucet

Telly—TV, television

Togs—swimsuit

Yellow Pages—directory of New Zealand businesses

Glossary of Styrian Terms

Halja—Hell

Gahvay—beverage similar to coffee

Se'nnight—seven nights; a week

Styrian—literally: Storm Rider

Teh—ten

Tehun—a troop of ten men plus their commander

Tehun-Leader—second-in-command

Other books in The Crystal Warriors Series

THE CRYSTAL WARRIOR
(Wulf & Chalcedony's story)

JADE'S CHOICE
(Malach & Jade's story)

OPAL'S WISH
(Danbur & Opal's story)

~*~

www.ingramcontent.com/pod-product-compliance
Lightning Source LLC
Chambersburg PA
CBHW021957170626
46808CB00001B/196